IN THE
MOUTH
OF THE
WOLF

IN THE
MOUTH OF THE WOLF

book **2** of the twin willows trilogy

NICOLE MAGGI

MEDALLION
P R E S S

Medallion Press, Inc.
Printed in USA

For Chris, the love of my life
and the best brainstormer I know

Published 2015 by Medallion Press, Inc.

The MEDALLION PRESS LOGO
is a registered trademark of Medallion Press, Inc.

Typeset in Adobe Garamond Pro
Printed in the United States of America
ISBN 978-1-60542-619-8

10 9 8 7 6 5 4 3 2 1
First Edition

ACKNOWLEDGMENTS

Although all the words on the pages in this book are mine, it is because of the help of many people that I am able to write them.

To my agent extraordinaire, Irene Goodman, for always believing in me. For the past ten years, no matter what has happened, no matter how low the lows got, you've always been on my side, and for that I am intensely grateful.

To my editor, Emily Steele, for her passion and belief in this series. To my copyeditor, Antonia Aquilante, for seeing the small stuff when I'm too busy looking at the big picture. To the incredible team at Medallion, especially Brigitte Shepard, Paul Ohlson, and Jim Tampa, for supporting me as an author, for promoting this series with such enthusiasm, and for answering all my naïve questions with such patience and generosity. To Michal Wlos for my stunning covers.

Deep gratitude to all those who nurture my writing, especially Barb Wexler, Anne Van, and Jen Klein. Much love to Lizzie Andrews for investing so much energy into this series, reading the book so quickly when I needed you to, and all our fabulous writing dates all over Los Angeles. Heartfelt love and gratitude to Romina Garber for our twin brains, your constant encouragement, and your enduring friendship.

Many thanks to the fantastic kid-lit community here in Los Angeles. Not only are you all great writers, but you are also the best drinking buddies an author could ever have. Huge thanks to the Class of 2k14 for your constant support, especially Tracy Holczer for all the margaritas and tater tots.

Thank you to the Republic of Pie in North Hollywood and Romancing the Bean in Burbank for keeping me happy with good coffee and great food while I write.

To my family for being proud of me no matter what.

And to Chris and Emilia, the two most important people in the world to me: There are no words. There is only endless love.

TABLE OF CONTENTS

CHAPTER ONE
The Arrival

Alessia

The tiny town of Twin Willows, Maine, looked like a toy village from five hundred feet in the air. Most people never got to see that view, but most people didn't have my ability. They couldn't pull their soul away from their body and transform into a Falcon as I could. They couldn't fly high into the air and see their houses in miniature. There were only two other people I knew who could do this. One was another Benandante like me, who transformed into an Eagle. The other was of my enemy Clan, the Malandanti. It took the form of a Raven, and it was currently bearing down hard on my tail.

I swerved around the tip of a pine tree, shaking needles loose in my wake. The Raven couldn't match me in speed, but its need for revenge spurred it on. Not long ago, I had broken both its wings in an all-out battle between the two Clans, and it clearly wanted to return the favor.

Moonlight shot through night clouds. The Raven appeared at the corner of my vision. Its silver aura gleamed. I dropped below the treetops. In the distance I saw the copse of birch trees, their bark ghostly white in the darkness. Just beyond it lay the Waterfall that was the source of all this conflict, the reason the Benandanti and the Malandanti were here in this dead-end, know-nothing town . . .

I heard the Waterfall before I saw it, rushing end over end. The silvery glow of the Raven disappeared. I didn't look to see where it had gone. The birch trees loomed in front of me. I soared between them. Through the brush, I saw the celestial light of the Benandanti that protected the Waterfall. Once I reached that, the Raven couldn't touch me.

A flash of silver blinded me. I screeched, blown backwards as the Raven blocked my way. Its little trick of turning off its aura was extremely frustrating—and useful. I needed to learn how to do that.

Alessia! Where are you? The voice of my Guide, Heath, rang through my head. The Benandanti communicated telepathically—a convenient, if sometimes annoying, power.

The Raven sniped at me. I circled up and away, out of its reach. *At the birch trees. The Raven's giving me some trouble—*

I'm coming. It wasn't Heath but the Lynx, another member of our Clan. Ever since we had regained control of the Waterfall, there were always two of us on patrol there, and we were not allowed to leave until our replacement showed up.

Far below on the ground, the Lynx appeared. I climbed, keeping the Raven's focus as it chased me upward. When it was just a feather's distance away, I stopped. *All right, jackass*, I thought, although the Raven could not hear me. *Let's see you catch me now.* And I dove.

Before the Raven knew what was happening, I was halfway to the ground. Falcons top two hundred miles per hour on a dive, and I was no ordinary Falcon. Not even lightning could catch me on a dive. I heard a swoosh behind me as the Raven plummeted after me. Just before I reached the ground, I veered sideways.

Too late, the Raven realized the trap I'd set. It was traveling too fast to stop and didn't have my control. As the Raven neared the ground, the Lynx leapt up and caught it in his mouth.

The bird thrashed and writhed but could not free itself from the Lynx's jaws. I knew the Lynx wouldn't kill it, but the Malandanti didn't trust us to be merciful. We certainly didn't trust them.

I'll get it out of here, the Lynx told me and bounded away, his powerful paws imprinting deep into the earth. But before he reached the other side of the birch trees, a huge black figure blocked his path. Jewel-green eyes flashed in the darkness. I pulled up short, my heartbeat pounding in my ears. For a moment, I was frozen, unable to think, unable to move, unable to breathe.

The enormous Malandante Panther lunged at the Lynx, who stumbled back but still hung on to the bird in his mouth. I shook myself into action and plunged toward them. A piercing cry tore from my throat.

The Panther looked up. Those emerald-green eyes widened at the sight of me.

I circled above the Panther's head. *Don't get too close*, the Lynx warned, but I knew something the Lynx didn't. The Panther wouldn't hurt me. That, I could trust.

Distracted, the Panther sidestepped. His path clear, the Lynx dodged forward, but before he could get past, the Panther jumped. In one graceful motion, the Panther knocked the Lynx off its feet and sprang into the air, catching me in his mouth.

I went limp, my body numb with shock. What was he doing? Had I been that wrong about him? The Lynx shouted something in my head, but I couldn't make sense of it, so jumbled were my own thoughts. Cold air swept through my feathers, waking my senses back up. I cringed, anticipating pain in every inch of my body. But the pain didn't come.

I blinked and twisted my neck to look up into the Panther's eyes. He was focused on the Lynx, but I could swear there was a warning there, something he was trying to tell me. Something crackled in my mind, like radio static, like he was trying to talk to me. Benandanti and Malandanti cannot communicate with each other, not telepathically, but I understood. He was holding me in such a way that he wouldn't hurt me—but only he and I knew that.

The Lynx backed up, drawing the Panther away from the Waterfall. Once clear of the birch trees, he opened his mouth, and the Raven tumbled out. With a loud squawk, the Raven streaked a talon across the Lynx's nose. The Lynx lunged and his jaw snapped shut, snagging a black feather from the Raven's wing. While the two of them sparred with each other, the Panther knelt in the snow and set me free.

I flew, testing my wings, feeling my bones and flesh for anything out of place. But everything was working, no pain at all. I fluttered in front of the Panther. Our gazes met for several heartbeats. Even though I was unhurt, my insides felt upside down.

Watch out! The Lynx's warning came just in time. I rocketed up as the Raven hurtled itself at me. *Get to the Waterfall,* the Lynx told me. *I'll take care of them.*

I rose, hovering for a moment. *I don't want to leave you two to one—*

And I don't want to leave the Waterfall with just one. Go. I'll be fine. The Lynx disappeared into the thicket. The Raven looked at the Panther before following, and I knew he was getting his orders too.

I winged my way through the trees toward the Waterfall. On the ground below, the Panther loped after me; I needn't have worried about the odds after all. But even so, I knew my first duty was to the Waterfall and its sacred magic—even if that meant sacrificing a member of the Clan.

The glow of the Waterfall brightened into brilliance. Before the Panther reached the water's edge, I plunged through the celestial barrier and spun to face him. He slid to a stop on the banks of the stream, watching me.

Heath stood on a wide, flat rock at the base of the Waterfall, his body rigid, ears tipped forward. *What happened?*

The Lynx drew the Raven away, I said, fully aware I was telling him only half the story. Heath's eyes moved from me to the Panther, who paced along the stream. He looked back and forth between us but didn't press me to say more.

I flew in slow, wide circles inside the perimeter of the barrier. As long as there was one of us inside, the Malandanti could not breach it, but one of them was always there, just beyond the magic, waiting. Waiting for us to slip up and make a mistake, waiting for a chance to lure us out and retake control of the magic. There had barely been a night without some sort of attack since we had won back the Waterfall, and I knew it was only going to get worse. But tonight was the first time that the Panther—I still could not think of him by his real name—and I had been on patrol at the same time.

And that could only get worse, too.

In the predawn light at the end of our patrol, Heath and I raced home. The Stag and the Eagle had taken over for us, and the Panther had still been at the edge of the stream, his green eyes wary and watchful. My wings felt heavy, as if I were still tied to the Waterfall even after I was miles away.

When we reached the farm, Heath veered toward his cabin on the other side of the pasture. I descended, my gut jolting as I skimmed over the charred remains of our burned-out barn. Remembering that night, I had a sudden, brutal wish that the Lynx had bitten that damned Raven in half when he had the chance.

Just beyond the ruined barn sat my house, still and silent and dark. My second-story window yawned open, beckoning me. Maybe I could catch an hour of sleep before my morning chores . . .

Transform and get to my cabin. ASAP.

My heart skittered. Ever since my dad had died a year before, frantic messages like that made me breathless. I tried to shoot back a question—*Why?*—but Heath's mind was closed off, already transformed back to human and unreachable to me. There was no chance for sleep now.

I glided in through the window, barely looking at my inert body on the bed before I dissolved into it with a burst of blue light. I lay on my back, breathing deep to steady myself back into my human form. When I was a Falcon, I was expansive. There was always a moment after I transitioned back when it felt as if my body could not possibly contain my soul.

I slid off the bed and tiptoed into the hall. It was still

night, but once the sun's first rays touched the hillside, my mother, Lidia, would be up and about. I glanced out the sunburst window over the front door as I eased downstairs; I had maybe an hour before day broke. If Heath was in real trouble, I wouldn't be back before Lidia woke.

As I hurried to Heath's cabin, the cold night air whipped through me. It felt harsh on my skin, so different than when I was a Falcon, covered in downy feathers. I neared the cabin, close enough to see through his brightly lit windows. Inside, Heath stood stock-still. A shadow moved across the wall opposite him. I stopped. Someone was in there with him..

Heath barely knew anyone in Twin Willows, and I had never seen anyone visit his cabin. A thrum started in my chest. I ran the last several yards to the cabin and pounded on the front door. "Heath! Are you—?"

The door opened, and I stumbled inside. A smooth, gentle hand caught me and pulled me upright.

"I hope you're steadier in the air than you are on your feet," said a laughing voice.

Amber eyes peered into my own. I stepped back so I could take in the whole person and then looked at Heath. "Who is this?"

The woman stepped forward and stretched a hand out to me. Her burgundy nails were long, manicured, and perfect. "I am Nerina DaVollo."

"Okay," I said, taking her hand. There was a callous at the base of her right middle finger. For some reason, that made me happy. "Should I know you?"

"No."

But as I stared at her, I realized I *did* know her. My eyes found the picture Heath had tacked up on the opposite wall. A gorgeous woman in profile, laughing. The woman I thought of as Heath's lost love because of the expression on his face whenever he looked at the picture.

It was Nerina.

I glanced between the picture, the real Nerina in front of me, and Heath, who stood motionless in the corner of his cabin. His face was pale and held the same expression I'd seen whenever he looked at the picture. I raised an eyebrow. He shook his head.

"But you know of me," Nerina said, either oblivious to Heath's and my silent exchange or choosing to ignore it. Her words clicked in my brain.

"The *Concilio*," I breathed. "You're from Friuli."

"*Si*." Nerina picked up her coat from the bed and shrugged it on. She flounced her snaky, dark hair out of the depths of the fur collar. I recognized the coat from a spread in *Vogue* that my best friend Jenny had been lusting over during a recent lunch period. Nerina turned to Heath. "Do you have a torch?"

He started. "A wha—? Oh. Yeah." He fished under the kitchen sink for a moment and came back up with a bright yellow, heavy-duty flashlight.

"What do we need that for?" I asked.

"I can't very well traipse through the woods in the

dark," Nerina said. "Who knows where I'll step? These are Louboutins." She kicked her booted foot out. How she'd made it over the snowy hillside in those spiky heels, I had no idea.

"Sorry—why are we going to the woods?"

"Darling, I can't possibly stay here." Nerina waved, indicating the tiny cabin. "People will ask questions. I need to stay out of sight." She tilted her head. "Catch up, dear. Your intellect was one of the reasons we Called you." She opened the door and switched on the flashlight. "You can bring the bags later," she said to Heath, and only then did I notice the three Louis Vuitton suitcases collected at the side of the bed.

I fell into step with Heath behind Nerina as she marched out into the night. The flashlight bobbed in her hand, jerking shadows over the dark ground.

"What is going on?" I muttered to Heath.

"She was at the cabin when I got back from patrol," Heath whispered. "I knew one of them would be coming here, but I didn't think it would be her."

I wanted to ask why and what their history was—I'd wanted to ask him that for ages—but now didn't seem like the right time to go digging into his personal life. Jogging ahead of him, I caught up with Nerina. "The Friuli site fell over two weeks ago. What took you so long to get here?"

Nerina didn't take her gaze off the pool of light guiding us into the woods. "I couldn't just show up at the

Venezia airport and board the next flight to America, darling. The Malandanti's own *Concilio* was tracking our every move."

"What about the Clan in Friuli? Are they okay?"

"They are all fine." She stopped and swung the flashlight back and forth. "One of us—the *Concilio*—stayed behind to assist them. This way," she said and pointed her light into a dense thicket of trees.

"How do you know? Have you been here before?"

She didn't answer me—just stepped over a patch of muddy snow. Somehow, her boots had stayed clean. I looked down. My Converse sneakers were so filthy you could barely tell they were once bright blue suede. Nerina flicked an errant leaf off her coat sleeve. She and Jenny obviously shared the same fashionista gene. It had skipped my mother's birthing room the day I was born.

"Here we are." We had reached the low wall that marked the edge of our property. Nerina walked its length, sweeping her light over the crumbling stones.

I planted my hands on my hips. "I could've gotten us here without the flashlight. I know every inch of this farm."

"You don't know this inch," Nerina murmured as she scanned the wall carefully, taking in every nook and cranny between the ancient stones.

"What are you looking for?"

"The door, of course."

The door? What door? Was she nuts? I shot a look at Heath, but he was focused on Nerina, his lips pressed in a thin line.

"Ah. Here it is." She set the flashlight on the wall, its light beaming upwards. Shadows skittered in its circular white glow. Nerina knelt beside the wall and reached her hand into a break between two large stones. She tugged, and there was a loud creak, like something awakening that had been asleep for a long, long time.

My breath caught. The ground below the wall shifted and moved. A narrow space appeared, big enough for a person to squeeze through.

A door.

"How," I said, squinting at Nerina, "did you know that was there?"

She grinned up at me, not answering as she lowered herself into the space. I peered into it. A staircase spiraled down—to what, I had no idea.

Heath grabbed the flashlight and disappeared behind Nerina. I looked up at the sky. The faintest line of pale blue stretched over the treetops. Daybreak was not far off. Pretty soon, Lidia would be awake. And where would I be? "Underground like a hedgehog," I muttered and lowered myself onto the first step.

At the bottom of the stairs, the space opened up into three rooms with concrete floors and walls. Retro furniture populated the rooms, a small but fully equipped kitchen and a comfortable sitting area. The bedroom was dominated by a vanity I could imagine Marilyn Monroe sitting at. But the bed was covered with a quilt that had a huge peace symbol stitched into the center.

"Whoa," I said. "I didn't know the DHARMA Initiative had a hatch here."

"Where's the button we have to push every hundred eight minutes?" Heath asked.

I put my hand over my heart and fluttered my eyelashes at him. "I've never been prouder of you than at this very moment."

"Ha, ha."

"What are you two talking about?" Nerina flung her coat over one of the orange plastic chairs in the kitchen.

"Haven't you ever seen *Lost*?" I asked.

"I have never been lost," Nerina said, smoothing a nonexistent wrinkle in her skirt.

"It's a TV show."

"The *Concilio* has better things to do than watch television," Nerina said with a sniff.

I clenched my jaw. If she was going to hole up in a secret hideout on *my* farm, she needed to drop the attitude. "So what is this place? And how come I never knew it was here?"

"Darling, I doubt anyone else alive knows this is here," Nerina said, running a forefinger along the kitchen table. Her fingertip blackened with dust. "We built it during the Cold War." A little laugh escaped, as if she were a baby bird learning to chirp. "After all, why do you think the Russians and the Americans were at odds to begin with?"

"Um, Communism?" I said.

Heath shot me a *watch it* look. I'd probably be in for a how-to-treat-your-elders lecture later. But Nerina wasn't much of an elder. I watched her go through the drawers in the kitchen. She looked barely older than me, maybe a few years younger than Heath.

Nerina moved on to the sitting area and started plumping pillows. Dust billowed. "Is this how you train her, *caro mia*? To be rude and impertinent?"

"Don't call me *caro mia*," Heath shouted so loudly that I jumped. "I am not your *caro mia*. The *Concilio* made damn sure of that—"

"Do not raise your voice to me—"

"You can't just barge in here and take over—"

"What did you expect—?"

"—and act like you're still my Guide."

"I am still your elder!"

"Stop it!" I threw up my hands.

They both looked at me. Heath's fair skin was mottled; even his hands were blotchy. Nerina had the same look on her face that my mother got when she was about to throw a full-fledged Italian fit.

I took a deep breath. "Look, I know you two have history, but, Nerina, if you're gonna be staying here, you gotta get along. I can't play peacemaker all the time."

Heath ducked his head. "She's right."

Nerina mumbled something in Italian.

"I'm not a child. I'm old enough to be a Benandante, so don't treat me like a kid." I gave her a little twisted half smile. "And, yeah, I speak fluent Italian."

"So I see," Nerina said, folding her arms.

"Besides," I said, "you're not much older than I am. I didn't realize the *Concilio* elders could be so young."

Nerina dropped her arms and looked at Heath. "You didn't tell her?"

"Don't start. She didn't need to know."

A little throb started at the base of my skull. "Know what?"

Nerina came around the coffee table and stood in front of me, so close I could see every nonexistent pore in her unlined face. "Do you not know what magic the Friuli site holds, *cara*?"

I shook my head.

She touched her face, as though to remind herself of what she looked like. "One taste of the juice from the sacred Olive Grove, and you will stop aging."

I swallowed hard. My throat felt dry. "When—? When did you stop aging?" I whispered.

"When I was eighteen." She smiled. "*Anno Domini* 1575."

CHAPTER TWO

Where Do They Keep the Self-Help Books for Sisters of Super-Villains?

Bree

I slammed the book shut and tossed it on the floor. Why were all the novels these days about emo girls who lusted after vampires/werewolves/angels/some-hybrid-supernatural-hottie that just made the rest of us feel bad about our own lives? I reached for the next book in the pile on the nightstand and read the back cover. It was about an anorexic girl. Who was in love with a succubus. I flung the book across the room, where it landed on the thick carpet with a soft thud. Who had possessed my body when I'd checked that out of the library? I looked over at the nightstand. The only book left was *Witchcraft of Italy*.

I stared hard at its ominous cover, black with the white silhouette of a witch flying by moonlight. Yeah, right. Witches didn't fly by night on their broomsticks. No, they were much more sly and insidious. They escaped through second-story windows and ran through the woods on four huge black paws. They lived in your house and slept one room over.

As if he could hear my thoughts, I heard a gasp. Barely audible—no way would my in-denial parents ever hear it—but I heard it. My senses were all too finely tuned these days.

I eased out from under the covers and tiptoed to my door. The hallway was cold and silent, the still-unopened boxes making uneven shadows along the wall. I crossed to his doorway in two gazelle leaps. His door was locked, but a quick jiggle with a hairpin fixed that.

Inside, Jonah sat on his bed, gasping for air as he clutched at his chest. Anyone else might have thought he was having a seizure, but I knew better. Shit, did I know better. I wished I didn't.

"Get . . . out." It was hardly a whisper.

I stood in the doorway watching him. Anger, disgust, and fear all raged for space inside me. That could have been me. That should have been me. *Thank God—or whoever—it wasn't me.*

I moved to the side of the bed. "Jonah." He looked up at me, and our gazes locked. In the depths of his green eyes, I saw something rare: shame.

It's not so cool being a supernatural hottie after you find out your girlfriend is your mortal enemy, is it? But I didn't say that. Instead I touched his arm and leaned over him, my long hair like a dark curtain around us. "Don't go," I whispered.

He shook his head. "No choice," he gasped out.

"There's always a choice."

"Not . . . for me." He fell back on the bed and went limp. An instant later, in a flash of silver light, the Panther stood on the bed, his huge paws wrinkling the bedclothes. He blinked once at me, then leapt out the open window. By the time I crossed the room, he was only a dim, silvery glow on the ground below.

I stood at the window for a long time. The air was cold as a witch's tit—damn, but Maine was cold, colder than any place we'd ever been. In more ways than one. Finally, I backed away from the window and dropped into Jonah's desk chair. I switched on his little banker's lamp and examined the stack of books on his desk. No vampires, werewolves, or supernatural hotties. Who needed to read about them when you were one? With a sigh, I picked up *A Clockwork Orange*. Mr. Foster, the English teaching assistant, had raved about it the other day. I flipped it open and read the first page. Oh yeah. This was much more soothing than vampires.

A loud thump against the window woke me with a start several hours later. *A Clockwork Orange* slid off my chest to the floor. The Panther stood on the windowsill, his bright green eyes narrowed at me. I scrambled to my feet and watched him. He stepped onto the desk, his huge paws knocking books aside, then sprang onto the bed. For a moment there were two Jonahs—the one I knew and the one whose life was a mystery to me.

A flash of silver light blinded me for an instant. When I could see again, the Jonah I knew was back. I folded my arms. "Nice night?"

Jonah ran his hands over his face. "I'm not in the mood, Bree."

I pressed my hand to my chest, my eyes wide. "Oh no! Did something happen?"

He glared at my sarcasm and pushed himself off the bed.

"I thought everything was sunshine and daisies in the land of the Malandanti," I said, following him to the closet.

"Just leave me alone." He grabbed a clean shirt and tossed it on the bed.

I blocked his path when he tried to get around me.

"Come on, Bree. Not this morning."

"Then when? What morning works best for you? Do the Malandanti have a secretary who keeps your calendar?"

"God, Bree." Jonah threw his hands up. "You're like a pit bull. You never let up." He sidestepped me and grabbed a towel from the back of his chair. "This is none of your business."

Why couldn't he see that everything he did was my business? He and I had shared a womb; that bond didn't go away after the doctor slapped our asses. I crossed swiftly to the door before he could reach it. "It is my business. It's my business now, and it'll be my business the day you don't come back through that window."

"That's not going to happen."

"Yeah, like it didn't happen to the person you replaced."

Jonah's eyebrows shot up.

I leaned back against the door. "What, you conveniently forgot that someone had to die before you could get Called?"

Jonah looked at the floor. "They could've died of natural causes."

"And next Christmas you won't get a pair of flannel long johns from Aunt Cindy. Wake up and smell the hazelnut latte."

"Maybe I don't want to wake up," he muttered. He bit his lip and turned his head.

I should have felt triumphant for getting him to admit it, but I didn't. Instead there was a sinking feeling in the pit of my stomach. I stared at him. He kept his face turned. Shadows swam beneath his skin. And suddenly I understood. "You saw her tonight, didn't you?"

CHAPTER THREE
The Graveyard Revisited

Alessia

Ever since I had become a Benandante, I'd had a love-hate relationship with school. Love, because it—particularly my friends—provided a great distraction from the life-and-death battle going on in my backyard. Hate, because it distracted me from the life-and-death battle going on in my backyard.

It seemed pointless to worry about my GPA when I might not ever get the chance to put it to good use. But I had to keep up appearances, and the pre-Benandanti Alessia was an honors student, an award-winning writer, someone who wasn't content to coast. I'd been coasting for months now, and that wave had had surprising longevity.

But that Monday morning after Christmas break, the wave finally ran to shore.

"Principal Morrissey would like to see you, dear," one of the secretaries said when I walked into the office. I worked there first period and assumed Morrissey wanted to give me another soul-sucking filing job. Not that I minded. My brain still needed time to wrap around the fact that I had a four-hundred-fiftysomething-year-old immortal living underground on my farm.

"Sit down, Alessia," Principal Morrissey said when I sidled into his office. He had an open file on his desk. I slid into the seat opposite him and saw it was my file.

I squirmed a little in the big comfy chair. Maybe I wasn't being given a soul-sucking filing job after all.

Morrissey steepled his fingers and fixed his gaze on my face. My skin grew hot and itchy. I felt as if I were back in third grade, when I had to go stand in the corner for passing notes with Jenny. It was the first and last time I'd gotten into trouble in school.

"Alessia," Principal Morrissey said, "I'm concerned about you."

I swallowed. "Um, why?"

"Well"—he looked down at the file—"your midterm grades aren't up to their usual standards at all."

Midterms had been the week after Jonah had broken up with me, after I'd transformed right in front of him. So, yeah. Not my usual standards. "That was a tough week for me."

Morrissey laid his palms flat on the desk. "Alessia, it's not like you to let a boy affect your grades."

My jaw dropped. "How—? How did you know that?"

He rolled his eyes. "I'm not sitting up here in an ivory tower. I know what goes on in this school—and this town."

I looked at my hands in my lap. "He's not affecting my grades."

"I beg to differ." Morrissey tapped the file. "You've gotten practically straight As throughout your entire high school career." His face softened. "Even after your dad died, which would've been completely understandable, but your grades stayed up. And now suddenly you're struggling to get a B. What's different? The boyfriend."

I pressed my lips together. The boyfriend wasn't the only thing different. But I couldn't tell Morrissey my schoolwork was suffering because I was out defending a precious magical site every night.

Morrissey closed the file. "I need to see an improvement the first half of this semester, or your mother and I will have to have a conference. Understood?"

I nodded. "Understood."

"Do you, Alessia? Do you understand? No boy is worth losing your academic status for. Or covering for in the office."

I looked away. "Sorry about that."

"I was young and in love once too." His brow furrowed. "But if it happens again, I'm going to have to give you detention."

"Okay," I whispered, focused on the edge of his desk. It was the first time I'd been in trouble since the third grade, and Morrissey had always been nice to me. My cheeks burned.

"Good. I think Mrs. Peterson has some filing for you,"

Morrissey said. He spun his chair around and stuck my file back into one of the drawers behind him. "And speaking of young Mr. Wolfe, would you please send him in?"

I froze, halfway out of the comfy chair. "What?"

Principal Morrissey swiveled back to face me. "He's back from his suspension. I hope that doesn't throw you off your game today."

I shook my head, not trusting myself to speak. I knew Jonah would have to come back from suspension eventually, but I had put off thinking about it at all. And after seeing him at the Waterfall last night . . .

My heart thudding, I opened the door to Morrissey's office. Jonah sat in one of the plastic chairs against the wall, his peacoat unbuttoned to reveal a grey T-shirt with Smokey the Bear and the phrase *Only YOU Can Prevent Forest Fires!* emblazoned on it. He rose when I came out of the office.

"Principal Morrissey wants to see you." I didn't meet his gaze. I walked right past him to Mrs. Peterson's desk and, though I heard him say thanks, I didn't turn around.

After first period, I counted the steps from the office to French class, feeling the weight of each one. Morrissey had for sure set Jonah on a strict course to good behavior, which meant he would be in the seat behind me in second-period French, his presence burning a hole in my spine.

Jenny caught up with me outside the classroom door.

As soon as she opened her mouth, I cut her off. "Jonah's back."

She linked an arm through mine as we went into class. "Well, you knew he'd be back after the holidays." She squeezed my elbow. "Do you want to switch seats with me?"

That was why Jenny was the best friend a girl could ever have. I leaned my head onto her shoulder. "No, that's okay. But thanks."

We broke apart as we reached our seats. Carly, the third member of our little foursome, slid into the seat in front of Jenny.

"Don't worry," Jenny said. "We'll shoot him looks of shame, won't we, Carly?"

"Yep!" She squinted. "What are we talking about?"

Jenny shook her hair out of a ponytail and threw her hairband at Carly. "Jonah! He's back."

"Oh!" Carly reached across the aisle and patted my hand. "Just ignore him."

Easy for her to say.

I pulled out my textbook and stared at it, the words swimming on the page with the effort it took me to not look at the door. Finally, just as the bell rang, Jonah ducked in. I forced myself to keep my head down as he brushed past me and dropped into his seat behind me.

Up at the front of the room, Madame Dubois could have been doing a cancan and I would have missed it. I had no idea if Jonah was staring at me, but the back of my neck sizzled. My hand moved across my notebook, conjugating verbs, but my mind was far away. Two miles, to be exact, at the Waterfall, flying circles inside the barrier under the watchful emerald-green eyes of the Panther. Jonah's eyes.

Madame Dubois called something out, and everyone shuffled and flipped through their books. I blinked and looked at my notebook. I had conjugated the verb *to ride* eleven times in a row. With a sigh, I ran a hand over my face. This was what Morrissey had meant. I would have to see Jonah every day, and I couldn't let him affect me like this.

A note slid onto my desk from behind, the sound of its landing hidden under the rustling of everyone's pages. I covered it with my palm, my fingers trembling. *Please be from Jenny*, I thought as I unfolded it. *Some easy platitude about hanging in there . . .*

But it was Jonah's block script that greeted me, not Jenny's curlicues and hearts.

I have information that you need to hear. Meet me in the graveyard at midnight.

At eleven forty-five that night, I sat on the edge of my bed, fully dressed, Jonah's note crumpled in my hand. All day, since it had landed on my desk, my brain had played tug-of-war. What information? Why did I have to hear it? Was it a trap?

That last thought was what kept me rooted to my

bed, sneakers half laced. Jonah was a Malandante. Everything I knew about them was evidence of their treachery, and though I didn't believe Jonah was deep-down evil, he was still one of them.

And yet . . . *he protected you.*

That was what Heath had told me, the night I'd learned what Jonah was, during an attack on the Waterfall. The Malandante Bobcat had nearly caught me, but Jonah had distracted him, giving me enough time to get away. And then last night, he had acted as though he was hurting me, but he hadn't. He had actually protected me again from the Raven.

I laced my sneakers the whole way up and stopped.

But just because he hadn't killed me, as the rest of his Clan wanted to do, didn't mean we weren't enemies. He was still one of them. He hadn't come to me asking for help to get out of the Malandanti.

My stomach turned over. Maybe that was what he was doing now.

Before I could think it through—before hope and fear could cancel each other out—I crossed my room to the door and tiptoed downstairs. Lidia had long since gone to bed, and I had snuck out of the house so many times in the last couple of months that it was second nature now.

The old wrought-iron gate still had the same creak it always had, but everything was different. The last time I had been here was *before.* Before Jonah had found out what I was. Before he had told me what he was. Before everything had fallen apart. I walked through the rows of gravestones. They, at least, were unchanging.

Icicles clung to the long, bare branches that brushed the top of my head as I wound my way to the bench. Our bench. I shook my head. Not our bench anymore. Nothing was ours anymore. We were separate. I had to remember that.

Jonah was already seated on the bench when I rounded the corner of the mausoleum. He looked up at the crunch of my feet on the snow-tipped grass. "You came."

I folded my arms and nodded, keeping my distance to several feet from the bench. "What information was so important you had to drag me out of bed at midnight?"

Jonah sighed and ran a hand through his hair. A large, black pen-ink tattoo circled his middle finger; I'd watched him draw it during biology class that afternoon. "Aren't you even gonna sit down?"

"Fine." I sat as far away from him as the bench would allow and hugged myself against the chill. Whether the cold came from outside or within, I didn't know.

"I can't believe how cold it gets in Maine," Jonah said after a few minutes of thick silence.

I looked at him. "Really, Jonah? *The weather?*"

"You're right—"

"Just tell me what you meant by your note, and then we can both go back to bed." I kept my focus on the frosted ground. Looking at him hurt, like staring at something so beautiful it broke your heart. He didn't speak for so long that I finally had to look up. Shadows veiled his eyes, but there was something in them that caught my breath.

"I still think you're wrong," he said finally. "About the Benandanti."

"Save your breath." Anger rose in me like soda bubbles. "I *know* you're wrong."

"Why can't you see—?"

"Is this what you came here to say?" I stood up. "Because if it is, you dragged both of us out of bed for nothing." I stared at him, my body suddenly numb. "Or did you? Did you drag me out here to keep me busy?"

"What do you—?"

"While the rest of your Clan attacks the Waterfall!" I backed away, every nerve alight with fear. I had to get out of here, get home, transform, and get to the Waterfall before they could—

"Alessia, stop!" In a blur, Jonah moved to block my path.

I froze. He was close enough now I could feel his breath on my face.

"I didn't bring you here to keep you busy. Get real. If the Waterfall were in trouble, you'd be Called."

I exhaled slowly. He was right, and I'd panicked for nothing in front of him. I clenched my fists at my sides. I couldn't let him see my weaknesses. Wasn't that a basic rule of warfare? "Then why did you ask me here?"

His eyes searched my face. "Uh, how's your mom?"

I blinked. "What?"

"She's okay, right?"

"She's fine." I tilted my head, trying to read in his face what he was getting at. But he gave nothing away. "Though she would be a lot better if Mr. Salter were around."

"What do you mean?"

My jaw tightened. "Mr. Salter. He's been missing since before Christmas. And I don't think it's a coincidence that the last time we saw him he was fighting with your father."

"Alessia, I have no idea where Mr. Salter is." Jonah balled his hands into fists. "You don't even know for sure that he disappeared. He probably just went away for a while."

"Yeah, right—"

"Look, I don't want to talk about Mr. Salter," Jonah said, his words tumbling out fast and angry. "I asked about your mom because—I think you should know—they're suspicious. They used the same magic on your mom that they used on the town, and it didn't work. And they're wondering why."

"Who's 'they'?"

He shook his head. "I can't tell you that."

I ground my teeth together. He didn't need to—I knew it was either his dad at the Guild or his Malandanti Clan. They were virtually interchangeable. "Why are you telling me this?"

"I told you—" He squeezed his eyes shut and opened them again. "I still care about you. I don't want you to get hurt."

"A little too late for that."

"God, Alessia!" Jonah turned away from me, then spun back, his eyes glowing against his pale skin. "You think this doesn't kill me? You think I don't hate this? I *loved* you! I still—" He clamped his mouth shut and inhaled sharply through his nose. "It doesn't matter why I told you, okay? I just thought you should know. Can't you just say thank you and be done with it?"

"Thank you." My voice shook. I was fighting to keep my balance. He said he still loved me. At least, I was pretty sure that was what he was going to say . . .

"You're welcome." Jonah straightened his shoulders. He rocked a little on his heels. "How come it didn't work? The magic?"

I bit my lip. I wasn't about to tell him about the amulet. "The Malandanti aren't the only ones who have magic, you know." As the words came out of my mouth, I realized they must be true. The Benandanti had to have magic, too. Why weren't we using it like the Malandanti?

Jonah crossed his arms. "I guess that makes sense."

"Doesn't it also make sense that the Malandanti burned down my barn?" We had fought over this point before. "If you follow the logic that they were suspicious of my mother? Besides the fact that I *saw* the freaking Raven there just before the fire?"

"I know." Jonah looked at the ground. "But you have to believe that I had nothing to do with it and didn't know anything about—"

"It doesn't matter!" Wind shifted through the

gravestones, as if the spirits below felt my anger. "Just because you didn't know about it doesn't mean you're innocent, Jonah. You're one of them. Whatever they do, you're a part of." He finally met my gaze, and we stood, inches but worlds apart, breathing heavily. "That's why we can't talk. Because you'll never convince me you're not just as evil as they are."

I backed away, my feet picking up speed until I rounded the corner of the mausoleum. I turned and ran, dry branches whipping against my face as I fled through the gravestones. It was a mistake to come here and face him. My heart had split open all over again.

Once through the ancient gate, I stopped and caught my breath. Jonah was nowhere to be seen; he hadn't followed me. I pressed a hand to my chest and closed the gate, its creak echoing down Main Street. It wasn't until I was halfway home that I really thought about what he had told me.

I stopped in the middle of the road and bent over, my head to my knees. I thought I might be sick.

Lidia was in danger.

They were coming after my mom.

CHAPTER FOUR
The Return

Alessia

Before the sun rose, I hiked over the hill and into the woods. Nerina had marked the hidden door to her hideout with a small cluster of stones, so it took me less than a minute to find, even in the dark. Light flooded into the predawn darkness when I pulled open the door. I figured that Nerina would still be jet-lagged and awake even at this hour.

"*Buongiorno?*" I called out. The smell of coffee grew stronger as I descended the staircase.

"*Pronto,*" Nerina answered.

When I got to the bottom of the staircase, I found a much different hideout than the one I'd seen a day ago. A cable-knit blanket was draped stylishly over the couch, and throw pillows had been arranged on the armchairs. An iPod dock sat on the end table, and the latest issues of *Vogue, Italian Vogue,* and *W* lay on the coffee table. I followed the scent of coffee to the kitchen, which had been tricked out with a very sleek, very silver, and very expensive coffeemaker, food processor, and convection oven.

Nerina sat at the kitchen table, papers and folders piled high in front of her. "Hello, *cara*." She was fully made-up and in high heels—at four o'clock in the morning. "Help yourself to some coffee," she said, waving a hand.

"Thanks." I opened the cabinet above the sink and pulled down a heavy ceramic mug. It looked brand-new. "Uh—where did all this come from?"

"Oh, I took a trip to Bangor yesterday while you were at school." Nerina came over to the coffeemaker and poured herself another cup. "I couldn't possibly be expected to survive on that antique that was in here." She took a sip and winked at me. "We Italians take our *caffè* very seriously. Sit, sit."

We sat at the table, drinking our coffee in silence for a few minutes. Nerina wasn't kidding; it was the best cup I'd had in a long time. I finished it and poured myself another. I was going on practically no sleep for the past two nights; it was definitely a two-cup morning.

"So what is all this?" I asked when I sat back down. I rested my hand on the top of a stack of folders.

"Everything I've collected on the Guild." Nerina sighed and ran a manicured fingertip over her bottom lip. "I had so much more, but this is all I had time to take before—" She swallowed and looked away.

I waited for her to say more, but she didn't. I picked up a bright yellow pamphlet from the table. The cover was dominated by a picture of two Africans in tribal dress standing in front of a sign that read Future Home of the

Guild Coffee Plantation. They were smiling broadly at the tall white man with his arms slung over each of their shoulders. My throat went dry. Mr. Wolfe.

I opened the brochure, and my stomach bottomed out. In the center picture, Jonah sat reading to a group of attentive African children. I dropped the brochure as if I'd been burned.

"What's the matter?" Nerina picked up the brochure and raised an eyebrow at me.

"Those people—" I cleared my throat. "That's the Wolfes. They moved here a few months ago with the Guild."

"Ah, yes." Nerina smoothed the brochure open on the table. "I know all about Mr. Wolfe. He's one of the Guild's gruntlings."

"What does that mean?" I crept my fingers over to the open brochure and traced Jonah's figure with my forefinger.

"That's what we call the employees who do the grunt work for the Guild. They go wherever the Guild sends them to do the dirty work. They aren't Malandanti; we're not even sure how much they know about the Malandanti. They're just people who have traded their consciences for a hefty salary and certain privileges."

"Privileges?"

"Well . . ." Nerina dug out a folder from the stack in front of her and flipped it open. "Before the Wolfes moved here, they lived in Fairfield, Connecticut."

I froze, my finger on Picture Jonah's hands.

"Their son got into a bad car accident, and the Guild made it—how you say?—go away."

"How—how did you know that?" I whispered. My voice felt paper thin, on the verge of shredding.

Nerina looked up from the folder. She focused on my finger on Picture Jonah and then on what must have been a stricken look on my face. "Is there something you'd like to tell me, Alessia?"

I knew I had to say something, but I didn't know how much I could. "That's his son, Jonah. In the picture. We dated for a while, but we broke up. Last month."

Nerina laid her hand on mine. "I'm sorry, *cara*. Love is never easy to lose."

I jerked my head up. It was the first time an adult had ever acknowledged that what Jonah and I had had was love and not some childish fling. Before I could stop myself, the rest of the truth tumbled out of my mouth. "I had to break up with him. He's a Malandante."

Nerina pulled her hand away and stood up. She walked over to the counter and pushed against it, her back to me. I clamped my palm over my mouth. Why the *hell* did I tell her that? What was I thinking? Honesty was not always the best policy. "Look," I said, "Heath knows about this, and he said as long as it doesn't get to me when we're at the Waterfall it would be okay and we didn't have to tell the rest of the Clan—"

"Alessia." Nerina turned around.

At the sight of her face, I pushed back my chair an

inch. She didn't look angry, just fierce, like whatever beast she transformed into lurked just beneath the surface of her skin. She came around the table and squatted next to my chair—not an easy feat in four-inch heels. "I know what it is like to love someone who is forbidden to you," she said, and for the thousandth time since she arrived, I wondered about her history with Heath. "I am sorry that happened to you."

"Uh, thanks." I looked down at our entwined hands. "I'm okay, though."

Nerina raised an eyebrow. "Is it definitely over?"

"Yeah. I mean, I saw him last night, but it is over."

"Last night?"

I thought I might turn to ash beneath her gaze. "Only because he had information for me."

"And what if that had been a trap?" Nerina rose and towered over me. "Alessia, there is no one who understands the power of the heart better than I do. But you cannot allow your heart to be so foolish. He is a Malandante. That is *finito*, the end of the story. You cannot be with him. Ever. *Capire?*"

"*Capire.*" I spread my palm flat over the brochure. "But I told you this for a reason. When I saw him last night, he told me the Guild is suspicious of my mom."

"Why?"

"Because the magic didn't work on her."

Nerina's brow creased in confusion.

"When Mr. Wolfe first came here, he gave a

presentation about the power plant they wanted to build over the Waterfall," I explained. "Most of the town showed up. He did something at the meeting, some kind of magic to make everyone agree to the plan. We—the Clan—figured it out." I tucked one leg up onto the chair and rested my chin on my knee. "But my mom didn't go to the meeting, so Mr. Wolfe came to the house. He tried to use the same magic, but it didn't work."

"Ah. Yes." Nerina dropped back into her chair. "The amulet."

I stared at her. "How did you know about that?"

She shrugged. "Because I put it there. When I was here, fifty years ago, building this." She waved her hand, indicating the whole of her hideout.

No wonder she knew where the door was; she'd been the architect. "You were here fifty years ago? Did you know my grandparents?" My nails scraped against the tabletop. "Did they know about the Benandanti?" *Did my father?* I couldn't quite give voice to that thought.

"So now the Guild wants to know why the magic didn't work in your house," Nerina mused.

It didn't escape me that she had pointedly ignored my last question. I decided not to press it; after all, she'd let me off the hook with Jonah when I knew I could've been in a lot more trouble about that. Besides, whatever had happened on the farm fifty years ago didn't exactly matter in the here and now. I pushed off the chair and paced the length of the little kitchen. "What if they suspect Lidia

Fremont Library

Customer name: Hsu, Lee Chou

Title: In the mouth of the wolf / Nicole Maggi
ID: 31357049827901
Due: 11-19-15

Total items: 1
10/29/2015 1:30 PM

LIBRARY HOURS
Monday & Tuesday 1-9, Wednesday 12-6
Thursday & Friday 11-6 Saturday 10-5
Sunday 1-5

TO RENEW:

VISIT US ONLINE AT
www.aclibrary.org or

BY PHONE
Call 510-790-8096

(For information on receiving Text Messages,
please see link below.
http://guides.aclibrary.org/sms. Standard text
rates apply)

of being a Benandante? They'll come after her—and it'll be all my fault." I rubbed my hands over my face. "What should I do? Should I tell her?"

"No." Nerina came over to me and put an arm around my shoulders. "It will just put her in more danger." She walked me into the living room and ushered me to the couch. "The amulet will protect her—and you—from any magic they try to do in the house. And if they use violence, they'll just raise suspicion."

"I don't know about that. They already burned down our barn."

Nerina grimaced. "Yes, Heath told me about that." She ran a hand through her hair. "Will it ease your mind a little if I tell you I'll watch out for her? Don't worry. I'll be stealthy so she doesn't suspect anything," she added with a wink.

"That would be great. Thank you."

Nerina got to her feet. "The sun is almost up, *cara*."

I didn't move. "Nerina, I've been thinking about something. Since I talked to Jonah."

"*Sì?*"

"Why *doesn't* the Benandanti use magic too? We must have it, right?"

Nerina walked in a slow circle around the coffee table, her heels clicking on the hard floor, and paused at the edge of the armchair. "The Benandanti most certainly has magic," she said quietly. She picked at an invisible thread on the armchair for a moment before facing me. "Alessia, I am going to tell you something that I would appreciate you keep to yourself. Until I tell the rest of the Clan."

"Okay." I sat up a little straighter. Heath and the others in the Clan—particularly the Stag—were always keeping things from me, saying I was too inexperienced or too impetuous or too something. Apparently Nerina had taken seriously my assertion the other night that I wasn't a child.

"Before the Malandanti attacked us in Friuli, the *Concilio* was"—she looked at the ceiling as she searched for the right word—"troubled."

My heart skittered a little. "What do you mean?"

She sank into the armchair and leaned toward me, her elbows digging into her knees. "We knew we were losing the war, but we disagreed on strategy. Although we controlled fewer sites than the Malandanti, we do have powerful magic—or at least the knowledge of it. But some of the *Concilio* didn't think we should use it."

"Why not?"

Her mouth twisted. "To do so, they said, would lower us to the same level as the Malandanti."

I shook my head. "But the war is already being waged on the lower level."

Nerina met my eyes. A hint of a smile pulled at her lips. "Alessia, I think you and I are going to get along very well." She stood up. "And now, you should really get home before Lidia finds you gone."

She walked me to the bottom of the staircase. I paused

on the first step. "Is that why the Malandanti were able to attack the *Concilio*? Because you were a divided front?"

"There are those in the *Concilio* who would deny that with their last breath, but yes, I believe it is." She flung her arms wide. "And look where it got us. We are more divided than ever."

The house was ablaze with light when I crested the hill on my way back from Nerina's. The sun had peeked over the treetops and gilded the grass. I held close the basket of eggs I'd collected from the hens. I hadn't been completely useless at three o'clock this morning; I'd thought to bring the basket in case I ran into Lidia on my way back.

I expected to find her at the stove when I came in through the back door to the kitchen, but instead, I glimpsed her rushing around the living room. "Mom?"

"Alessia! Good. You're back." She skidded into the kitchen, one shoe on, the other clutched in a hand. "Have you seen my shoe? I can't find it anywhere!"

"Uh, Mom." I set the basket of eggs on the table. "You're holding it."

She stared at me for a second. Then she looked down at the shoe in her hand. "Oh, *mio Dio*," she moaned and hit herself lightly in the head with the shoe. She sank into one of the chairs at the kitchen table and pulled the shoe on. "I need my coffee."

Nerina's got a fresh pot in her underground hideaway.

"Do you want me to make some?"

"No, *cara*, I don't have time." She stood, tucking errant strands of hair behind her ears. "I have to go."

"Where? What's going on?"

She heaved a deep breath. "He's back. Ed—Mr. Salter. Barb called me this morning. They found him wandering down Main Street about an hour ago."

Barb was Jenny's mom. She always seemed to know everything happening in Twin Willows—much the same way her daughter always knew everything going on at Twin Willows High. "What do you mean, 'found him'? Is he—?"

Lidia grabbed her purse from the counter. "He's okay. Physically, anyway. Barb says—" She pulled her keys out of her bag and turned to me. "Barb says he can't remember anything."

My insides went cold. "I'm going with you."

"*Cara*, no—you have school—"

"Not for another hour and a half. You can drop me off. Where is he?"

"At the Sands's."

I followed Lidia out to the car, my mind whirling. Mr. Salter returned this morning, just hours after I'd yelled at Jonah about his disappearance. I couldn't believe that was a coincidence, not when I knew, in my gut, that the Malandanti had been responsible for Mr. Salter going missing in the first place.

The drive to Jenny's house took less than two minutes—not nearly enough time for me to figure out how to question Mr. Salter without giving any of my secrets away. As we walked up the steps to the front door, I hung back from Lidia and pulled out my cell phone.

> *Mr. Salter's back. Will text you later with more deets.*

I found Heath's number in my contacts and hit Send.

Jenny's home was the kind of place where you could walk in without knocking and be greeted at six o'clock in the morning with a cup of coffee and a muffin. I think that was why my mom got along with them so well; their hospitality reminded her of her neighbors in Italy. So we opened the front door, called out good morning, and found everyone in the kitchen.

Mr. Salter sat at the table, his hands wrapped around a mug of steaming coffee. His eyes glowed when he saw Lidia and me, and he half rose out of his chair. "Hey, Jacobs gals. Feels like it's been forever."

Lidia hugged him tight before he sank back into the chair. "Where were you, Ed?"

He shook his head and looked into his mug. I met Jenny's gaze across the kitchen. She was perched on top of the counter, kicking her legs against the cabinet underneath. I sidled around the table and hitched myself up next to her. Barb handed me a muffin. It was still warm. I was about to bite into it when Jenny muttered under her breath, "It's gluten-free." I set the muffin on the counter and focused on Mr. Salter.

"I think I was at my cabin—you know, up north?"

He hunched one shoulder. "But I don't remember. It's all fuzzy. And I only use that cabin when I go hunting."

"So?" Lidia accepted a cup of coffee from Barb and settled into a chair at the table.

"If I was hunting, where's all the game?" Mr. Salter's mouth pinched. "I've never gone out for a week and come back with nothing to show for it."

"We'd never call your hunting prowess into question," Jenny's dad, Jeff, said. Gentle sarcasm lilted his voice.

I looked over at him. He stood against the sink in the corner of the kitchen, tapping his fingers on his thighs. Being a vegetarian, Jeff was always ribbing Mr. Salter about his hunting.

"So if you weren't at your cabin, where would you have gone?" Lidia asked.

"I don't know." Mr. Salter's eyes shifted from each of us, his cheeks ruddy under our intense scrutiny. He pressed two fingers against his temple. I noticed his hand shook. "I don't know."

"Mr. Salter, do you remember if you talked to anyone? Right before you left?" I asked.

"The last thing I remember is spending the night at your house because of the snowstorm," Mr. Salter said.

I licked my lips. "What I remember is you fighting with Mr. Wolfe."

Everyone looked at me. "What does that have to do with anything?" Jeff asked.

"Well," I said, tiptoeing over my words, "first my

mom protests the Guild's power plant. Then our barn burns down." I pointed at Mr. Salter. "He gets into a fight with one of the Guild's top men and disappears for more than two weeks."

Jenny bumped against my side. "You really are turning into a conspiracy theorist, aren't you?"

"No," I said, sharper than I intended. I forced a shrug. "It just seems like a lot of . . . bad stuff has happened since the Guild came to Twin Willows."

Jeff coughed. "It's a little far-fetched—"

"But not out of the realm of possibility," Barb said. A look passed between them, something deeper than I could read.

Jenny hopped off the counter. "I'd love to stay and fight corporate America, but we gotta get to school."

"I'll drive you," Barb offered.

"Lidia," Mr. Salter said, "will you come to my store with me? I can only imagine what's piled up in there."

"Of course." Lidia patted Mr. Salter's hand, holding it there a little longer than necessary.

I watched this little exchange, my brow furrowed, until Jenny tugged on my arm. "See you later, Mom," I said.

"Have a good day, *cara*." She blew me a little kiss and turned back to Mr. Salter.

"How weird is that?" Jenny said after we'd gotten out of the car in front of the school. "Losing your memory? I thought that only happened on soap operas."

"Yeah, it's pretty weird." I chewed at my bottom lip

until I tasted blood on my tongue. It wasn't that weird—but Jenny didn't know what I did.

The Malandanti ruled a site in the Congo that had the power of controlling minds. And I was pretty sure that making someone lose his memory for two weeks fell under the heading of Mind Control.

Lidia was still at Mr. Salter's store when I got home from school. There was a message on my cell telling me she'd be home in time for dinner. I forced myself to focus on homework while I waited for her. The last thing I wanted was for Principal Morrissey to call her in for a conference and tell her how behind I had fallen.

But it was close to impossible to maintain my focus in school when I had Jonah sitting in front of or behind or next to me in almost every class. We didn't exchange a single word, and he didn't try to pass me a note, but his constant presence was like a brick wall I kept bumping into. So when Lidia came home, only about half my homework was done.

"How's Mr. Salter?" I asked while she bustled around the kitchen, making dinner.

She shook her head and dipped her wooden spoon into the sauce that simmered on the stove. "Not great."

"What, the sauce? Or Mr. Salter?"

"Mr. Salter. Ed." Lidia laid the spoon in its little cradle on the countertop and faced me. "Imagine how you would feel if you simply could not remember what happened for the last two weeks."

"Yeah, I'd be pretty freaked out." I moved my books to one side of the table and got up to get plates and silverware.

"Well, that's what he is—as you say, freaked out." She turned off the gas on the stove and poured the sauce over the hand-rolled cavatelli waiting in a bowl on the counter. As she carried the bowl to the table, there was a knock on the back door, followed by a creak as it opened. "*Buonasera*, Heath. You're just in time."

"*Buonasera*, Lidia, Alessia." Heath slid into the chair nearest the door. "Thanks for inviting me."

"*Pffft*." Lidia sat down. "You're always invited for dinner. You know that."

In the months that Heath had been working at our farm, he had become more like family. Especially to me, since he was my Guide. And Lidia loved having another mouth to feed.

Lidia and Heath talked all through dinner about the farm and plans for rebuilding the barn once the weather warmed. After dinner, they sat in the living room drinking coffee while I tried to finish my homework. Finally around ten, Lidia excused herself to bed. Heath said good night and ducked out the back door.

But as soon as Lidia was upstairs, he snuck back in. "Don't get too comfortable," he said.

I raised an eyebrow, but before he could explain, my

rib cage tightened. I tried to gasp, but no breath came. My life, my soul, literally squeezed out of me. Heath flung open the door. Wind gusted in, flipping the pages of my biology textbook. *I still have a chapter to read*, I thought, and then I was gone, flying out the door while my body slumped over my unfinished homework.

CHAPTER FIVE

The Meeting

Alessia

The stars looked close enough to touch as I soared toward the woods. Heath's white figure streaked through the brush below. *Why were we Called?* I asked.

Before he could answer, a voice echoed in my mind, one that I had never heard before. *I Called the entire Clan.*

I looked around for the source of the voice, but the blackness of the night enveloped me. *Who said that?*

I did.

White light flooded the darkness. I wheeled, blinded by the brilliant glow. I blinked several times until my eyes adjusted. Then I blinked again, certain that what I was seeing was a hallucination.

The creature that hovered above me—me, the Falcon who could fly as high as the stars—was not like any kind of animal I had ever seen before. It galloped across the sky on legs that looked like a lion's, but its wings unfurled against the darkness just like mine. The creature dipped and came level with me. Its head was that of an eagle, and its sharp eyes were unmistakable. *Nerina?*

Her laughter filled my mind. *Yes, it's me.*

Wh—what are you?

A Griffin, silly.

Yeah, silly me, for not recognizing a Griffin. Considering they didn't exist. *Um—how did that happen?*

The Concilio *all transform into mythical creatures,* Heath said.

Before I became immortal, I turned into a simple lioness, Nerina explained. *But once I tasted the magic, I became this.* She fluttered her enormous wings, buffeting me backward in their wake. *I must say I liked the upgrade.*

King of beasts *and* birds? Yeah, I wouldn't object to that either. I trailed behind her as she loped over the treetops. Her movements were power and grace combined—just like Nerina in her human life. As jarring as it was to see a mythical being come to life, it suited her perfectly.

We passed over the copse of birch trees near the Waterfall, and Nerina dropped toward the ground, grazing the bare branches with her paws. *It's just past these trees,* I told her.

I know, dear.

Sorry—I just figured it's been a while since you've been here—

She laughed again, the sound like church bells inside my head. *When you are on the* Concilio, *all of the sites live inside you. We cannot survive without them, and they cannot survive without us.* As she spoke, the sound of rushing water grew louder, as though it ran through my own veins. *Though it has been many years since I was last here, I can find the Waterfall with my eyes closed.*

We broke through the brush and veered left, soaring over the creek that flooded into the Waterfall. The misty veil surrounding the site glittered and danced like a living thing. I dove through the barrier ahead of Nerina. On the ground below, the rest of the Clan gathered, their auras reflecting off the barrier. I landed on a branch that dangled over the pool below the Waterfall. I turned my head upward.

There was a collective gasp from the Clan as Nerina emerged through the veil. She circled above the Clan and floated down to earth impossibly slowly.

Someone likes to make a big entrance, I thought.

You're not kidding, Heath muttered.

I started; I hadn't meant anyone else to hear that. But apparently Heath was the only one. Everyone else was too distracted by the fantastical Griffin in our midst.

Nerina landed on the muddy bank of the pool, just below the branch where I perched. She folded her great wings around herself, and I was reminded of a picture I'd seen in my French textbook of the gargoyles that populated Notre Dame. The others clustered around her, though Heath hung back, keeping himself outside the bubble of her aura.

Thank you, friends, Nerina said when everyone had settled, *for the warm welcome. It heals my soul to be amongst the finest of the Benandanti.*

I rolled my eyes. Mentally. Falcons can't actually roll their eyes. I know, because I tried once, and it felt like my eyeballs were going to pop out of my head. But really, Nerina was laying it on a bit thick. The finest of the Benandanti? She probably would've said that to whichever Clan she landed in.

Heath tilted his head up, his look piercing. I shifted from one claw to the other. I was sure I'd closed my mind off this time, but it was almost as though he knew what I was thinking anyway. He snorted, puffing a white cloud of air, and settled back on his haunches.

What happened in Friuli? asked the Stag.

My attention slid back to Nerina. She cocked her huge eagle's head and blinked at the Stag. *For centuries, the* Concilio Celeste *has been safely hidden away in the hills of Friuli*, she said. *But nearly three weeks ago the Malandanti, and their* Concilio Argento, *found us.*

How? It was the Eagle. She was perched on one of the Stag's antlers.

We don't know, Nerina answered. She stood and paced in a small circle, the tips of her wings drawing spirals in the mud. *It happened so fast that there was no time to contemplate how we were betrayed.*

The Lynx stretched out his front paws. *What about the others?*

One of the Benandanti from the Friuli Clan was killed.

A collective sorrow clouded my mind. My gaze flickered to each member of my Clan. I never wanted to know what it would be like to lose one of them.

A search has been started for her replacement, and one of the Concilio *stayed behind to aid them.*

And the rest of the Concilio? Heath spoke for the first time. *Where are they?*

In the very brief time we had before we had to flee, Nerina said, *we agreed to scatter to each of the Clans.*

And why did you choose to come to Twin Willows? Heath asked. The line of his jaw was tense as he stared at Nerina. *Why this Clan?*

The Stag swung his head toward Heath, nearly unseating the Eagle. *What does that have—?*

I came to this Clan, Nerina interrupted, *because it is the one best positioned to set my plan into motion.*

Everyone stilled except the Stag, who stepped toward her. *What plan?*

Nerina trotted to the very edge of the pool. She unfurled her wings, stretching them so wide they seemed to encompass the Waterfall and the barrier of protective magic. *The Malandanti are wholly focused on this site. It is the last holdout against them. They need it to gain the power granted by controlling all seven sites.*

We know this, Heath said, and I could feel his impatience like a slippery eel in my mind.

And they have shrouded their presence here behind the veil of legitimacy, Nerina continued, ignoring Heath. She met the Stag's eyes with a calm stare. *We must shred that veil.*

The Guild, he breathed.

Yes. Nerina tucked her wings back against her body. *The Malandanti relies heavily on the Guild—to secure their footing in the communities surrounding the sites and to do their dirty work once there. If we take down the Guild, we will deal a blow to the Malandanti that they will not recover from.*

But the Guild has offices all over the world, said the Lynx. *How can we take them down from here?*

The entire company is focused on Twin Willows right now, Nerina said. *This is the seat of their power. I would not be surprised if the* Concilio Argento *shows up here soon.*

The branch crackled beneath the strong grip of my talons. The Malandanti's *Concilio* in Twin Willows? That would be catastrophic. I fluttered my wings and looked at the other Clan members. None of them seemed surprised by this news; apparently it had already occurred to them that the *Concilio Argento* would show up any day now, and I was just catching up. I tucked my wings back in.

Is this what the Concilio *agreed on before you left Friuli?* the Stag asked.

Nerina turned to the Stag. *We did not have time to discuss this particular issue.*

That wasn't exactly an answer. *We disagreed on strategy,* she'd told me earlier that day. I ruffled my feathers. Well. It seemed Nerina was taking advantage of the chaos that had rousted the *Concilio* from their nest to put forth her own agenda. *The Guild is a huge, multimillion-dollar, Fortune 500 company,* I said. *How on earth can the six of us bring them down?*

It won't be easy. Nerina padded toward me and stopped just beneath my branch. *And everyone will play a part. I want all of you to come up with at least one good, viable idea.*

I stared at her. She didn't blink or look away, but I didn't need to read her mind to know what was going on behind those large, clear eyes. She had no idea how to topple the Guild, and she needed the rest of us to figure it out for her.

We'll meet again in a week. Nerina swung her gaze away from me and faced the Clan. *Any questions?*

Yes, Heath said. *How exactly—?*

Good. In bocca al lupo, Nerina said, giving the blessing that all Benandanti used. *May the wolf hold you in its mouth*. The crystalline magic of the barrier illuminated her as she passed through it. I shot a look at Heath, whose blue eyes were narrowed to slits as he glared at Nerina. I tracked him through the woods toward the farm, trying to break into his thoughts, but he had turned them off.

Something silver flashed against a snow-covered pine as I brushed through its needles. I wheeled, peering into every corner around me, but nothing was there. Rising up to the treetops, I tried to reach Heath again, but he was still shut down. A spark of silver winked again.

I veered away from the farm, my feathers cold. Something was following me, and I was pretty sure it was the Raven. That damned aura trick. If it followed me home, it would know who I was. My heart jumped, and I dropped several notches. Below me, Heath's pale form streaked through the trees. If it followed Heath home, it would know who he was, too.

Heath! Heath! I tried to break through to him. No answer. I climbed, my eyes razor focused for another tell-tale glimpse of silver. There it was, just below me, tracking Heath's path . . .

An ungodly sound filled the air, like a hundred different animals screaming in unison. The Raven uncloaked, quivering in midair mere feet away from me. The sound ripped across the forest again. Nerina burst through the trees. Her aura lit up the world, shimmering like a thousand prisms. In the glow of her light, the black feathers of the Raven looked white.

Nerina pounded through the air toward the Raven. For a moment, the Raven hung frozen in shock at the sight of this unearthly creature. I almost laughed at its confusion. But it shook itself into action and bolted toward Nerina, its dark eyes focused on her throat.

I raced behind Nerina, but she reached the Raven before I did. She dodged its attempts to strike her with the grace of a boxer and a ballerina rolled into one. The Raven rushed her. She swiped one of her enormous paws, and the Raven tumbled out of the air, disappearing into the trees below.

What the hell? Heath's thoughts came roaring through.

The Raven was tailing you, Nerina replied. *You need to pay more attention. The Falcon was trying to warn you, and you weren't listening.*

Now they know you're here! Heath headed west, taking the long way back to the farm in case the Raven was still lurking. *You should've stayed hidden!*

They were bound to find out sooner or later.

Later would be better, Heath snapped. *You can bet their own* Concilio *will be here in a matter of days.*

Their own Concilio *was probably on their way anyway, long before they knew I was here,* Nerina said. *They need the Waterfall, and they will muster all their force to get it.*

It was rash, insisted Heath. *You should have—*

Stop! I sliced through their thoughts. *The Raven already suspects we're connected to the farm, and my mother is already in danger. Nerina is right.*

Nerina reversed her course, heading back to the Waterfall. I dipped low, skimming the trees just above Heath as I followed him home. *What was that about?*

She shouldn't have done that. He sounded like a six-year-old, in trouble for roughhousing in the sandbox. *Her being here is the one element of surprise we had, and now it's gone.*

Give it up, Heath. I floated over a branch. *Your attitude toward her is just making you look bad.*

He tilted his head up. *Who's the Guide now?*

I'm serious. We came to the stone wall that bordered the farm. Heath jumped it in one long, graceful leap, the frozen earth crackling beneath his paws as he landed. Somewhere below was Nerina's hideout, filled with expensive appliances and plush throw pillows and all the information she could gather on the Guild. *Besides, I'm far more interested in her plan.*

Or lack thereof?

So he had noticed that too. We crested the hill and passed the ruins of the barn. The light in the kitchen was still on, the back door still open. Heath's body lay in the doorway, with mine slumped over the table just beyond. With a burst of bright light that I hoped wouldn't wake Lidia, we transformed back to human.

I grabbed my coat from the peg by the door and walked with Heath back to his cabin. "So she really has no clue what she's doing?"

Heath sighed. "It's not that. It's just—Nerina tends to make grand plans, which is great, but then she has no practical way of making them happen."

"She thinks big." I folded my arms and hugged myself. "And she needs us to think small." I walked to the window and peered out into the night. The Raven had almost found us out. Even the skies weren't safe for me anymore. I bid Heath good night, walked back to the house, and tiptoed up the stairs and down the hall to my mother's bedroom. I rested my palm on her closed door. If they found out who I was, I knew they'd go after Lidia before they'd come for me. They would make me suffer first.

I turned away from the door, my mind reeling in a dozen directions. Nerina had the grand plan, and I needed the small puzzle piece that would fit into her big picture. But what could I do? I was just a kid. Or at least, I had thought I was before I had been Called. I had grown up a lot in the last couple of months, and I had learned that kids could do a lot more than people gave them credit for.

People underestimate kids. It was true. I climbed into bed and drew my knees up to my chest. It also meant kids could get away with a lot more. Kids could fly under the radar. Nobody suspected kids. In the dark, an idea formed in my mind. I was a kid; Jonah was a kid. And there was one other kid who linked us and could be the key to everything.

CHAPTER SIX

Why You Should Never Talk To Your Twin Brother's
Ex-Girlfriend

Bree

I stood across the street from the school, wondering if I should ditch. I mean, what the hell was the point? There was not one person on this planet who could convince me I needed algebra to survive in the real world. When the Malandanti came calling at my door, they weren't interested in whether I'd read *Wuthering Heights*. And it had taken a skill that I hadn't learned in school to dodge their clutches.

I took a deep drag on my cigarette. The smoke tasted delicious in the morning chill. Kids milled on the lawn in front of the school, but no one seemed to notice me on the other side of Main Street. And that was just fine. You know how people are always asking which superpower you'd rather have—flying or invisibility? Well, I knew what it was like to fly, and I didn't need it. But invisibility? Now, that would come in handy.

"Hey, Bree."

I dropped my cigarette. "Jesus," I hissed, spinning around.

Alessia Jacobs had somehow sidled right up next to

me without my noticing. Great. I stepped off the curb and walked toward school. Guess I wasn't ditching after all.

Alessia jogged to keep up with me, like a freaking puppy dog.

"What the hell do you want, Alessia?"

"I need to talk to you."

"I'm not talking to Jonah for you. No way am I stepping into the middle of that pile of dog shit."

"This isn't about Jonah."

I stopped and cocked my head at her. "Really."

"Really." She laid three fingers over her heart. "I swear."

The warning bell rang. God, I did not want to face first-period English. "Meet me in the auditorium in ten."

"Don't you have a class?"

"Do you want to talk to me or not?"

Kids streamed past us into the building. I could see Alessia itching to join them, like the goody-two-shoes joiner that she was. "Fine," she said and dissolved into the throng of students.

I waited for the second bell before I ducked inside. The hallways were claustrophobic with activity. Josh Baker cornered me outside the auditorium. He leaned in close, his breath hot on my neck. "You in the mood for a free period?"

Free period was Josh's code for let's-find-an-empty-supply-closet-and-make-out. I was definitely not in the mood for a free period. I laid my palm on his chest and ran my finger down to his navel. "Meet me after school."

"I got practice." He slipped his hand under my coat. "Come on, skip English."

Well, I *was* skipping English but not to make out with him. I danced just out of reach of his groping hands. "Skip practice."

"You know I can't."

He caught me by the waist.

I gyrated my hips into him for a moment, my lips at his ear. "Well, then you're out of luck, aren't you?"

The second bell rang. Josh gave a little groan as I pulled away from him. I blew him a kiss and slipped into the auditorium, hiding behind the door until I was certain he hadn't followed me inside. I shrugged my coat off and smoothed my shirt where Josh's wandering hands had wrinkled it. He was getting too easy to lead around on a leash. The last thing I needed was a *boyfriend*.

I tossed my coat on the floor of an alcove at the back of the auditorium and settled in, stretching my legs in front of me. The door opened with a creak.

It took a minute for Alessia to locate me. "Hey," she said, sitting down next to me.

"So what the hell is this about?"

She dug into her backpack and pulled out a Ziploc bag. "Want a biscotti?" she asked, holding the bag out to me.

A sweet almond scent wafted out of the bag. I drew one out and bit into it. "Oh, my God," I said with my mouth full of cookie goodness, before I could stop myself. "This is amazing."

"Yeah, my mom's a really great cook." Alessia nibbled on the edge of her biscotti. "They're better when you dunk them in coffee, but you don't want the crap they serve in the office."

We ate our biscotti in silence. I reached for another, then pulled my hand back. What, she thought she could bribe me with a few tasty cookies? The girl had kidnapped me, for Chrissakes. I folded my arms over my chest. "What do you want, Alessia?"

She brushed crumbs off her sweater and tucked her knees up to her chest. "Um, I have something to ask you. And you can say no, but—"

"No."

Her cheeks reddened. "Can you at least hear me out?"

"Are you freaking kidding me?" My voice echoed in the rafters of the auditorium. Alessia glanced around, but I didn't take my focus off her face. "You kidnapped me, dragged me into that whatever-it-is-you-call-it on your farm, and then tried to attack me. And now you're asking me for a favor?" I pushed myself up on my hands and started to get to my feet. "You're outta your mind."

"Bree, please." She grabbed my arm, forcing me to sit down. "I know what I did was wrong, and I am so, so sorry. I was upset and got totally fixated on the—the Panther—and you got in the middle of it—"

"Because you put me there—"

"And I'm just so sorry." She lowered her gaze so all I could see were the tops of her wet eyelashes. "If there was a way to make it up to you—"

"You can leave me the hell alone." I got to my feet.

Alessia put a hand on my ankle.

I looked down at her. "I'm serious."

"So am I." She raised her eyes. "You wouldn't be helping just me. You'd be helping Jonah."

My breath caught, the taste of smoke and biscotti trapped on my tongue. Slowly, I sank to the floor. "I'm listening. Talk fast."

Alessia swallowed. "We need to take down the Guild."

I didn't need to ask who she meant by *we*.

"And I think one of the best ways to do that is to have someone on the inside."

I shrugged. "Yeah, so?"

She didn't say anything, just swallowed again and searched my face.

My stomach squirmed. "You mean *me*? No. No way."

"Think about it." Alessia leaned toward me, her eyes gleaming. "You're perfectly positioned. You could tell your dad you're interested in the company. He could set you up with an internship or something. No one would suspect you—because you're already connected to the Guild."

"And then what? We brush-pass on our way to biology? Secret meetings under the bleachers?" I shook my head. "This isn't Hollywood, Alessia. These are dangerous people."

"But you would be protected. No one would suspect you, because of your dad."

"And if they found out, not even my dad could

67

protect me." I stood up and stepped back so she couldn't grab my ankle again. "You have a lot of nerve asking me to do this. Especially since I don't owe you anything."

"You're right. You don't owe me anything." Alessia rose and leveled her gaze at me. "But you owe it to Jonah."

Who the hell did she think she was? I slammed my locker shut so hard I heard the books inside tumble off the top shelf onto the floor. I gave the locker an extra kick for good measure and stomped down the hall. Several people scattered out of my path, shooting me dark looks, but I ignored them. Whatever. I didn't need anyone's approval at this place. And I certainly didn't need Alessia-freaking-Jacobs telling me what I should or shouldn't do.

You owe it to Jonah. My ass. If anyone owed anybody anything, he owed it to me for keeping his little secret for as long as I had. He owed it to me for all the times I had saved his skin when he'd go on a bender during the drinking days. A little dart of guilt pierced my gut. *You didn't save his skin when it mattered most,* said that slithery voice inside me. I stomped harder to shut it up. It wasn't my fault what happened in Fairfield.

With my head down, I rounded a corner and smacked into something very solid. "Watch where you're going!"

"Uh, Bree," said a laughing voice, "you're the one watching the floor."

I looked up into the face of Mr. Foster, the teaching

assistant for my English classes. "Sorry. Bad day."

He put a hand on my elbow. With most other teachers, it would've been creepy, but with Mr. Foster, it was actually genuine. "You want to talk about it?"

Sure, dude. My brother's ex-girlfriend just asked me to infiltrate a dangerous organization and spy on them. Let's discuss the Shakespearean themes in that scenario. "No."

He cocked his head. "We missed you in class this morning."

"Yeah, uh—something came up." I looked over his shoulder, beyond to the door that was my escape from this claustrophobic building.

"Well, stop by my classroom after school, and we can go over what you missed." Mr. Foster dropped my elbow. Little creases appeared at the corners of his eyes as he smiled at me, making him look older than he was. "You're a bright girl, Bree. There's no reason for you to fall behind."

"Okay, I'll stop by." I knew there was a slim-to-none chance in hell that I actually would, but the kind look on his face almost made me want to. "See you later." I stepped around him and hustled to the door. Above me, the bell went off, announcing I was officially late for government class. Whatever. Let Clemens report me. Then both the Wolfe twins could be known as screw-ups.

Outside, the wintry air was cold and biting. I stood under the shelter of an overhang and lit a cigarette. The smoke burned my throat with a delicious heat. *You owe it to Jonah*. Fuck her. I blew a ring of smoke and watched the wind tear it apart. She really knew which button to push. I had to give her credit for that at least. She wasn't a total idiot. Not about that, anyway. Funny how she could be so blind about Jonah, but she had me pegged.

I dropped the cigarette, ground it out with my heel, and started walking. I circled the school, around the back to where the track was. And there, under the bleachers, hunched over like a gargoyle, was my brother. I stopped and watched him turn the pages of his book. A hard wind cut across the field; at the same exact time, Jonah and I tugged our coats closer to our throats.

Alessia Jacobs had no freaking idea what it was like to have a twin. It was as though I were standing here in my own skin yet looking across the track field at the other half of myself. How dare she ask me to turn against myself? How could she possibly think that by betraying Jonah, I would be saving him?

"No way in hell," I whispered. That was my answer to Alessia. She could choke on it for all I cared.

CHAPTER SEVEN

The Magic from Angel Falls

Alessia

Bree skipped government class, and I didn't see her for the rest of the day. I toyed with the strap on my backpack as Jenny and I walked home. Bree was probably going to tell me to screw off, and I really couldn't blame her. It had been a long shot to ask her anyway.

"Lessi. Earth to Lessi!" Jenny shook my arm. "God, you haven't heard a word I've said, have you?"

I sighed. "No. I'm sorry."

Jenny rolled her eyes at me. "You know, it's getting old, you being spaced-out all the time."

"I know. I'm sorry. It's just that—"

"Save it. You're lucky I'm so patient, or I would have given up on you weeks ago. Melissa and Carly are just about ready to kiss you off."

I stopped in my tracks. "Are you kidding me?" I kicked at the road and started walking so fast that Jenny had to trot to keep up with me. "After all the crap I've put up with over the years, they're ready to throw me over because I've been distant for a few weeks?" Jenny reached for my arm, but I danced out of her way. "That's bullshit. Seriously."

"Come on, Lessi, give them a break. They're worried about you."

"Oh, really?" I hunched my shoulders. "If they were so worried about me, they'd be asking me what's wrong instead of threatening to end our friendship."

"They're not—" Jenny threw her hands up. "Look, don't get all riled up, okay? We're all just worried about you, and it's frustrating, because you're not talking to us."

I rubbed a hand over my face. "I've had a lot going on, and I don't really want to talk about it." *Actually, I'm not allowed to talk about it*, but I couldn't say that. "Can't you guys just—I don't know—be supportive of me? Silently?"

Jenny linked her arm through mine. "You know we're not very good being silent about *anything*."

I snorted. "Well, try."

When I left Jenny at the turn-off to her house, I watched her walk down the road for a minute before I continued toward the farm. Despite all the other people who had come into my life over the last few months, I needed my friends. I needed the old familiarity of their company and the way they knew everything about me.

My gut twisted. Well, not everything. And that was the problem.

The house was blissfully empty when I opened the door. A note from Lidia on the kitchen table said she'd be at Mr. Salter's until late, helping him with inventory at the store. I held the note for a moment, a little twist in my gut. The kitchen felt cold and empty without Lidia bustling from stove to counter to sink as she cooked dinner. I knew Mr. Salter needed help, but I still felt abandoned.

However, Lidia's absence did open up a world of possibilities. I wasn't on patrol so I had the whole evening luxuriously in front of me. I could catch up on homework that I had fallen woefully behind on, turn on my instant messenger and chat with Carly and Melissa, and be asleep by nine.

But my body had other ideas. As soon as I had settled on my bed with my books spread out in front of me, the pillows beckoned. *I'll just rest my eyes for a moment*, I thought and lay back against the headboard.

An unearthly scream broke the stillness of my bedroom. I jerked awake. Daylight was gone, and the only light in the room was the soft blue glow of my clock. It was nearly ten. I sat up and pressed a hand to my pounding heart. What had I been dreaming about? The scream seemed to come from inside my head . . .

I heard it again, a piercing, animalistic shriek, coming from inside my brain. I clapped my hands over my ears, but at the same time, my chest tightened. My heart churned as it tore me away from my body. I scrambled off the bed and flung open the window an instant before I transformed.

Outside, the night was clear and cold. I hung in the air for a moment, listening. But no other voices invaded my mind. Why had I been Called? On instinct, I turned toward the Waterfall, but before I could open a link to the Benandanti on patrol there, the scream rang through my head again.

This time, a picture accompanied the horrible sound. A huge expanse of green, crisscrossed with red-and-white stripes. I spun around and mounted the wind. It felt incredibly wrong to fly away from the Waterfall, but something—or someone—was Calling for me, and I knew where to find them.

Main Street of Twin Willows lay quiet and sleepy. Soft light seeped into the street from Mr. Salter's hardware store, and one of the waitresses was just locking up at Joe's Coffee Shop as I flew over. I swerved toward the school and skimmed over the rooftop. Unnatural light flickered from beyond the building. For an instant, it looked like the clear, celestial blue of a Benandante's aura, but then something red distorted it.

Another scream echoed through my brain, and the light crackled. I dove over the side of the school toward the football field. The white stripes gleamed on the dark grass, but something blocked the bright insignia in the center of the field. The light flashed again, and in that moment of illumination, I saw who had Called me.

The Lynx lay on the ground, writhing in the shadow of a huge figure. Bloodred bands wrapped around his aura, twisting it this way and that. With every twist, the Lynx yelped. The figure raised its arms—God, it was a *human*—and the bands obeyed the gesture, tightening around the Lynx. His aura ebbed, and the bands grew brighter. The Lynx moaned, an eerie, inhuman sound. I wanted to shut my ears to it. The figure threw his arms above his head, and the bands doubled in size. The Lynx fell silent. That was far more ominous than any moan or scream.

I shrieked, and the dark figure turned.

Watch—out, the Lynx warned me, his voice raspy.

I shot up but not fast enough.

A scarlet band whipped through the air and dragged me down. A sickening sensation swept through me, as if someone were trying to pull my heart out through my mouth. I fell toward the earth, completely weak and helpless under the power of the fiery red band. My aura dimmed. I felt my soul shudder and weaken. I beat my wings in a vain attempt to stay aloft, but I could barely move them an inch.

I hit the earth with a hard thud and lay there, stunned. The figure raised his arms over my head. Another band slithered around me. Pain sliced through me; I was being torn in two by something worse than a knife. My aura sputtered, and the band glistened. That evil man was drawing power from my aura, stealing the life out of me . . .

Out of the corner of my eye, I saw the Lynx struggle upright. He dragged himself toward the figure whose focus was on me now. I could hear the Lynx's panting in my mind, feel the effort it took him to move. With a painful push of energy, the Lynx swiped the hooded man with one of his enormous paws.

The figure fell backward with a cry, and the bands around me disappeared. My aura flickered once and roared back to life. I twitched my wings and flew low to where the hooded man lay. The Lynx took another swipe at the man and hobbled backward.

I rushed at our attacker, but he was fast. He sprang to his feet and dodged me as I dove for him. I tried to snag his hood—I had to know who was under there—but he feinted to the side. He held up his hands, light slithering between his fingers. Time seemed to stop for an instant; I blinked, and the hooded man was gone.

What the—where the hell did he go? I wheeled over and over, trying to see where the man had gone. I skimmed through the bleachers, but they were empty, save for the icicles that gleamed in the moonlight. *How did he do that?*

Magic.

The broken tone of the Lynx's voice made me halt.

He used—magic.

I swept down to the field where the Lynx lay. His side heaved with the effort to breathe. The glow of his aura was fractured, tiny cracks splintering the blue-white light. *What did he do to you?*

The magic . . . from the . . . Angel Falls site, the Lynx panted. *It has . . . the power to . . . suck out . . . your life force.*

Your aura, I breathed. The cracks were multiplying before my eyes, the light leaking away from him. This was magic way beyond my understanding. My wings fluttered, lifting me a few inches off the ground. *I'm going for help.*

The Lynx lifted his head off the ground. *No. Please . . . stay. I don't want . . . to die alone.* He rested his head back down and closed his eyes.

My heart felt squeezed in a too-tight fist. I landed softly next to the Lynx's head. *Don't say that. You're going to be fine—if you let me go for help. The Griffin—she'll know what to do."*

By the time . . . you Call her . . . I'll be gone. His voice in my mind was graceful and quiet, like he was trying to comfort *me.*

No! I closed my eyes and opened them again, unable to deny what was right in front of me. The Lynx's aura was bleeding out from him, disappearing with every passing second. I thought of the Lynx's human form, asleep on his bed or couch or favorite comfy chair in his house, never to wake up. No way was that happening on my watch. I opened my mind to Call Nerina and Heath, but I had never Called anyone before. I didn't know how.

It's okay, the Lynx said, hearing my confusion in his own head. *I knew . . . a long time ago . . . that I would . . . lay down my life . . . for the Benandanti.*

I landed and pressed in close to the Lynx, my head buried in his fur. I knew that falcons couldn't cry, but inside I was swimming in an ocean of tears. *It's not fair.*

I knew . . . what I was getting into . . . when I was Called. The Lynx's breath rattled. *Before I go . . . I want to know—who are you?*

There was never a better time to break a rule I thought was dumb anyway. *Alessia Jacobs.*

There was a catch in my mind as the Lynx gasped. *So young. Too young.*

Apparently not. The Lynx's breathing slowed more and more. I stayed pressed against him even though I knew I could do nothing. *And you—who are you?*

Sam. Sam Foster. I jerked my head up. He was a teaching assistant at the school, a grad student who was Heath's age. I wasn't in his class, but I knew him by sight. All this time, passing him in the halls, and never knowing what we shared.

Will you do something for me? His thoughts seemed fainter in my mind, as though he were speaking to me from very far away.

Yes—anything.

He opened his eyes. They were glassy and unfocused. *Tell the Clan . . . I don't regret . . . anything. And promise me—* His breath came in snatches, with the space of many heartbeats in between. *Promise me . . . you won't let them win.*

I will. I promise. I hopped back a little so he could see me; it suddenly seemed important that the last thing he saw in this life was a friend, a comrade, the shining blue light of a fellow Benandante.

Thank you. His voice in my mind was fading, just like his aura. *In bocca al lupo, Alessia.* His aura flickered once more, like a candle being blown out, and went dark.

CHAPTER EIGHT
The Ascension

Alessia

I let out a keen that echoed across the field. I still wasn't sure how to Call the others, so I simply opened my mind to the vast, cavernous void of the universe and flooded it with my grief.

Within moments, the voices of the other Benandanti tumbled into my brain, crying and questioning. Too many thoughts overlapped for me to pull apart and make sense of. I silenced them all with one answer. *The Lynx is dead.*

I closed my mind off to their grief and listened to the wind. Beside me, the Lynx's body was still warm, and if I didn't think too hard, I could imagine that he was sleeping. I had a horrible brief memory of my father, lying in his casket in the funeral home . . .

A voice broke into my mind's cave. *Where are you?*

It was Heath.

At the school. The football field.

Nerina and I are coming. The other two must stay at the Waterfall. Heath's voice dropped, low and soft. *Just stay strong, Alessia.*

I didn't know how to do that when my feathers felt so heavy I thought I might collapse under their weight. All I wanted was to lie down beside the Lynx and make this all go away. In my mind's eye, I kept seeing the Lynx on the collapsed bridge, the first night I had ever seen any of the Benandanti. He was so graceful, so much power in his sleek body. How could he suddenly be gone?

Bright light pierced the darkness. I jerked upward, spreading my wings wide over the Lynx. But the light was blue and white, the friendly auras of Heath and Nerina. She descended from the air over the field as he raced through the open space in the bleachers. I fluttered down to the ground and folded my wings in tight. But not even my own warmth could banish the cold that snaked through me.

Heath slowed. His footsteps heavy, he padded around the Lynx. A small, sad whine escaped his throat. He lay on his belly and pressed his nose to the Lynx's, as if he were trying to breathe life back into a place that couldn't hold it anymore.

Nerina landed nearby and walked to us, her long wings dragging in the stubby grass. Her graceful neck arched over the Lynx as she surveyed his body, then turned to me. *What happened?* she asked, her voice gentle.

He Called me, I said. *I don't know why he Called just me—*

He didn't, Heath said. *He tried to reach the rest of us, but he was too weak. You were the closest in proximity.*

I heard again the scream that had woken me up, that

had dragged me out of bed. *When I got here*, I continued, *there was someone else—a man—*

Nerina cocked her head, her fierce eyes fixed on me. *What did he look like?*

I—I don't know. I tried to remember every detail of the hooded figure's appearance, but all I could see were his hands, raised, twisting bloody bands of magic around the Lynx.

Ah, Nerina breathed. She stepped back and paced in a long arc around the Lynx's body. I blinked, and she looked at me. *No*, she said, *keep the picture of him in your mind.* She was reading the image, looking for details in my memory.

After a long moment, I asked, *Do you know who he is?*

No, but I know what he is. At the exact spot where the man had disappeared, she sniffed the air. *I can sense the remnants of magic. Angel Falls, is that right?*

Yes. My feathers rustled as a shiver ran through me. *That's what the Lynx said. Before he—*

Heath snapped his jaw. *So it's true. They're using mages, just as you suspected.*

Yes. Nerina looked at the Lynx's lifeless form. *And now I have proof.*

I looked between them. *Excuse me, but what are mages?*

People who are skilled in magic, Heath said. *They aren't Malandanti in that they can't transform—*

But they aid the Malandanti by using the magic culled from the sites, Nerina continued for him. *It is an ancient tradition amongst the Clans—and once upon a time the Benandanti used mages, too.*

Why don't we? I unfolded my wings. *If the Malandanti are using them, we should be too! We could have prevented this.* I pushed off the ground, letting the tips of my wings brush the Lynx's silver fur as I rose.

Nerina watched me as I flew in a circle above her head. *My dear, you are—as they say—preaching to the choir.* Her eyes gleamed like two dark halos. *I have long argued that we needed to bring back the mages, but I was outvoted.*

I beat my wings hard against the cold and soared away from the center of the field. Now I understood what Nerina had meant when she said the *Concilio* had disagreed on strategy. And their unwillingness to "lower" themselves to the Malandanti's level had gotten the Lynx killed. I swept over the top of the bleachers and turned toward the school.

Alessia. Heath's voice slowed my flight. *We need you here.*

I just want to go home. I wanted to be back in my safe skin, away from this place. I didn't want to look at the Lynx's body anymore, the empty shell where his soul should be—

Wait a minute. The Lynx's body was Sam Foster's soul. How had it not just disappeared when he died? I turned slowly back to the field. *Heath? How—?*

Exactly. That's why we need you back here. We need at least three Benandanti to perform the ritual.

I glided down to where Heath stood, next to the Lynx.

Nerina trotted in a circle around the three of us. Particles of light fell from her wingtips as they trailed along the ground, illuminating the earth. When the glowing circle was complete, she stepped inside. *You go there*, she said, directing me to the Lynx's right. I hovered just above the ground, my wings jittery—exactly what was this "ritual"?

Heath took position at the left and Nerina at the Lynx's head. The moment we were all in place, the light multiplied, stretching out to form a protective bubble around us.

Nerina bent her head to the Lynx, her beak brushing his throat. All at once, his aura flared to life again. I jerked, my heart in my throat, and thought for one crazy-happy instant that Nerina had the power to resurrect the dead.

The Lynx's aura spilled over on itself and encircled his body. The light shifted and moved, a million crystalline beams dancing as one. Buoyed by his aura, the Lynx's body rose, higher and higher, until it hung above our heads. I stared at it, frozen with wonder. What was happening?

Something tugged on my heart, gentler than the Call but still with that bittersweet ache of breaking apart. I looked over at Heath. A thread of shimmering blue-white light had separated from his aura and was feeding into the cocoon that surrounded the Lynx. The same thing was happening to Nerina. I twisted my head and saw that my own aura was offering up to the Lynx, gifting a small piece of my essence to him . . .

Slowly, the Lynx disappeared, swallowed by the

brilliant cocoon. Then, like a supernova flaming out at the end of its life, the cocoon of light shattered into a million pieces. They fell like snow around us. When the last particle of light had fallen, the bubble that surrounded us dissipated and blew away on the wind.

He's gone, Nerina whispered. *His soul has ascended.*

We were silent for a long moment. As small as that thread of my aura had been, I felt its absence, a hole inside me that nothing could fill.

Nerina turned to me, her eyes gentle. *It hurts, doesn't it?*

Why? My voice wavered, my mind crying where my eyes could not. *Why do I feel so lonely?*

Because a piece of you has been lost. All members of a Clan are connected; when one dies, part of you dies. Until we find a replacement for the Lynx, we will not feel whole again.

I knew it could take months to find a new Benandante; I could not imagine feeling like this for that long.

Heath trotted over and nudged me with his soft, wet nose. *It's okay,* he said softly, speaking to me alone. *We have each other.*

It would have to be enough. But as I flew home on the cold wind, icicles on my feathers, I wasn't sure it was.

CHAPTER NINE

Aw, Crap

Bree

I knew it was going to be a bad day when I got downstairs in the morning and found my mother smoking a cigarette in the kitchen. She smoked only under two conditions: my father was out of the house, and she was mad at one of her kids.

She stubbed the cigarette out in an old, chipped ashtray and blocked my path to the refrigerator. "I got an e-mail from your school."

I loved how she called it *my* school, like it was *my* decision to go there.

"They said you skipped your government class yesterday."

And my English class, but I guess they'd given that one to me as a freebie. "I had something to do." I reached around her to open the fridge and pulled out an apple.

Mom sighed. "What could you possibly have to do, other than be in class?"

I shrugged. "Save the world?"

She searched my face, her eyes unreadable. "Is that a joke?"

"If you want it to be."

Mom grabbed my arm, hard. "Bree, you are on warning from Principal Morrissey. And that's *not* a joke. I thought things were going to be different here. I thought we had decided to start over here."

I yanked my arm out of her grasp. "No, *you* decided that. Not me. I never wanted to come here." I slammed out the front door, ignoring her as she called after me, and headed up the driveway.

Footsteps pounded after me. I spun around, but it was just Jonah. "Guess who's the bad twin today," I said, not slowing down.

He fell into step beside me. "I could use a break."

"I didn't do it as a favor to you." I glanced at him out of the corner of my eye. *You owe it to Jonah.* I clenched my jaw. I had already decided to say no; why was her stupid voice still in my head?

"What did you do?"

"Skipped class." I smirked. "I know, that's small-time for you."

"Hell, yeah." Jonah elbowed me. "You hang with the big boys, and I'll teach you how to skip a whole semester."

"And still get a B, right?" I nudged him back. "Jonah?"

He wasn't listening; he was squinting down Main Street. I followed his gaze. There was a crowd outside the school, much larger than the normal milling-around-before-the-bell crowd. As we got closer, I could see bright yellow police tape stretched across the front steps. "Whoa."

We picked up our pace. When we reached the edge of the crowd, Principal Morrissey came out through the front doors of the school, a police officer and a janitor trailing behind. They bent their heads together for a few minutes while the officer took notes on a little pad in his hands.

I grabbed a blonde chick I knew from my Spanish class. "What's going on?"

"A teacher died in one of the classrooms," she said, her eyes wide. "I guess the janitor found him early this morning."

"Which one?"

"I don't know—down the English hallway."

I rolled my eyes heavenward. "Which *teacher*, genius."

She pulled away from me. "You are such a bitch, Bree." And she flounced away, her ponytail swinging, without telling me who had died.

I turned to Jonah. His face was pale, his bottom lip bleeding from where he'd evidently bit it. "What's up?"

He swallowed and looked over my shoulder.

I spun around, not surprised to see Alessia standing right behind me. What was surprising was the fact that her face was streaked with tears, her eyes overly bright. My gut squirmed a little. "Wha—?"

"Get out of my sight," Alessia growled. I stared at her for a second before I realized she wasn't talking to me. She was talking to Jonah. "I can't stand to look at you right now."

I expected him to protest, but he must have read

something in her face that I couldn't see. Without a word, he skirted the crowd and went around the side of the school, no doubt to seek refuge under the bleachers. Guess he was taking over the role of Bad Twin after all. I turned back to Alessia. "What the hell is wrong with you?"

She met my eyes and sniffled.

I felt that squiggle in my gut again. "The teacher who died—he was one of yours, wasn't he?"

She nodded. A fresh tear spilled onto her cheek.

"Who was it?"

She took a deep breath. "Mr.—Sam. Sam Foster."

I felt a punch right through my rib cage, hard and fast. "No." My feet backed up of their own accord, across the sidewalk and the lawn, until they couldn't carry me anymore. I sat down on the cold ground. On the opposite end of the lawn, the janitor gestured with his hands while the officer listened. Everything seemed stark and separate, like puzzle pieces that just wouldn't fit together. "I saw him yesterday. I talked to him. How can he be—?" I shook my head, unable to finish the sentence.

"It happened last night." Alessia knelt in front of me. "I was there. He was killed by the Malandanti."

The breath left my body.

I saw again the look on Alessia's face as she'd told Jonah to get out of her sight.

"Was it—? Tell me it wasn't—"

"He wasn't there." She glanced aside, as if she could feel his presence even though he was nowhere to be seen.

"But I don't know that he wasn't involved."

"No." I shook my head so hard that a hot crick shot up my neck. "He wasn't. He couldn't be."

"Yes, he could!" Alessia grabbed my arms, her fingers digging deep into my biceps. "Don't you get it yet? People are *dying*, Bree!"

"But it's not my fight!" I wrenched away. "I don't want to be involved. I just want to stay—"

"Stay where?" She leaned forward on her hands to peer into my face. "In the middle, where you could get squashed like a bug? Yeah, that's a lot safer than choosing sides."

"But I could be next," I whispered. "I could be the next Sam Foster."

"Yeah." Alessia looked straight into my eyes, her gaze unflinching. "Or it could be Jonah."

God, I had underestimated her. I had completely overlooked how calculating she could be, knowing the exact thing to say. I hated Jonah more than anything at that moment, hated the random event in nature that had caused us to share a womb. I did owe it to him, for being the other half of myself. And for Fairfield. I had failed him then, and I had felt that failure in my own soul. If I failed him now, I would lose myself.

"Okay," I said, fast before I thought of the million other reasons to say no. "What do you need me to do?"

Alessia glanced at the school. There were still kids and teachers milling around outside. It was well into first period; no way were we having classes today. Alessia rocked back onto her feet and stood up. "Come with me."

I fell into step with her as we walked quickly away from the school. God, if unassuming Mr. Foster was a Benandante, there were sure to be Malandanti running around the school, too. I stared at the janitor as we passed him on the sidewalk. Was he the asshole who'd killed sweet Sam Foster? Or the policeman taking his statement? I looked around wildly. It could be anyone.

I wrapped my arms around myself and followed Alessia all the way to her farm. It wasn't until we reached the top of her driveway that I stopped and broke the silence. "Um, no."

Alessia squinted at me. "No, what?"

"No way am I going back to that creepy cheese cave with you." I crossed my arms. "I'm not going to fall for that twice."

"We're not going to the Cave." Alessia started down the driveway, breaking into a slow jog. After a moment, I followed.

When we came around the side of the house, I halted. I had only seen the ruins of her barn at night. In broad daylight, it was a hundred times more depressing. "Jeez. I didn't realize how destroyed it was."

Alessia touched one of the charred posts that stuck up out of the ground. "The Malandanti did this."

I cocked my head. "Are you sure?"

She kicked the post. "I chased one of them away from here right before the fire started. I'm sure." She jerked her head toward the hillside. "Come on. We're going to the woods."

As we hiked over the hillside, I tried not to think about all the fairy tales in which young maidens were lured into creepy, dark woods to have their hearts cut out. I glanced at Alessia. She *had* seemed sincere the other day when she'd apologized for the Cave incident. And she did love Jonah. That much I could see all over her face.

The ground was hard with patches of old snow as we passed under the tall trees. Bare branches clacked overhead in the chilly wind. A little ways into the woods, we came to a crumbling stone wall.

Alessia stopped and ran a hand lightly over the moss-covered stones. "You might want to move to your right."

"Why?" I asked but did it anyway.

Alessia pushed on the wall. A trapdoor opened in the ground at the exact spot where I had been standing.

My jaw dropped as a staircase appeared, spiraling into the earth. "What the hell?"

Alessia grinned. "Pretty cool, huh? Not even my mom knows about this." She started down the staircase. I looked all around. Not a soul in sight, not even a squirrel. This was a thousand times worse than the Cave. At least someone else knew about that place. I could disappear down this staircase and never come up, and no one would ever know. What was Alessia smoking that she thought I'd just follow her down the rabbit hole?

She peeked up from the bottom of the stairs. "Are you coming?"

"Uh—" I pulled my scarf off and flung it over the stone that Alessia had pushed to open the trapdoor. A crumb for the search posse. "Yeah."

The air warmed and thickened with each step down. When I got to the bottom, I was in one of the coolest rooms I'd ever seen. The walls were deep and shockingly red, and the roots of some ancient tree spanned one of them. Modern furniture was tastefully arranged, with splashes of color on a throw pillow or a rug here and there. The whole room beckoned, inviting me to stay for a long time. And the air smelled like coffee and cinnamon. It didn't feel like a murder room . . .

A tall, curvy woman who looked like she modeled for Botticelli rose from the velvet couch. "Alessia," she said in a delicately accented voice, "who is this?"

"Nerina," Alessia said, bouncing on the balls of her feet, "I've found us a spy."

CHAPTER TEN
The Bad Idea

Alessia

I stood under the tree on the school's lawn, staring at the front doors. Was there anything more pointless than school right now? The thought of sitting at those little desks made me want to scream. There was no way I would make it through the whole day . . .

"Hey." Jenny nudged me. "Coming in?"

I sighed. "Yeah." Nerina had told me yesterday that it was important to keep up appearances, and unfortunately, going to school fell under that heading. She'd said this to both me and Bree. I shook my head a little, prompting a strange glance from Jenny. It was bizarre to think of Bree in the same breath as Nerina.

At the top of the steps, I turned to look back at Main Street. Half a block away, Bree walked toward the school, a cigarette dangling from her mouth. My gut hollowed out; Jonah was just behind her, his collar turned up against the cold. I watched as Bree took the cigarette away from her lips and said something to her brother. My fingers tapped fast against my thigh. I still had no idea whether I could trust her, whether she was telling Jonah *right now* how I'd asked her to betray him . . .

That was the nature of spies, I was learning. You had to trust them even though their entire job was based on lying.

I followed Jenny through the double doors. "See you in French." That was another punch to my gut; I'd have to see Jonah in French, too, and I didn't yet know how to be in the same room with him.

The mood in the office was strained and sad, with everyone trying desperately to act normal even though they were all upset about Sam. I exiled myself to the corner with the shredder and a stack of papers almost as tall as me. Half an hour later, I was clearing a jam when a voice muttered in my ear, "We're in business."

My hand slipped and hit the Shred button. I jerked back as the machine rumbled back to life, spitting out bits of paper onto the floor. "Jesus!" I punched the Stop button and looked up.

Bree stood over me, her hand splayed over the stack of unshredded paper.

"I could've lost a finger."

Bree shrugged. "But you didn't." She glanced around. "Can we talk?"

I motioned for her to sit next to me and positioned the shredder in front of her so she was blocked from the secretaries' views. I turned the shredder on and fed it continuously, the noise covering our voices.

"My dad practically did cartwheels when I told him I wanted an internship at the Guild," she said. "I think I actually saw a tear in his eye."

"Okay. Is he setting it up?"

She nodded. "He said he'd get me in next week. I'll have an ID badge and everything. All-access pass, baby."

"Awesome." At least one thing was going right. "I'm sure Nerina will have instructions once you're in."

Bree traced the edge of the papers waiting to be shredded. "What's her deal, anyway?"

I paused and looked at her. Nerina had told her about the *Concilio* and the hierarchy of the Clans, but I didn't know how much I should tell her beyond that. "What do you mean?"

"I mean, she's, like, our age. How did she get on the Council thingy?"

"*Concilio.*"

"Whatever. I mean, how much experience can she have? Unless she got on the Council by . . . you know." Bree made an incredibly crude gesture with her hands.

I glared at her. "Actually, she has quite a lot of experience."

Bree snorted. "What, did she get Called when she was like five?"

"She looks pretty good for her age, doesn't she?"

"What do you mean?"

I leaned across the shredder so that I was an inch away from her. "She was born in 1557."

It was with a great sense of pleasure that I watched the blood drain from Bree's face. I sent the last papers through the shredder as she sat stock-still. The bell rang, and I grabbed my bag. "See you later," I said cheerily.

She was still sitting there when I crossed in front of the office windows.

My sense of satisfaction slipped away with each step I took toward French. Maybe he wouldn't be there. Maybe he didn't want to see me as much as I didn't want to see him . . .

But when I rounded the corner into the classroom, he was already sitting in his usual seat, right behind my usual seat. I looked around wildly; maybe someone would switch seats with me. People bustled around me, filling up the chairs that were my only salvation. Finally, I swallowed hard and walked to my seat.

The moment I sat down, a note landed on my desk. I slammed my palm on top of it and crumpled it into a tiny ball. Under the cover of the bell, I twisted around and dropped it on the floor next to Jonah's feet.

"Oh, come on, Alessia," Jonah whispered.

I stared straight ahead. Out of the corner of my eye, I saw Jenny shoot me a glance, but I didn't look at her. The words on the blackboard blurred until I couldn't read them. Behind me, I heard Jonah sigh. My shoulders relaxed a little, and I actually started to pay attention to Madame Dubois.

"Please translate the sentences on page one-sixty-five," she said. "Then pass your work to the student in front of you for review."

I nearly banged my head on my desk. Why couldn't she have told us to pass to our right or our left? *Why was my luck so crappy?* I rushed through my own sentences and passed them to Carly, who sat in front of me. Remembering what Jenny had told me, I gave her a shy smile, which she returned. "Sorry," she mouthed with a nod toward Jonah. I shrugged as if to say, *What can I do?* Like the sight of his handwriting didn't make me want to cry.

After a moment, Jonah's work landed on my desk. I picked up my pen, ready to correct the crap out of it.

I know you're upset.
I can't imagine what you're going through.
I SWEAR I DIDN'T KNOW.
Please talk to me. Please.
The graveyard. Midnight. Tonight.

Was he insane? How stupid did he think I was? I dug my pen in so hard it tore the paper.

Upset is an understatement.
You have no idea what it's like to watch someone die in front of you.
You're a liar. You're a liar you're a liar you're a liar
The thought of talking to you makes me sick.

I flung the paper over my shoulder. Within thirty seconds, it was back on my desk.

I'm not lying. I SWEAR.

I set pen to paper again.

PROVE IT.

His answer was instantaneous.

Fine. Graveyard. Tonight. Midnight.

Well, I'd walked right into that one.

"You have to get your mom to change her mind about Paris." Jenny dipped one of her fries into the little puddle of ketchup on my plate. "It won't be any fun without you."

I looked up from the ketchup doodle I was making with one of my own French fries. I had no idea why I'd bought them; I'd lost my appetite the second Jonah's note landed on my desk. "How'd we get on this topic?"

Melissa flicked a crumb at me. "If you paid attention to our conversation, then you'd know, wouldn't you?" She grinned at me, but I felt the bite in her words.

"Sorry." I pushed my fries away. "I just have a lot on my mind right now."

"And a trip to Paris is the perfect cure for that!" Jenny waved a fry around before popping it into her mouth. I snorted. She was trying to keep us all light and happy and friends, and I had to love her for that.

"Well, unless Lidia gets amnesia or a brain transplant between now and spring break, don't count on it," I said.

Jenny crossed her arms. "Then I'm not going either."

"Don't be a drama queen."

"I'll take your place," Melissa said. She took Spanish, a decision she cursed after finding out about the Paris trip.

"What am I, chopped liver?" Carly said to Jenny. "I'll be there."

"I know," Jenny said, plucking a grape from Carly's Ziploc bag. "It would just be so much better if we were all going." She looked at Melissa. "Including you."

Melissa sighed. "I wish I could switch to French. You know what the big Spanish class trip is this year?" She slumped in her chair. "The Puerto Rican Day parade in Bangor."

Carly laughed.

Melissa shot her a dirty look.

I tapped her foot with mine. "I feel your pain, sister."

"It's totally unfair," Jenny said, though I wasn't sure if she was talking about Lidia or the Puerto Rican Day parade. "But I have an idea to make up for it."

"What's that?" Carly asked, popping a grape into her mouth.

"I think we should go away for a weekend." Jenny looked at each of us in turn. "Just the four of us."

There was a pause while we all took this in. I chewed at my lip. I didn't want to be the first one to shoot it down.

"My parents would never go for that in a million years," Melissa said.

I breathed a sigh of relief and opened my mouth to

say how I would never be able to go either. But before I could speak, Jenny said, "Well, I was thinking we could go to Western Mass to look at colleges." Her eyes sparkled. "Amherst and Williams for sure, and maybe some others. That way, we could sell it as an educational thing."

"You know," Melissa said, "my parents might actually buy that."

Jenny looked at Carly, who finished eating a couple of grapes. "I could tell them I need backups for Juilliard," she said, "which I do considering I'm never gonna get in. And Williams does have a good music program."

All three of them turned to me. I shoved a bunch of cold fries into my mouth and took a really long time to chew and swallow. How could I tell them I couldn't go to college? *Sorry, guys, I have to stay here to protect a magical Waterfall. The fate of the world depends on it . . .*

I looked at their faces, shiny with hope and the promise of an unforeseeable future. While I, meanwhile, saw my own future stretched out before me like one long, narrow road, stuck in this town forever. The fries tasted like sawdust in my throat. Suddenly, I wanted to go away with them more than anything. My desire for it was tangible, burning in my belly. I couldn't go to Paris. I couldn't go to college. At the very least, I could go to Massachusetts with my three best friends. The Benandanti owed me that. "Yeah," I said. "Let's do it."

"You really think your mom will go for it?" Jenny asked

me later when we were walking home from school.

"Go for what?"

She bumped me with her hip. "The girls' weekend, silly. You think Lidia will let you do it?"

"I don't know. I hope so." It wasn't Lidia I was worried about, though. It was Nerina. And Heath. One Clan member down, a Malandante mage on the loose, a spy to oversee . . . Yeah, it wasn't exactly the best time to be jaunting off for the weekend, and who knew if things would be even worse by the time the weekend getaway rolled around? "I'll figure something out." All I could hope was that I could sell it to Nerina as a need-to-keep-my-cover deal. Then I'd worry about Lidia.

"By the way," Jenny said, "what was up with Jonah in French class today?"

My throat went dry. "Wha—what do you mean?"

"The note." She raised an eyebrow. "I mean, he wasn't actually passing you the assignment, was he?"

I shook my head. I desperately wanted to talk to her about Jonah and get her advice. I could talk to Heath about the Clan. I could talk to Nerina about the *Concilio*. God, I could even talk to Bree about the Guild and the Malandanti. But I couldn't talk to anyone about Jonah. Not one single soul. I swallowed hard. "He wants me to meet him tonight."

Jenny stopped in her tracks. "You're not going to, are you?"

"I—I don't know." I really didn't.

"Lessi . . ." Jenny ran a hand through her hair.

Somehow, the gesture made her blonde locks even shinier. "Do you think he wants to get back together?"

"No. *Definitely* not."

"Then what does he want?"

To convince me he's not a murderer. "Um, I'm not sure."

"Well, it's your decision," Jenny said and started walking again. "But I don't know if it's a good idea."

"Oh, it's a bad idea. I have no doubt about that." I looked sideways at her. "Doesn't mean I'm not going, though."

Jenny laughed. After a moment, I joined in and linked my arm through hers. I hadn't laughed in days; it felt strange and good all at once. Even if I was just pretending the only complication in my life was a weirdo ex-boyfriend, it felt good.

"Be careful," Jenny told me when I left her at the turn-off to her house. "And text me details!"

Yeah, right. I could just picture that text.

J not a murderer! 😊 *But still evil.* 🙁

I waved at Jenny until she got to the top of her driveway, then sprinted the rest of the way home.

I didn't have patrol, so I could conceivably sneak out and get to the graveyard. I paced around and around in my room, wearing the rug thin. Was this my life now? Even when I didn't have patrol, I was either plotting to bring down the Guild at Nerina's or sneaking out to see Jonah or—

I squeezed my eyes shut.

Or getting Called by a dying Clan member.

I looked at my bed. There was no way I was going to sleep tonight anyway. I might as well occupy my time with something worthwhile. And finding out whether Jonah had anything to do with Sam's death was definitely worthwhile. At least to me.

The iron gate was slicked with ice when I pushed it open. Smoke-colored clouds covered the moon, and inside the cemetery was pitch-black. I wished I'd thought to bring a flashlight.

I held my hands out, groping for obstacles. As I turned down one row, I stubbed my toe on an old marker, half-sunk into the ground with age. "Dammit." My breath rattled as I waited for the throbbing to subside. This was a mistake. I should have stayed home and tried to get some sleep.

"Hey," a voice muttered in my ear.

I yelped and jumped back, but a hand clamped on my elbow and turned me around. Jonah's pale face loomed out of the darkness.

"What the hell is with you and your sister?" I said. "Did you both take a class on sneaking up on people?"

"Ssshhh." Jonah dragged me into the shadows of a tall mausoleum. "I think I was followed here."

"Are you kidding me?" I yanked my arm out of his grasp. "I'm outta here."

"No, please." The urgency in his voice stopped me. He looked around the corner of the mausoleum. "I don't see anyone. I'm probably just being paranoid."

"Jonah, this is such a bad idea. I shouldn't be here. You shouldn't be here. We should not be meeting like this."

"I know, but—"

The loud snap of a twig shut him up fast. I flattened myself against the mausoleum wall. After a moment, I slid to the edge of the cold marble and peeked out.

Nothing but wind and frost occupied the row between the headstones. I looked around for the telltale light of a Malandante—or a Benandante—but there were only shadows. Still, knowing there was a mage out there, I couldn't trust what I couldn't see. I turned back to Jonah. "We should leave."

"Let's go to the school. Under the bleachers—"

"No."

Jonah flinched at my sharpness.

I inhaled deep. "That's where *it* happened. I'm not going back there."

His eyes met mine, and my breath hitched. His irises were ripe with concern, his gaze like the embrace we couldn't share. I knew I should leave, right now, but when he looked at me like that . . .

"Come on," I said softly. "I know someplace we can go."

He followed me away from the mausoleum. I didn't go back to the front gate; if someone *was* following Jonah, they'd be watching what they thought was the only exit.

But I didn't grow up in Twin Willows without learning some of its secrets.

When we reached the far corner of the graveyard, I felt along the tall, iron fence until I found what I was looking for. One of the rails was bent, the victim of a drunk driver's crash eleven years ago. "After you," I said to Jonah. I turned and swept my gaze all along the silent cemetery. If someone had followed us, they were invisible. I squeezed through the gap in the fence.

"Where are we?" Jonah asked.

"In the mayor's backyard."

"What the hell are we doing there?"

"Nothing. It's just where that gap in the fence lets us out. Follow me." There was a light on in the house; apparently, our fair mayor was a night owl. We edged around the lawn, careful to stay in the shadows.

"This is the town hall," Jonah said when we reached the back door of the building next to the mayor's house. "This is where we're going?"

"Yes." I stretched up onto my tiptoes and felt along the top of the door frame. Years ago, Jenny and I had discovered they kept a hide-a-key up there for whoever was running the early-morning AA meetings. We'd held many a candlelight séance in the basement rec room. I led Jonah down there and stood on the threshold for a moment. It had been years since I had been down here, but the faded carpet, the rickety tables pushed against the walls, the cabinets filled with games and toys—it was all the same. Nothing ever changed in Twin Willows.

Except I was here with Jonah. That was different.

"There should be candles and matches in the cabinet over there," I said, pointing.

A faded, reflective yellow-and-black Fallout Shelter sign on the wall spoke to the room's past purpose, but now I wondered what emergency would bring the whole town down here in the future.

Jonah lit two pillar candles and carried them to the center of the carpet. We sat down cross-legged, facing each other, the candles in between us.

"Okay," I said. "Talk."

"Alessia, I'm really sorry about Mr. Foster. Which one was he?"

I hesitated before answering. "The Lynx."

Jonah looked at his lap. "Which Malandante was it?" His voice was low.

I froze. "What do you mean?"

He wouldn't look up. "Which Malandante killed him?"

I stared at him. Did he really not know? Jonah was good at masking his emotions, but he wasn't so great at acting an emotion he didn't feel. And he didn't seem particularly shut down right now.

I leaned toward him. "Look at me."

He raised his head.

I searched those deep green depths for any hint of pretense. I couldn't find any. But still . . . "You really don't know?"

"Know what? Which of my Clanmates committed

murder? No, I really don't know."

"Wow. You sound kinda down on the Malandanti."

He exhaled hard. One of the candles flickered. "Just tell me which one."

I sat back. "Relax. It wasn't one of your Clanmates. No, it was the crafty little mage you guys employ to do your dirty work."

"Huh?" Confusion clouded his face. "A mage? What's that?"

Okay, now he was acting. He had to be. "Like you don't know."

"Alessia, I really don't." He balled his hands into fists and pressed them against his thighs.

"A mage is someone who can work the magic from the sites," I said softly. "The Lynx was killed with the magic from Angel Falls."

"Well, then, how can you possibly know it was the Malandanti? The mage could have been hired by anyone."

"You're kidding, right?" I pinched my forehead. "Who else wants to kill the Benandanti? Who else even *knows* about us?"

"People like Bree who have refused the Call, for one," Jonah shot back. "You have no proof that this mage guy is connected to the Malandanti."

"And you have no proof that he isn't." My fingernails dug painfully into my palms. "You really had no idea?"

Jonah grabbed my wrists and held my fists in his hands. The candlelight cast shadows on our skin.

"Alessia, whatever you think of me, you have to believe that I didn't know."

I looked down at our hands. It felt as if an electrical current ran through the connection of his body to mine, into my very core. I wanted to believe him. I needed to believe him. But doubts still swirled in my head. "How could your *Concilio* decide something like that without telling your Clan?"

Jonah hunched his shoulders. "They might not have."

"What do you mean?"

His grip on my hands slackened. "I— They don't tell me everything."

I swallowed, trying to keep my face neutral. *Of course* the Malandanti ran their Clans less democratically than the Benandanti did. Why was this a surprise to me?

Jonah looked past me, to the faded *What To Do In An Emergency!* poster on the wall. "I'm sort of on probation right now."

"*Probation?*"

"Yeah." His chest moved up and down, as though each breath cost him a great effort. "They— My Guide was kinda pissed that I didn't, um, hurt you when I had the chance."

I thought back to that night when the Panther had caught me in his mouth. One tiny movement of his jaw, and I would have been dead. I shivered. Jonah had saved my life . . . at the risk of his own, it seemed.

"Sorry," I whispered, then clamped my lips together.

Sorry for what? That he hadn't killed me? That he was now in trouble for not killing me? That wasn't *my* fault. I drew my hands slowly out of his and tucked them into my own lap.

Jonah leaned toward me. "I'm not sorry," he breathed. Even if I wanted to look away from those green eyes, I couldn't. "Alessia—"

"Don't. I believe you. But just because you didn't help kill Mr. Foster, just because you didn't kill me—it doesn't change anything. You're still one of *them*—"

He jerked back. "You're right," he said, unfolding himself to a standing position. "We shouldn't be meeting like this." The candle flames wavered in his wake.

A gust of wind blew through the rec room when he opened the door. The candles went out, and the door slammed shut, leaving me in utter darkness.

CHAPTER ELEVEN
The Dinner Party

Alessia

The bell chimed over the door to the hardware store, giving me a warm little jolt as I walked in. It had been over a month since I'd stepped inside, and even though Mr. Salter hadn't reopened, it felt good to be there. Like at least one thing in my life was returning to normal.

"In here," Mr. Salter called from the office. I slid behind the counter and stopped in the doorway to the office.

Mr. Salter sat at the desk, the glow from the ancient PC reflected on his face. My mother stood over him, pointing at the screen. "Now click on that with the mice."

I rolled my eyes. "You two are like the blind leading the blind." I jerked a thumb at Mr. Salter, who obediently rose from the chair to let me sit. "What do you need?"

"Sales receipts," Mr. Salter said. "There's a folder somewhere . . ."

I found it on the desktop and opened it. Scrolling down the list, I asked, "What do you need these for?"

"Trying to see if any of them jog my memory," Mr. Salter said.

Lidia rubbed his arm, and he covered her hand with his, lingering there a little longer than friendly support called for.

I pressed my lips together and faced the screen. "Okay, the last receipt was from December thirteenth. The day of the blizzard," I said. I leaned in. "No, wait. There's a receipt from the next day, the fourteenth."

Mr. Salter bent over my side, squinting at the computer. "That can't be right."

"Why not, Ed?" Lidia asked.

He flicked his gaze to her and back to the screen. "Because it was a Sunday. Right? I'm not open on Sundays. And I definitely wouldn't have been open that Sunday. Not with the snow and all."

"Well, there's a receipt." I scrolled down the page, reading line by line. "'NA Moth. Quantity, one.' Time stamped eleven in the morning." I looked up at him. "What's NA Moth?"

"That definitely can't be right." Mr. Salter nudged my shoulder. I got out of the chair, and he slid into it. He pulled the screen to the edge of the desk, so close his nose was almost pressed against it. "It stands for naphthalene mothballs. I haven't stocked those in years. They're illegal."

"Maybe you hit the wrong button on the register by mistake," Lidia said.

"Maybe." Mr. Salter leaned back in the chair. "The time stamp makes sense, though. I left your house that morning around nine or ten and came back here. That's the last thing I remember clearly."

"Maybe someone knocked on the door, needing something in an emergency," I said. *Like a henchman from the Guild.* "You would have opened up for that."

"Yeah, I guess." Deep lines grooved into his forehead. "And if the register did make a mistake in what the item was, that would explain it. But still . . ." He shook his head. "I don't remember."

Lidia put an arm around his shoulders. "We'll ask around town, see if anyone bought something that day. Someone else may remember for you."

He smiled up at her, a tired but sweet expression like he used to give his late wife. Seriously, what was up with him and my mom? I tapped my foot against the leg of the desk. "Is there anything else you need me to do?"

"I'd like to reopen tomorrow," Mr. Salter said. He stood up. Lidia and I followed him back out to the main store. "But the place needs a good cleaning."

I surveyed the register counter, which was covered in dusty piles of unopened mail. "I'll start there."

"And I'll do the floors," Lidia said, heading for the broom in the corner by the door.

Mr. Salter turned on the little radio by the register, and we cleaned to the sounds of country music for over an hour. I had one more stack of mail to go through when a shadow darkened in the corner of my eye. I looked up. Just outside the plate-glass window, Bree stood, a plume of cigarette smoke crowning her head.

I glanced around, but Lidia was mopping the back of the store, and Mr. Salter was in the office. Moving fast, I slipped out the front door, hoping the music would cover the sound of the bell.

I shivered when the cold air hit me. "What's up, Bree?"

She dropped her cigarette and ground it out with her heel. "I got some information for your girl."

I rolled my eyes. "She's not my girl."

"Whatever. I have information."

"It's about time."

Bree stuck her hands on her hips. "It's only been two weeks since I started my internship." She jabbed a finger in my face. "You think spying is so easy, then *you* do it."

"Oh, relax." I looked back into the store, but Lidia and Mr. Salter were still out of sight. "I can take you to Nerina tonight." I hugged myself and rubbed my arms. "Unless you'd rather go without me?"

"Well, I would, except I'd probably be stuck outside that godforsaken wall looking for the godforsaken secret passage for three days."

I grinned. It was nice to know she needed my help, even if she couldn't say it. "Meet me outside my house—by the barn—at ten thirty."

"Fine." Bree peered into the hardware store. "The prodigal son returns, eh?"

I waved her off. "See you later, Bree." I ducked back inside. Warmth and twangy music washed over me, along with the smell of pine cleaner and sawdust. I pushed away from the door and headed to the counter. "Find anything else?" I called into the office.

"No," came Mr. Salter's voice, a moment before he appeared in the doorway. He leaned against the frame. "But I think I remember that Sunday sale."

"Really?" My heart crept into my throat as I turned to him. "What do you remember?"

He scrunched his face up, as though the act of remembering was strenuous. "Well, it was like you said. Someone knocked on the door, and I opened it."

"Who was it?" *Say it was Mr. Wolfe or his creepy assistant or someone wearing a Guild baseball cap . . .*

"Not someone from Twin Willows, that I remember." Mr. Salter rubbed a hand along his jaw. "Said he got stuck in the storm. I'm pretty sure he bought towrope, though, not an illegal pesticide that I don't carry."

"Well, you must've hit the wrong key on the register," I said, turning back to the last stack of mail. "Like Mom said."

"Yeah, maybe." Mr. Salter disappeared back into the office.

I shuffled the envelopes hard against each other. So it wasn't Mr. Wolfe or someone I knew for sure was connected to the Guild. But that didn't mean the Guild wasn't involved. I mean, some stranger shows up in Twin Willows right before Mr. Salter's memory goes missing? That couldn't be a coincidence.

I froze. A stranger . . . a lost memory . . .

The Guild had used mind tricks before. Tricks they

pulled from the power of the Congo site.

And just *who* had the ability to wield that power?

A mage.

Bree was sitting on our front stoop when Lidia and I pulled into the driveway at dusk. I clenched my jaw as I opened the car door. Why couldn't she ever follow directions? Was it so hard to remember *barn* and *ten thirty*?

"Who's that, *cara*?" Lidia asked, coming around the other side of the car. Behind us in the driveway, Mr. Salter slowed his truck to a stop; Lidia had invited him over for dinner.

"Bree Wolfe. She, uh, is— We're working on a project for school. I forgot that she was coming over."

Lidia put an arm around my waist as we walked toward the house. "Wolfe, eh?"

I sighed. "Mom, don't start. She doesn't have anything to do with the Guild's power plant."

Lidia squeezed my side. "Actually, I was thinking more that she is Jonah's sister."

"Oh." I shrugged. "I tried to get a different partner, but Mr. Clemens wouldn't let me switch."

"What's the project?"

Really, with the twenty questions? "It's, uh, on the local economy. So I'm going to show her the farm, tell her how we operate and stuff." That gave us a good reason to be out in the barn. I had to pat myself on the back; I was getting better at lying.

Bree got to her feet as we approached. Her gaze shifted to Lidia's arm around my waist. She shoved her hands in her coat pockets. "Did I mess up the time?"

Was she kidding? I still wasn't always sure with her. I gave her a big smile. "No, I forgot. But my mom is about to make dinner."

"You're welcome to stay, Bree." Lidia unlocked the front door and let us all in. "Ed's staying, and I'm sure Heath will be up, too."

"Who's Heath?" Bree muttered to me.

"The guy who helps run the farm. He lives in a cabin on the edge of the pasture, so he's over all the time."

And sure enough, no sooner had we all hung up our coats than the back door opened, and Heath dodged in, bringing a wisp of cold air with him. "Saw you guys pull up," he said, unwinding a scarf from around his neck. "Can I help?"

"Why don't you light a fire?" Lidia asked. "It's freezing in here."

Bree wandered around the living room, her fingers trailing over the back of the sofa, the lamp shade, the end table. At the mantel she stopped. "Who's this?" she asked, pointing to a photo of a smiling man and woman standing in front of the barn.

"My grandparents." I came closer so I could peer at the picture too. "My dad's parents. I never knew them. They died in an accident when I was a baby. That's why we moved back here from Italy, to run the farm after they died." I touched the glass lightly, as though somehow I could reach through time and space. My grandparents looked so kind and loving.

"They look happy," Bree said, echoing my thoughts. "Sorry they're dead."

I rolled my eyes at her tactlessness. "Come on. Let's go into the kitchen."

As we bustled about getting dinner ready, Bree sat on one of the kitchen chairs, one foot tucked under her. She seemed to take everything in—how my mother held out the wooden spoon for me to taste the sauce, how Heath pulled vegetables out of the fridge to chop without being asked, how Mr. Salter brought some of his stored venison to thank us for helping him out that afternoon. When I came over to set the table, Bree took the dishes out of my hands. "It really does take a village, doesn't it?" she said.

"What do you mean?" I asked, going back to the island for the glasses.

"It seems like people really stepped up," Bree said. "With your dad gone and all." She shrugged, placing a fork very deliberately next to one of the plates. "It's a nice reminder that not everyone is always just looking out for themselves."

I leaned toward her. "They're just here for the food. I mean, you tasted the biscotti. Wait till you taste her venison marsala."

Bree snorted. I left her to set the rest of the table and went back to the stove. As I did, I saw my kitchen through her eyes, the old-fashioned appliances, the worn tile, the cluttered counters. And yet, the room was filled with a soft golden light and the warm, comforting smell of a good homemade meal. I remembered the few times I had been in her kitchen. Everything was stainless steel and spotless, and her mother was always trying to cook something with a fancy French name. Maybe there was a deeper reason she'd shown up at my house five hours early.

We sat down to our venison and ate in silence for several minutes. Lidia took a sip of wine and leaned back in her chair. "So, Bree. How are your father's plans coming along?"

I pressed my palms against the edge of the table. "*Mother.*"

"What?" Lidia raised her eyebrows innocently. "I'm just making conversation."

"How would I know?" Bree said, twirling her fork in the air. "It's not like I talk to my dad or anything."

Lidia set her wineglass down, her face painted with a look that said she was about to light into someone.

I chewed as hard as I could to get rid of the food in my mouth, but Heath cut in before me. "Their plans for the power plant have stalled, haven't they?"

Bree narrowed her eyes at Heath. "How would you know?"

I froze. Heath knew because the Malandanti no longer controlled the Waterfall, but Bree had no idea that Heath was a Benandante. Heath reached for his water. "Well, they didn't break ground when they were supposed to, did they?"

"*Ringraziare Santa Maria* for that," Lidia said.

"Yeah, it would've sucked, having these woods destroyed," Bree said. She fixed her gaze on Heath's face. "Especially that really pretty waterfall."

Crap. She didn't miss a trick.

"What waterfall?" Mr. Salter asked.

"There's a waterfall in the woods," Heath said.

"Really?" Mr. Salter paused, his fork halfway to his mouth. "How far in?"

"About half a mile," Lidia said.

I swung my gaze to her, my mouth open. In all the years I'd gone there with Dad, she never once acknowledged that she knew about the Waterfall.

"I can't believe I never knew that," Mr. Salter said. "I've gone hunting not far from there."

Lidia looked at me. "Did you know about it?"

"Dad took me there," I said softly.

Mr. Salter glanced at Lidia. A sad, sweet smile flittered on her face. She got that way whenever my dad came up in conversation. "Of course he did," she said. Her voice was thick. "He loved those woods."

"What about you, Heath?" Bree asked. "How did you find it?"

I wanted to stab her under the table with my fork.

Heath stared at her across the table, his face placid. "I like to wander."

I hoped that was the end of it.

After dinner, we helped clean up, then hung back as the adults meandered into the living room.

"Uh, I'm going to show Bree the Cave," I said.

"Be careful in the dark," Lidia said. "Take the lantern."

I pulled on my coat and grabbed the old kerosene lantern from its hook just inside the basement door. Bree followed me outside and caught my arm after I closed the door. "I thought we were going to see Nerina. You're nuts if you think I'm going back to that creepy Cave with you."

"Well, I don't know what to tell you." I handed Bree the lantern and slid my phone out of my back pocket. "If you'd gotten here when you were supposed to, my mother would be in bed, and we could go to Nerina's and not worry about anyone seeing us. But, no, you had to change the plan."

I sent a quick text to Nerina.

"Hey, not my fault that my mother had a meltdown of epic proportions this afternoon, and I had to leave my house." She bit her lip and looked away.

I stuffed my phone into my pocket. "Sorry to hear that."

"Yeah, well." She exhaled hard and looked back at me. "She wanted to make lobster Thermidor, but when she went to the store, they were out of lobster. How a store in *Maine* can be out of lobster, I have no idea—"

"It's out of season right now. The lobstermen don't

get enough this time of year, so some of the smaller stores don't carry it."

"Well, it would've been nice to know that ahead of time. Apparently she threw a hissy fit so big that the store manager had to call the police. My dad had to go pick her up." Her eyes searched my face, as if she wwas challenging me to laugh or pity her or tell her what a jerk her mother was. I stayed silent. Bree swallowed hard and glanced back at the farmhouse. The lights made warm pools on the cold ground. Bree stepped into one of the pools of light, her face illuminated. "I bet your mom has never done that."

"That, no. But she once refused to pay for a meal at an Italian restaurant because they used jarred sauce."

Bree laughed. I took a step back; I didn't think I had ever heard her laugh spontaneously. It was a full, rich sound. "I guess everybody's parents have issues," she said, hiccupping.

"I guess so." We stared at each other, both of us on the verge of smiling.

The back door creaked open and slammed shut behind Heath. He stopped short when he saw us. "Evening, ladies."

Bree pointed at him. "Why don't we just meet at his cabin?"

My heart skipped about a dozen beats. "What?"

"You said he lives in a cabin on the edge of the pasture, right?" She shrugged. "Why don't we just meet there?"

"Excuse me?" Heath stepped into the pool of light.

"Meet about what?"

"Oh, please, like you don't know." Bree rolled her eyes. "You're practically wearing a T-shirt with your animal alter ego on it."

Without thinking, Heath and I rounded on her, backing her out of the light and into the shadows of the burned-out barn. For the first time since I'd brought her into this whole thing, I saw fear in her face, a realization that maybe she'd finally gone too far. She put her hands out in front of her, palms toward us as we advanced on her. "Look, I'm not going to say anything. It's just—it's obvious, okay? I mean, to me. Not to anyone else, I'm sure—"

"Was it because I knew about the Waterfall?" Heath asked.

Bree nodded. "Among other things." She stopped and held her ground. "I mean, come on. You show up on Alessia's farm right before she's Called?" She looked at me, suddenly seeming to realize who she was again. "Please tell me that didn't get past you either. And I doubt Nerina's hanging around here because she wants to be BFFs with Alessia." She spread her arms wide. "This is Benandanti Central, isn't it?"

I glanced back at the house, but through the windows, I saw that the kitchen was empty. Lidia and Mr. Salter were probably hanging out in the living room, oblivious to what was going on right outside the farmhouse walls. Whatever was going on with the two of them, maybe having him around to distract her wasn't such a bad thing. Beside me, Heath relaxed. I sighed and pulled out my phone again. "I'll tell Nerina to meet us at the cabin."

CHAPTER TWELVE

Sometimes You Have to Take Pleasure in the Little Things

Bree

Heath's cabin was tiny. Seriously, how did anyone live in such a small space? It was, like, one room. I guess he was trying to get the college dorm experience without actually going to college.

Alessia set the lantern on the table in the center of the room and settled into one of the hard wooden chairs. They looked about as comfortable as the chairs at school. No, thank you. I helped myself to the bed, rearranging pillows to create a little nest. Heath seemed mildly annoyed at my redecorating but didn't say anything. We all sat in awkward silence, staring at each other for several minutes until the door whooshed open, and Nerina swept in. A cloud of expensive perfume—Shalimar, I think—swirled in after her.

Heath coughed, and I stifled a laugh. Yeah, he didn't seem like the type to appreciate fine perfume. He seemed like the type of guy who'd take his girlfriend fly-fishing.

Before Nerina could say anything, Heath stood up. "Bree knows."

"Eh." Nerina waved a hand. "She would have had to learn sooner or later anyway."

"Are you kidding me?" Alessia stomped a foot. "'Eh'? That's all you're going to say?"

"I figured it out," I said loudly. "It's not like someone spilled the beans—"

"You don't get it," Alessia said, her voice low but sure. "If the Malandanti discover Heath's identity, it won't take them long to connect the dots to me and my mom."

"Your mom's not involved."

"That doesn't matter!" Alessia got to her feet and paced around the table. "They'll think she is, and they'll hurt her. They already destroyed our barn—"

I hugged myself. I understood her desperate need to protect someone she loved. It was how I felt about Jonah. Wasn't I doing all this to keep him safe? "I won't say anything."

She looked at me from across the room, her hands on her hips.

I exhaled hard. "You don't trust me."

"It isn't a matter of trust." Nerina stepped in front of Alessia, cutting off our eye contact. "It's a matter of your being found out, and the information getting . . . forced out of you."

Whatever. I could withstand torture. I did that every day at school.

"There's nothing we can do about it now," Heath said. "She knows, so that's that."

"Yes, that's that." Nerina shot Alessia a pointed look.

Alessia shook her head slightly and retreated to her chair.

Nerina walked to the bed and settled next to me. "Tell us how your internship is going."

Finally. Back to the good stuff. "The first day was super boring. I had to watch, like, a hundred videos about how great the Guild is. But then on day two, things got interesting."

"How?" Alessia asked, crossing her arms.

"I got invited to a meeting, but it became obvious—to me, at least—that it was a meeting for the employees who have no idea what the Guild really is, while the real meeting was being held elsewhere."

"Any idea what was going on at the real meeting?" Heath asked.

I shook my head. "But it was big. All the executives were locked in a conference room on the top floor for more than two hours. If we'd had some sarin gas, we could've solved our problems in one fell swoop."

"So the question is," Nerina said, "how do we get you into one of those meetings?"

"I don't think it's that simple." I shifted on the pillows. "The assistants don't get invited to the meetings. Well, except Perfect Pratt."

"Who?" Nerina and Heath asked at the same time.

"Mr. Wolfe's assistant," Alessia said.

I cocked my head. "Way to be on the ball, Alessia."

Alessia stretched a hand out and fingered the grooves

in the wood table. "I've seen them together. There's a weird dynamic between them. Have you noticed that?"

"Yes." I leaned forward. "They're attached at the hip."

"It's not just that," Alessia said. "It's almost as if your dad—"

"—is the assistant, and Pratt is the boss." I nodded, my hair falling into my face. "Yeah. I've seen it. But I can't get close enough to figure out what's really going on."

"You can't get close enough?" Heath asked, his lip curling. "He's your *father*."

"Not while we're at work, genius. My dad practically ignores me while I'm there. And Pratt . . ." I toyed with a loose thread in the quilt on the bed. "I don't think he trusts me. He keeps me at a distance from my dad. It's like he knows there's something more to my sudden interest in the company."

Nerina tucked her legs up against her and leaned her chin on her knees. "So forget your dad for now. He's not the only executive there that you can get information from."

"True." I pushed myself off the bed. "Thanks for the powwow, guys."

"That's it?" Alessia stood up and blocked my path to the door. "That's all? You call this big meeting, you show up at my house *hours* early, you learn another Benandante's identity, and all you give us is that the executives were locked in a room together? Are you kidding?"

"Hey, you're getting my services for free, so don't complain." I sidestepped her and put a hand on the door.

"Although, there is one more thing."

"What?"

I turned and looked past Alessia, right to Nerina. "It might interest you to know there's a room in the Guild offices that can't be unlocked."

"So get a key," Alessia snapped.

I shot her a bored look, then focused on Nerina. "I think you know what I mean."

If Alessia's eyes had been lasers, Nerina would have been blown to bits. "What does she mean?"

Nerina stood. "She means, no key can unlock that room. It has been bound with magic."

I met Alessia's stunned look with a sweet smile. "It's nice to know someone's on the same page as I am," I said and practically skipped out of the cabin.

CHAPTER THIRTEEN
Magic Can Suck Me

Bree

I had barely gotten ten steps across the pasture when Nerina's voice came to me in the night air. "*Un momento*, Bree."

I spun around. "My parents are expecting me home."

Nerina came closer, her face lit by stark moonlight. Her eyes gleamed. "There's no need to lie to me, Bree. I'm not your enemy."

I opened my mouth, then closed it again. Nerina put an arm around my shoulder. I stiffened a little before realizing that I didn't want to shove her away. She turned me gently toward the woods, and we walked slowly, her arm still around me. Like the way Alessia's mom had her arm around Alessia's waist earlier. The way my own mother hadn't done in years.

Nerina leaned her head toward mine. "I was like you once. Angry at the world for what I saw as its offenses against me personally."

I hated it when adults said stuff like that to me: *I know exactly how you feel.*

Actually, you don't.

But coming from Nerina, who looked my age, it was easier to stomach. Still . . . "When was that? Back when you were a mere teenager of a hundred seventy-five?"

Shadows slashed across her face, fragmenting her features. "I was a real teenager once, you know, before I was immortal." Something flickered deep in her eyes, something dark that disappeared too quickly for me to read. "Back then, I made many mistakes. Some I am still atoning for."

"Well, you have all of eternity," I said, but my gut twisted a little. I'd made mistakes too, but I didn't have all of eternity to make up for them.

Nerina sighed. "Eternity, yes. A concept that is very different in practice than it is in theory."

"Yeah, the world must get super boring after a couple hundred years."

"Boring? No. But an immortal life sometimes feels too long." She glanced at me. "But it's not exactly a gift you can give back."

"You could've gotten yourself killed in battle."

Nerina stopped and stood in front of me. "Ah, but you see, I may be tired of immortality, but I am not ready to die."

We walked in silence for a minute while I digested that conundrum. When Alessia had first told me Nerina was immortal, I had thought how cool it must be, to see the world change century after century, to not only be a witness to all that history but also be a part of it. Then I started to really think about what it meant to live that long. Watching people you love die while you never age a day . . . That was freaking depressing. And after four hundred fiftysomething years, I would be *exhausted*.

The shadows deepened as we passed into the forest. I looked up at the trees that hid the moon. With practiced ease, Nerina tapped the stone and opened the door to her lair. When we got to the bottom, I settled into the leather chair while Nerina worked the shiny espresso machine. I pulled a luxe cashmere throw onto my lap and smoothed a hand over its soft cable-knit. "This place wasn't like this when you got here, was it?"

"Of course not. Someone who didn't care about thread count stayed here before me." The espresso machine hissed and steamed. Nerina turned the knobs and lowered the pitcher of milk with the deftness of a trained barista. Seriously, it was as if she'd worked at Starbucks for twenty years. The one time I had tried to use an espresso machine, I'd wound up with steam burns on my wrists.

Nerina made a tray with two lattes and a plate of biscotti and carried it into the living room.

I picked up one of the lattes. I hadn't had a decent one since we'd moved here. "So, uh, what's this all about?"

"I want to hear more about this room at the Guild."

She didn't waste time. I reached for one of the biscotti. "Did Lidia make these?"

"No, they're store-bought."

Ugh. I pulled my hand back and took a sip of latte. It was way better than the excuse-for-coffee they sold at

Joe's. Over the rims of our cups, Nerina's gaze fixed on my face. I let her stare at me while I drank half my coffee and leaned back into the plush leather of the armchair. Finally, I lowered my cup. "I don't know what else to tell you. It was a room. With a door. That was locked."

"By magic."

"Yeah, so?"

"How did you know?" Her voice was soft and slightly sweet, as if she were trying to coax a shy kitten out of a closet. "That the door was locked with magic?"

I shrugged. "I don't know. I just knew." I squirmed in my seat and went for a biscotti even though I knew it was going to be bad.

"But how did you know, Bree?" Nerina tilted her head. "The door wasn't glowing, was it? There wasn't a distinct, telltale sign of magic, was there?"

"I guess not." I was right; the biscotti was tasteless. I dipped it into my latte to at least give it a coffee flavor. "I mean, that would be pretty stupid, with all those non-Malandanti assistants running around."

"My point exactly." Nerina set her cup down on the coffee table. "The magic isn't obvious. It's only obvious *to you*."

I stilled, the coffee-drenched biscotti halfway to my mouth. That was true. No one gave that office a second glance—no one except me. And it wasn't as though there was a big Do Not Enter sign on the door. There was nothing unusual about it. I just knew that every time I passed it, I got a feeling up my spine. And when I'd reached for the doorknob . . .

"It repelled me," I said. "I couldn't even touch the knob." I dropped my half-eaten biscotti into my coffee and put it on the table. "Why? Why did it do that to me and no one else?"

"My guess is the door is masked," Nerina said. "A non-magical person probably doesn't even know it's there, or if they do, the spell subtly directs them away. But a magical person—"

I leaned forward, away from the comfy pillows. "Um, I'm not magical."

"Yes, you are, Bree." Nerina smiled, her eyes soft. "You were born with the caul. You were Called by the Malandanti. You have more magic in you than the average person does. That's how you can sense the door."

"But I refused the Malandanti." I picked at an imaginary pill on the chair's arm. "Shouldn't the magic go away once I refuse the Call?"

"No." Nerina took a sip of her coffee. "That magic never goes away. You were born with it. It's like an innate talent for a musical instrument or languages. It's part of you. Though I do believe it has manifested in you more strongly than in any other Refuser I have ever seen." She shook her head slightly. "Maybe because you're younger or because of your connection with your twin brother."

When Jonah and I were kids, we used to have a made-up language we spoke only to each other. It pissed off my mother something fierce. She was always convinced we were talking about her. (Half the time we were.) As we got older and realized we were two separate people and not two halves of the same being, we stopped using our language. But even now, every once in a while, I found myself thinking in that language. It never left me. And even though we never spoke those words to each other anymore, I knew Jonah remembered it too. We didn't need to speak it out loud; we only had to look at each other to know what the other one was thinking.

"Do you mean," I said slowly, "that somehow I'm feeding off the magic he has, because he's a Malandante?"

Nerina tucked an invisible stray hair behind her ear. "That could be part of it. I've never seen a case like this before. So it is new territory for me, too."

"Did you know this before? When Alessia first brought me in?"

"No, but I did suspect once she told me you were Jonah's sister." A little clock next to the sofa chimed, like fairy princess bells. Nerina glanced at it. "Oh, *cara*, it is getting late. You should be getting home."

"Are you kidding me?" I resisted as she came over and pulled me to my feet. "You tell me I'm magical, and you want to send me home? No way—I need to know more."

"And you will. Just not tonight." She propelled me to the stairway leading back to the world. "Come back tomorrow. You and I will be meeting regularly from now on."

The second I emerged aboveground, the door closed,

leaving me alone next to the ancient wall. What the hell was I supposed to do now? Go home? I leaned against the stones and wound my scarf back around my neck. Even though the ground was solid again, with no sign of the world beneath it, I felt as if the earth were still shifting under my feet, ready to knock me onto my ass at any moment.

I hated that. I needed to be back in control. I dug into my coat pocket and pulled out my phone. "Hey, Josh," I said when he answered. "You busy?"

The good thing about Josh was that he was never busy. He'd never been confronted with a girl like me, someone who booty-called *him*. This town was filled with too many girls who'd had The Rules drilled into them by their prudish mothers. Fortunately, my mother was too busy throwing fits in grocery stores to do that. So I had fun instead of sitting by the phone wondering why the hottest guy in school wasn't calling me.

"Pick me up at the corner of Walnut and Main Street," I told Josh.

"I, uh, have someone with me."

Well, well, well. I walked toward the edge of the woods, the hard ground crackling under my feet. "I'm not into three-ways."

"But I can't just—"

"That's fine." I lowered my voice to a husk above a whisper. "I'm sure she'll be able to give you everything I do. Just like I can find someone else to give me everything you do."

There was a short pause, so short I actually felt a little bad for the girl he was with. "I'll be there in fifteen minutes."

That was more like it. I climbed over the fence that lined the Jacobs farm and broke into a run until I reached the road. Solid ground was much easier to deal with.

Josh had a hulking SUV with a back row of seats that conveniently folded down. Seriously, how clueless were his parents? It screamed sex car. But despite its comfortable roominess, the windows steamed up remarkably fast. I sat up and pushed my sweat-soaked hair off my forehead.

"Where you going?" Josh murmured, his hand creeping up my naked back. "I'm not done."

"I am." I slid out of his reach—another convenient feature of the big car—and dug for my phone in the pile of clothing shoved against the folded-down seats. I thought I'd heard it go off before, but I'd been too preoccupied to check.

Sure enough, there was a missed call—a number I didn't recognize—and a text from the same number.

> *Come to the lair after school.*

I didn't need ten guesses who sent it. I hadn't heard from her since the other night at Alessia's, and *now* she calls me? How did she know this was my afternoon off from

my Guild internship? And I had chosen to spend it doing . . .
I glanced over my shoulder at Josh.

The phone buzzed in my hand. *School let out over an hour ago. Where are you?*

"Come on, babe." His murmur had turned into a whine. "My turn . . ."

I'm on my way. I hit Send and held the phone up. "Sorry. Gotta go." I sorted out my clothing from Josh's— I'd become an expert in getting dressed in the back of a car—and climbed over the middle row to let myself out.

Nerina was waiting by the wall. She had on a long plaid shawl, artfully arranged over her shoulders. Her arms were crossed, and she tapped a to-die-for boot against the bottom stones. "I didn't think you'd remember which stone to push."

"Good thinking."

She made no move to open the door. "What took you so long to get here?"

Did she really think she could pull attitude with me? "I had things to do."

"Apparently." Her gaze swept over my rumpled skirt and skewed sweater.

I looked down. Damn. It was on backwards.

"Apparently you had *someone* to do," Nerina muttered.

Oh, no, she didn't. "Hey," I said, louder than was necessary since we were the only two people here in the middle of the woods, "I don't have to be here. I am under no obligation whatsoever to help you. So if you're going to stand there and judge me, you can go to hell."

Nerina caught my arm as I twisted away. "I'm not judging you." Her voice had a bite to it that I hadn't heard before. It made me face her. "I'm trying to understand you." She shook her head. "I don't understand why you want to waste your time, energy, and talent on boys who aren't half as smart as you are."

I tossed my hair. "How do you know I'm not screwing the captain of the mathletes? He could be a genius for all you know."

Nerina raised an eyebrow. "But he's not, is he? He plays sports and drives a big car. Am I right?"

Eerily so. But I wasn't going to give her the satisfaction. I pressed my lips together.

Nerina snorted. "I thought so." She punched the trick stone, and the doorway creaked open. "I've seen your type before," she said as we waited for the ground to stop moving. "Sex is the only thing you can control, and you control it with a vengeance."

I watched her descend the stairs, fighting the urge to hightail it out of the forest. People had tried to peg me before—and a few school counselors probably had—but no one had had the guts to say it out loud. No one wanted to talk about the fact that I was having sex and had been for a number of years. No one wanted to have *that talk* with me. They just wanted to hand me a couple of condoms and be able to say they did their jobs.

They only wanted to cover the *how* and ignore the *why*.

I took a deep breath and followed Nerina down into her lair. "Is this why you called me here? To lecture me on how I should be saving myself for marriage?"

"Please." Nerina pulled her shawl off and flung it on the back of the armchair. "If I followed that rule, I'd be a virgin. Can you imagine being celibate for nearly five hundred years? No, thank you."

The laughter that bubbled up inside me was so unexpected it almost knocked me off my feet. I doubled over, a stitch in my side, gasping for breath. When I straightened, Nerina was perched on the arm of the chair, her face red with laughter too. It took several minutes for both of us to calm down. When we did, Nerina looked at me. "I don't want to lecture you. I want to show you that there are many paths in life—not just the one you've chosen to go down. You have options." She stood up. "But what I really want to show you today is this."

Nerina knelt on the plush rug in front of the coffee table. I fell to my knees beside her. For an instant, I flashed back to the last time I was in church, how much I hated being told how to live. I looked sideways at Nerina. I couldn't imagine a less priest-like person.

Nerina placed her hands on the coffee table. Only then did I see it—a huge, ancient book. It was bound in cracked leather with raised gold lettering that I tried to read, but it was in a language I didn't know. "What is that?"

"One of the only things I was able to save," Nerina whispered, "from the attack on my home in Friuli." She stroked the cover with such gentleness that I felt I should leave them alone.

The cover creaked when she opened it, and when she turned the pages, they seemed to speak in hushed tones. I could practically feel the magic coming from the book. "Is there a spell inside that can break into the room?"

"Yes." Nerina stopped turning the pages and slid the book slightly to me. "This one."

I bent over the coffee table. The letters on the page were handwritten in centuries-old ink, the corners illuminated in gold and red. "Is that Italian?"

Nerina shook her head. "Latin."

Of course. A dead language. "How the hell am I supposed to read it?"

"You aren't." She grabbed my wrist and brought my hand to the book, hovering my palm just above the page. "You feel it."

The instant she brought my flesh in contact with the book, cold electricity shuddered through me. I tried to pull away, but the book wanted me. I could feel its desire, how it needed to give me its knowledge, how it longed for someone to understand it. I clutched at the table with my other hand. "Wha—what is that?"

"It's magic." Nerina was smiling, her eyes dancing. "Most people would touch those pages and feel nothing. "But you—I knew you were different."

The book's power swept over me—God, it was like an orgasm. I curled my fingers into a fist and drew it back. I swore I heard the book sob, as if it missed me. And I missed it too, with a gnawing separation in my gut. I squirmed on the rug and pushed back from the table. "I have to go."

"No, you don't." Nerina laid her hand on my elbow. I stilled. "Don't run from what you can't control. You are more powerful than you know. Embrace that."

I swallowed hard and searched her face. For what, I didn't know. I just knew I felt pulled in two directions. I wanted more of what the book had to offer, what Nerina had to offer, and yet I wanted to walk out of here, text Josh, and not have to think about any of this. "I don't know if I'm ready to do this."

"Ready?" Nerina shook her head. "What is ready? Do you think I was ready when I was Called? When I became a Benandante? Or when I became immortal? Do you think I was ready to live forever?" She leaned toward me. "Were you ready when you were Called? Do you think Alessia was?" She shook her head. "No one is ever ready for the big moments in life, Bree. That's not what's important. What's important is the courage with which we face what we aren't ready for." One corner of her lip curled up. "What is the saying? 'Courage is not the absence of fear. It is—'"

"'Feeling the fear and doing it anyway,'" I finished for her.

We stared at each other for a long moment.

I looked down at the book. Slowly, I raised my hand and lowered it onto the page, pressed my palm flat against the thick paper. I let the magic swirl through me. "What do I need to do?"

"This spell needs two people to perform it," Nerina said. "One of them must be a Benandante." She placed her hand next to mine. I had a brief, strange memory of pressing my palm flat like this next to Jonah's and tracing them in fourth-grade art class. I shook my head, and the memory danced away. Nerina tilted her head toward mine. "You and I are going to learn this spell and break into that room. Together."

CHAPTER FOURTEEN
The Embrace

Alessia

Moonlight spread out across the Waterfall, thin and wavering in its reflection on the water. I flew in slow circles above the pool, watching my reflection below. My wings itched to take me beyond the perimeter of the site, but Heath was prowling outside the barrier. I had to remain inside.

I knew why he had volunteered to take the outside watch. He was worried Jonah would be on Malandanti patrol and I would get distracted.

He wasn't wrong.

Jonah had taken to skipping classes again, so I barely saw him at school. There were no more surreptitious notes in French class or sidelong glances in biology. I shrugged it off to Jenny and told Heath, "Of course not," when he asked me if I'd spoken to Jonah.

But I needed to see him, like I needed to breathe. I knew I shouldn't want to. I hated him with every fiber of my Falcon's being. But the Alessia in me . . . She was a different story.

And so, every night I was on patrol, I asked to sweep the perimeter, hoping to catch a glimpse of his other self. Even though I knew if I did see him, it would hurt worse than any mage's spell.

Apparently Heath had caught on. *I'll take the outside watch*, he told me when we reached the Waterfall that night.

I can do it, I replied. *I don't mind*. As if I were martyring myself.

I know you don't mind. Heath pranced down the rocks, hugging the edge of the magical barrier. *Since you seem to be so keen on it lately*.

He was on to me. *Fine, whatever*. And now I was stuck inside the barrier, like a figure inside a snow globe.

I dipped just inches above the water. I would never touch it deliberately; I didn't need to see the future. Not the version the water showed me, anyway.

Low growling broke the stillness. I swerved toward the sound. Just beyond the shimmering veil that protected me, the Panther stood in the shadows, his green eyes glowing. A sound escaped me, a strange twitter I'd never made before. I fluttered backwards and forwards, drawn by those eyes but bound by my duty.

A loud bark snapped whatever thread had spun between me and Jonah. *Stay there*, Heath commanded. He bounded across the banks of the pool. Jonah sprang out of the shadows, his eyes wide as they shifted between me and the White Wolf. For a moment, he was frozen as Heath rounded on him. They faced off with each other, black and white, like the yin and the yang. Heath moved closer to Jonah.

Don't! I couldn't help it; the word escaped me before I could stop it.

Stay where you are, Alessia.

Don't hurt him. I flew right up to the edge of the magic, the tips of my feathers brushing the mist.

Heath swung his head toward me, his blue eyes icy. *Don't you dare move, Alessia. Don't you dare.*

Switch with me.

What?

Switch with me. Let me deal with him.

You'll let him go.

And you'll kill him. Which one of us is right?

I won't— Heath's eyes narrowed at me.

I held my breath.

Quick, before I change my mind. He leapt into the mist at the same time I dove outside of it.

At the top of the Waterfall, Jonah turned, his sleek body so black that I didn't know where he ended and the darkness began. His Clan was itching for a kill, but I knew I was safe. If I hadn't taken Heath's place, I wasn't so sure he would be.

I flew up over the Waterfall, leveling out at the creek that ran into it. Jonah chased me, splashing down off the rocks and into the water. I drew him into the forest, so deep I could no longer see the glittering veil that protected the site. I kept my mind open in case Heath needed me to return, but every other ounce of me was focused on the Panther.

At the base of a tall pine tree, Jonah stopped, his ebony coat shiny with sweat, his sides heaving. I landed on a branch several feet above his head, showering needles onto the ground. Jonah reared up onto his back legs and pressed his front paws against the tree trunk. He growled, a guttural sound that I felt in my belly. I arched my gaze down to him. He scraped the bark and growled again.

He was calling me.

I floated down one branch closer to him.

He dropped to all fours and paced beneath my perch. Every time he changed direction, he looked up at me, his green eyes deep as the forest in spring.

I lowered down one more branch.

He threw his head back and keened to the sky. My blood froze.

I opened my wings and let the wind carry me all the way to the ground. Jonah backed up to the base of the tree and lay on the ground. I picked my way over to him, each step slow and deliberate. When I was within a few inches of him, he opened his front paws. It was not a threat. It was an invitation.

I came within the circle of his paws and furled my wings around my body. He rested his head against my back. Our auras shifted to envelop both of us, silver and blue meshing into one. Something flickered in my mind, as though his own emotions were entwined with mine, as though his love for me could break through the barrier that kept us from communicating with each other. If someone were to see us—

I closed my eyes. However screwed up it was, I was in the arms of the boy I loved, and nothing else mattered.

Hours later, Heath and I joined each other again when the Eagle and the Stag took over patrol. I soared high above the snow-tipped trees, hoping my distance would give him a hint that I didn't want to talk.

No such luck. *Where were you all night?*

Keeping Jo—the Panther away from the Waterfall. Doing my job.

Hmmph. I could feel his disapproval in every corner of my brain. I tried to turn off my thoughts, but he broke through before I could shut down. *Alessia, you need to be very, very careful.*

I know that—

I don't think you do. Deep down, I don't think you understand how dangerous this is.

I plunged through branches at a dizzying speed until I was right above him. *How can you possibly say that to me? I watched the Lynx die. I know what kind of danger we're in.*

Then why did you go chasing him? Heath slowed and raised his long white snout to me. *You're playing with fire. I warned you that I will go to the Clan with his identity—*

Cold leaked through me. *Are you going to?*

Heath tossed his head, his snowy fur mussed by the

wind. *Yes. I'm going to tell Nerina.*

Ha. *She already knows.*

He slid to a stop and let out a short bark. *What?*

I told her weeks ago. I circled Heath's head. *She was actually pretty understanding.*

I can't believe you did that.

Why not? I had to talk to someone about it, and you made it clear the subject was off-limits. I spun, my razor-sharp gaze on Heath. *She understands what it's like to be in love. Not like you—*

Heath lunged at me so fast he almost got a mouthful of feathers. I dodged backwards just in time, my wings clumsy with shock. His eyes were like icicles.

What the hell, Heath?

How dare you. How dare you! He shouted so loudly in my head that it hurt.

I blinked at him, torn between scratching his eyes out and getting the hell out of there. I chose the latter. *I don't know what the hell is wrong with you, but I'm going home. Good night.* I glided away, suddenly exhausted. It was inching toward dawn, and I had to get up in a few hours.

Wait. Alessia, please wait.

I didn't turn, but I slowed enough that he could catch up with me. When he was directly below me, I looked at him.

He glanced up, then back at the ground again. He padded to a stop and drooped his head. *You can't imagine what it's like. Being around her all the time and not able to be with her.*

I landed hard next to him, kicking up dirt and twigs. *Are you even listening to yourself? You just described my entire life.*

Heath's sides heaved, his breath a white mist in the cold air. Finally, he lowered his head. *Yeah. Yeah, I guess I did.*

I don't get it. I hopped a little closer to him. *You're a Benandante. She's a Benandante. Seems like the perfect arrangement.*

Except that she's immortal, and I'm not.

So?

So . . . someday I'm going to grow old and die, and she's not.

It didn't seem like that big of a problem to me. But as I really thought about it, really put myself in that situation, I stilled. That would suck. Well and truly suck. *But couldn't you at least be together for the present?*

Heath started walking. I lifted off the ground and floated next to him, letting the wind keep me aloft. *Yes, we could have. But the* Concilio—*they didn't think that was such a good idea.*

I don't see how that's really any of their business.

Heath snorted again. *I said the exact same thing. But Nerina—* *You have to understand. The* Concilio *is her family.*

Oh, I understood. *La famiglia.* It was the most important thing to an Italian. You do not go against the family. My mother had drilled that into me since I was old enough to speak. If Nerina's family told her to break up with Heath, she would obey. I dipped and rose next to Heath as he walked. *That's why they sent you here, isn't it?*

To separate you and Nerina?

Yes. His steps were heavy, his paws covered in mud. *They wouldn't even let me communicate with her when I got here.*

You must really hate me. I glided higher, near the middle branches of the trees. *For being the reason you had to leave.*

Oh, Alessia. Heath shook himself, as though he were shedding a cloak, and bounded over to me. *I don't hate you. And they would've come up with any reason to get me out of there. It wasn't about you.*

I could see the stone wall up ahead. I swung around and faced Heath fully. *So you get it now? You get what I'm going through with Jonah?*

Heath met my gaze calmly. The deep blue of his eyes seemed to hold me, as if I were trapped in frozen water.

Alessia, I've always gotten what you're going through with Jonah. That's why I'm telling you to be careful. Because I know just how much it will damage you if you're not.

CHAPTER FIFTEEN
Mission Impossible, Interrupted

Bree

I stood in front of my closet in my bra and panties, clothes strewn on the floor all around me. What the hell did one wear to a break-in? I would kill for that catsuit I'd seen at the naughty shop in Bridgeport before we'd left Connecticut. I knew I should've bought it. It would have come in handy right about now.

Not to mention it was like twenty below outside. I needed something sleek and slinky but warm. I should've listened to my mother when she tried to buy me long underwear.

I glanced at the clock. After eight. Shit. I had to hurry. I dug out my dark-wash skinny jeans, tucked them into my knee-high black boots, and pulled a charcoal-grey turtleneck over my head. Not exactly Catwoman, but it would have to work.

I inched my door open and stuck my head out into the hallway. Loud bangs rang up from downstairs. My fingers curled on the door frame, scratching the wood.

Mom was having a manic fit in the kitchen. Pots crashed against each other as she experimented with making chocolate. I'd seen an arsenal of strange materials laid out on the counter earlier. I could picture her now, hair flying, face spotted with liquid chocolate. Well, this was one night when her crazy obsession with perfection would work to my advantage.

I slipped out into the hall and took one last look at my room. I had my music on low, the lights off except the dim lamp on the nightstand . . . and the pièce de résistance, the Bodyform pillow that really looked like a body in my bed. I'd perfected the art of arranging pillows to look like me years ago.

When we lived in a house in California that was all on one floor, it had been a cinch to sneak out. This house, not so much. The stairs creaked, and you had to pass through the wide-open expanse of the kitchen and living room to get to the front door. I'd have to get through the kitchen to make it out the back door now. There was a chance my mother would be too busy playing mad chocolate scientist, but I wasn't going to risk it. That left a second-floor escape. There was only one, out the bathroom that Jonah and I shared. You had to climb out onto the porch roof and then shimmy down a tree. But desperate times called for desperate measures.

I gazelle-leapt across the hallway to the bathroom, but before I could disappear inside, Jonah's door opened. I turned, my heart thudding as if I'd been caught in the backseat with a boy. "What's up, Jonah?"

"Nothing." He narrowed his eyes at my outfit. "Are you going out?"

I shrugged. My outer body felt disconnected from my insides. "Yeah, I'm—meeting Josh."

"Seriously? That jackass?" His lip curled. "You can do a lot better than him."

"And your awesome track record in relationships qualifies you to give me advice . . . how?" I sidestepped into the bathroom, the door frame splitting my vision. I could see only half of him, the other half wavering in and out of sight. I wondered, did that other half even exist?

Jonah snorted. "Like you've never given me advice without being asked for it."

"Night, Jonah."

"Come on, Bree." He stepped into the hallway. Now I could see all of him. Whole. Human. The Panther lay hidden, dormant, somewhere inside. I shook my head slightly; I didn't want to be reminded of that other half of him. Not tonight. Not when I was setting out on a mission to destroy it.

"I have to go."

"Just stay in tonight." His tone froze me. It was the old Jonah, the one who used to talk to me in a made-up language. I stared at him. *Did he know?* "You can do without Josh for one night. Just stay in—with me. We could play Risk, like we used to."

I searched his face. He examined the paint on the

wall and wouldn't let me meet his eyes. Either he knew what I was up to or he was trying to grasp at something old and familiar, when it was him and me against the world instead of me against him.

Whichever it was, I didn't have time to figure it out. I had one night to get this done, and Nerina was waiting for me.

I crossed to him quickly and touched his arm. "We'll play Risk tomorrow. I promise."

He nodded, still not looking at me. I backed away until I reached the bathroom and shut the door. Inside the darkened room, I leaned against the counter and bent over until my forehead touched the cool marble. A hot lump spread from my throat to my chest to my belly. I knew what I was doing could save Jonah. But I was also betraying him.

I took a deep, ragged breath and straightened up. Fast, before I could change my mind, I opened the window and climbed out. The cold air froze in my throat and nostrils as I breathed in and out, in and out. I focused on one thing at a time—avoiding the loose shingle, knowing the exact notch in the tree to put my foot in, how far I had to slide down before I could jump to the ground. When I got there, I couldn't help it; I looked up. Jonah stood in his window, his figure a dark outline against the soft light in his room. I wasn't sure if he could see me, but I raised my hand and saluted him.

I'd been spending so much time at Nerina's that I could find my way there in the dark. I knew the exact stone to push and how many counts it took for the door in the ground to open up. I knew the door would already be closed above my head when I reached the bottom of the stairs.

Nerina stood in the living room, pulling on a pair of black leather gloves. A tight black cap covered most of her hair. She was dressed much like I was: tight jeans, tall boots, dark turtleneck. Her gaze swept over me, and she planted a hand on her hip. "We look like twins."

"Well, I wasn't exactly sure of the proper attire." On the chair next to her, I spied the book. "Are you taking that?"

"*Sì.*" Nerina turned in a small circle. "I think I have everything we need."

"You think? Be sure."

She shot me an annoyed look but did one more check. As she switched off the lamp next to the sofa, a creak echoed above our heads. The secret door was opening.

"Heath and Alessia always call or text before they come over," Nerina said. Her eyes were wide, fixed on the top step where any moment someone's foot would appear.

I backed up slowly until I was right next to Nerina.

She tore her gaze away from the staircase and reached down under the sofa. When she straightened, she held an iron crossbow in her hands. It was loaded.

"Whoa," I breathed.

"Get behind me."

I did as she asked. I wasn't about to mess with a chick carrying a crossbow. She raised the weapon to shoulder height and aimed it at the stairway. The door stopped moving. A footstep thudded on the top step. First, a pair of Chuck Taylors appeared, then two legs in corduroy, then an entire person as he got to the bottom step. I relaxed a little. I mean, what bad guy wears Chuck Taylors?

"Are you Nerina?" he asked, somewhat breathlessly.

"Who's asking?" She didn't lower the crossbow.

The man pushed his little wire-rim glasses up his nose. "I'm Aaron. I'm from the Redwood Clan."

"Prove it."

I wanted to kick her. The guy was wearing a sweater-vest, for Chrissakes. And he probably weighed all of a hundred twenty pounds soaking wet. Nerina's oversized Fendi bag might've weighed more than he did.

Aaron pushed up the sleeve of his shirt to reveal a silver chain-link bracelet. I bit back a gasp. It wasn't unlike the one Jonah always wore. The one that contained his caul. I tensed as he slipped it off his wrist and walked toward Nerina, holding the bracelet out to her. *"In bocca al lupo."*

Keeping the crossbow pointed at him with one hand, Nerina took the bracelet into her other hand. She brought it close to her mouth and whispered something I couldn't understand. The bracelet glowed blue, so bright it emitted a hum. She gave it back to Aaron and lowered the crossbow. "Welcome, friend." She opened her arms, and they hugged as if they had known each other all their lives.

"How did you do that?" I asked.

Nerina stepped back from Aaron. "I asked the bracelet to reveal itself—and it did. It contains the caul of a Benandante." She placed the crossbow on the coffee table. "From the Redwood Clan? How did you find me?"

"Dario sent me." Aaron pushed his glasses up again. "I'm the head of my Clan, and when Dario first arrived, we revealed our identities to each other. He said that if anything were to happen I should come to you, and he told me where to find you."

"Who's Dario?" I asked.

"What's happened?" Nerina ignored me, her eyes searching Aaron's face.

"We've retaken the Redwood site," Aaron said. "It's back under Benandanti control."

"That's good, isn't it?" I stepped next to Nerina, but neither she nor Aaron even looked at me. This being ignored thing was really getting on my nerves.

"Why didn't Dario come to tell me this himself?"

"He's been captured." Aaron swallowed, his Adam's apple bouncing. "By the Malandanti."

Nerina clutched at the back of the armchair. "How long?"

"Last night. I got on the first plane I could." Aaron ran a hand through his hair. "We think we know where he is. And we think he's still alive—"

"He is," Nerina murmured. "I would feel it if he weren't."

I looked at her. She had made reference to this connection between the Benandanti, how they fed off each other's energies, like how I fed off the book. "Can't you just do that telepathy thingy with him?"

Nerina shook her head. "It's too far. And the Malandanti have ways to block that." She took a deep breath and reached for Aaron's hand. "What do you need me to do?"

"Rescue him," Aaron said. "I can't do it on my own. And the rest of my Clan needs to be at the site. We're under constant attack by the Malandanti there—"

"But wouldn't the Malandanti be busy with Dario?" I asked.

This time they both looked at me.

"It's the Malandanti's own *Concilio* that's captured Dario," Nerina said. "Isn't that right, Aaron?"

He nodded.

"Wow," I said. "They bring in the big guns for the important people, I guess." I tossed my hair. "Okay, so you'll leave tomorrow. But we need to go—"

"What?" Aaron snapped.

I glared at him. Dude in a sweater-vest pulling attitude with *me*?

"We need to leave now," he said. "There's a red-eye out of Bangor in two hours."

"Hold up, Batman," I said. "Nerina and I were just about to leave for a super-important, top-secret mission. So step back, buddy."

Aaron puffed himself up, like a scrawny peacock

about to make a play for a hen way out of his league. I squared off in front of him. Bring it on, Chuck Taylors. But Nerina placed a palm lightly on his chest, and he deflated a little. Then she turned to me. "I'm sorry, Bree. It will have to wait."

"But it can't! The executives are all out of town, just for this one night. This is our only chance in who knows how long—"

"If I wait until tomorrow, Dario could be dead." Nerina's voice was quiet, but it cut through me like the arrow resting in the tip of her crossbow. "Or, worse, tortured. He can withstand a lot, but we need to find him before he's forced to give up information." She took my hands and looked me in the eye. "Please understand. Dario is my family. I must go to him."

I didn't say anything. She took that for acceptance and dropped my hands.

"I'll just be a moment," she told Aaron.

While Nerina threw a few things in a bag, Aaron and I stared at each other in uncomfortable silence. For a chick with so many designer clothes, she packed faster than I thought was humanly possible.

I followed them up the stairs, my brain clicking as though it were stuck between two gears. When we emerged into the night, Aaron said, "My car's up on the road," and they took off, skirting around the pasture so no one would see them cut across the farm.

Nerina didn't even say good-bye; they barely looked

at me as they left. I watched them disappear into the darkness, my insides seething.

I stomped through the woods back to the farm. One night. One freaking night when the Guild executives were definitely not in the office. I knew that for sure, because I had booked all of their flights to New York. They were there for a huge meeting with the international offices, and their building in Bangor would be empty.

One freaking night, and it had to be the exact same night Redwood Guy showed up.

I passed the chicken trailers and kicked the side of one, making the chickens inside squawk in protest. When I got close to the barn, I stopped. Nerina hadn't even said how long she'd be gone. I guess you couldn't put a time limit on rescuing your buddy from the bad guys, but still. Three days? A week? Two weeks? In that time, the Malandanti could wreak some serious havoc. In three days, the Malandanti could get wind of Nerina's absence. In a week, they could decide to attack the Waterfall. In two weeks, Jonah could be dead.

I hugged myself and looked past the barn to the farmhouse. The upstairs lights were on. Alessia was probably doing her homework, like a good little schoolgirl.

Wait a second. The gears in my head locked into place and started spinning. I needed a Benandante to perform the spell . . .

And there was one, sitting twenty feet away.

CHAPTER SIXTEEN

The Break-in

Alessia

A soft but insistent pinging against my window jerked me out of the reverie I'd fallen into over my biology book. It was a sound I hadn't heard in a long time. When we were younger, Jenny used to do it all the time until Lidia caught her and told her to use the front door, for *Santa Maria*'s sake.

I slid off my bed and shoved the window open. A pebble bounced off my forehead. "Dammit!" I leaned out the window and looked down.

Bree stood on the ground, about to take aim again. She caught sight of me. "I need to talk to you," she stage-whispered.

I pointed to the driveway to indicate that I'd come down.

I drew back into my room. *Now* what? Was she back for more biscotti? It wasn't even nine. Lidia was still up. This had better be good.

I tiptoed down the stairs and out the front door in my socks.

Bree stood under the eaves of the house, half-hidden in shadow.

"Not exactly the best time for a house call."

Bree rubbed her gloved hands over her arms. "You think we could go inside? It's like Alaska out here."

"Fine, but be quiet. My mother is still awake."

We crept up to my room. I shut the door and shoved a throw blanket into the crack between floor and door just to be safe. When I turned around to face Bree, she was just inches from me. "We have to break into the Guild tonight."

"*What?*"

She sighed and pinched her forehead. "Nerina and I were supposed to break into that room—the one locked with magic—tonight. But she . . . had to leave, and I need a Benandante in order to perform the spell, and it's the one night when they're all away and so we have to go. Now."

"Wait." I waved my hands in front of my face. "Nerina *left*? Where did she go?"

"Some guy from the Redwood Clan came. He said they reclaimed the site, but the Malandanti captured one of them. Dario. The *Concilio* dude."

I tried to process all of her words, but everything was jumbled. "We reclaimed the Redwood site? I have to tell Heath." I turned toward the door.

Bree grabbed my upper arm, hard. "No." The sight of her face stilled me. Her cheeks were flushed, her eyes bright. Her hair was plastered to her forehead with sweat even though it was drafty in my room. I had never seen her like this. "How much simpler can I make this for you? All the executives at the Guild are in New York. The offices are empty. There's no chance of my dad or anyone walking in on us. It *has* to be tonight. But Nerina left me high and dry. You have to help me."

I drew my arm out of her grasp, my mind whirling. This had *bad idea* written all over it. Then again . . . Nerina was handling the Redwood issue. If she needed Heath to know about it, she would get in touch with him. Besides—I remembered now—he was on patrol tonight with the Stag. And if all the Guild executives were out of town . . .

"Just let me change my clothes," I said and went to my closet. What the hell did one wear to break into a super-secret magic room?

We barely made the last bus to Bangor. Bree wanted me to "borrow" Lidia's car, but I convinced her that was a terrible idea. I wasn't sure how we were going to get home from Bangor, but we'd have to cross that bridge when we got to it.

I tried not to think about the last time I'd taken the bus to Bangor. The day I had skipped school with Jenny, when I had still been normal. And then, coming home that night, the world had turned upside down, and my life had been changed forever.

I leaned my forehead against the cool glass window

and peered out into the night. Darkened fields gave way to soft residential streetlamps. The buildings grew closer and closer together until we were on the outskirts of the city. The bus stopped in the middle of a block populated with tall office buildings. Bree nudged me, and we slid out of our seats.

"You girls gonna be okay here?" the driver asked, squinting down the desolate street.

"We're meeting my dad," Bree said, giving him a sweet smile. "He works in this building."

"Well, okay, then." The door swooshed to a close behind us, and the bus pulled away from the curb.

I planted my hands on my hips. "Now what?"

"Come on." Bree marched around the side of the building to a small, silver door marked Employees Only. She checked her watch, then waved a card in front of the electronic pad next to the door. I heard a click. She pulled the door open, and we slipped inside.

The fluorescent lights in the hallways were turned down to half, giving off a soft, bluish glow. I shivered. It almost looked like my aura. I looked around, my gut turning over on itself. I was inside the Guild. I was in the beating heart of the Malandanti.

"The office is on the third floor," Bree whispered. "We should take the stairs."

"Why?"

"To get to the elevators, we'd have to pass the security desk."

"So?"

She rolled her eyes. "There's a security guard sitting there, genius. I'd rather not explain to him why we're here."

I grabbed her arm. "There's a security guard? Jeez, Bree." The back of my neck itched, as if I were being watched. I looked up. Sure enough, above my head, a camera angled down on the hallway. Its red light felt white-hot on my face. I flattened myself against the wall. "Can they see us?"

"Not at this moment. The angle changes every three minutes." She pulled me toward a door labeled Stairs. "I timed our entry so the camera wouldn't be focused on the door."

"Nicely done."

"Please. Give me some credit." Another wave of her pass got us into the stairwell. "I have this worked out perfectly."

We jogged up the two flights of stairs. When Bree swiped her card to get us onto the third floor, I briefly wondered if there was a link from her card to security that would alert them to our presence. I followed her out into the hallway and pushed the thought out of my head. We were in too far to back out now. I only hoped she had a plan in case we were caught—because I sure didn't.

The floors up here were marble, the walls painted a white so bright it glistened. Sleek, black doors with frosted glass windows lined each side of the hall. Far down, opposite us, the hallway opened into a large reception area with an enormous, curved black desk. The words *The Guild Incorporated* hung over the desk, seemingly in midair, but when I squinted, I saw there was actually a glass wall behind the desk, and the words were painted in sharp, deep black on the clear glass. Everything was so stark, all black and white and marble. Totally at odds with an organization that sold its message as the deepest shade of grey.

"Which door is it?" I asked.

"The fifth one on the left."

I moved to go down the hall, but Bree flung an arm out and knocked me back. "Wait!" She pointed above the first door. A camera perched like a predatory bird, facing away from us. "It will turn this way in about ninety seconds. Be ready to move." She looked at me, and as she talked, I kept my eyes fixed on the camera. "We will only have three minutes to perform the spell before the camera catches us. That includes getting to the door."

"Well, are you going to tell me what I have to do?" I'd asked her repeatedly on the bus ride here, but she said my part was simple and to just chill out. Like that was going to happen.

Bree peered at her watch. "All you have to do is transform. Sixty seconds to go."

"*What*?" I stepped away from the wall. "I have to transform? Why the hell didn't you tell me that?"

She glanced up from her vigilant clock watching. "What's the big deal? It's like second nature to you, isn't it?"

"Yes, but—" I spread my arms wide. "Look where we

are! Transforming here would be like waving a giant 'I'm a Benandante' flag. Do you know what—?"

"*Move.*"

I shut my mouth and ducked. We ran along the wall, passing beneath the camera at the precise moment it switched directions. I counted the doors—one, two, three, four, five—and stopped.

I could feel the magic seething from the room. The door practically hissed with power. I put a hand up to it, but Bree swatted it away.

"Don't." She swung to face me. "I need you to transform only for a moment. All I need is the energy burst that happens at the moment of shifting—that's what will fuel the spell."

I wondered what would have happened if Nerina had been here. Had Bree seen what she transformed into? That would have been an inconvenient shock.

Bree positioned herself in front of the door. "Are you ready?"

"Are *you?*"

She grinned at me. "Always am, sweetie darling." She raised her hands, palms down. "*Now.*"

I pulled myself apart and watched my body crumple to the marble floor as I soared toward the ceiling. My wings beat with joy of their own volition; despite the crazy dangerous thing we were doing, it was still exhilarating to transform and be free. I flew in a small circle, the tips of my wing feathers grazing the ceiling. My aura filled the hall, bouncing off the marble like sunlight through a prism. I took a little dive and rose again, blood pumping through my veins. This was my life, my reason for—

"Okay. You can transform back," Bree said.

I blinked. The door was open. With a twinge of sadness, I sank back into my body and stood. "That was fast."

"With ten seconds to spare." She jerked her chin toward the camera, still facing away from us. We hurried into the room and shut the door.

We leaned against the door for a moment, surveying this forbidden room that it had taken an ancient spell to get into. It didn't look so special. File cabinets lined one wall, and a sleek computer sat on a small desk in the center of the room.

Bree reached into her pocket and fished out two miniature flashlights. She handed one to me. "Get to work."

"What are we looking for?"

"You start on the files. I'm gonna see if I can get into the computer."

I aimed my little light toward the cabinet immediately to my right. I expected the files to be locked, but when I pulled on the drawer, it slid right open. "Guess they figured the magic on the door was enough security."

"Or the spell broke the magic inside the room too," Bree said without looking up from the computer.

I made a face at her back and stood on tiptoe to peer into the drawer. It was filled with boxes of pens. I slammed the drawer shut and was about to move to the next cabinet when I paused. Why would the Guild use up space in their precious magic room with *pens*? That made no sense. I rolled out the drawer again. When I looked inside, it was filled with staplers.

"Bree," I said, "there's a spell on these cabinets."

She straightened and walked toward me. When she was a foot away, she stopped. "I can feel it now," she muttered.

"Feel it?" I had felt the magic on the door but not in here. It must have been a subtler spell, a kind of magic that only someone with skill could undo. I stared at Bree. Was that what she was? Was that what she was doing with Nerina every night? Was Bree . . . a mage in training?

"Stand back," she said. "I want to try something."

I moved behind her and watched her raise her hands to the cabinet. Her lips moved without sound. The cabinet flashed, and Bree stumbled back a step. "Shit," she said.

"I hope no one saw that."

Bree swung around. "I'm doing my best, okay?"

"Hey, I could just leave," I said, even though I really couldn't. "I didn't have to come."

She clenched her jaw and faced the cabinet again. This time she placed a palm flat against the beige metal and murmured something under her breath. The drawer sighed with a wisp of silver smoke. Bree pulled it open. "That's what you're looking for," she said.

I gripped the sides of the drawer and looked inside. Several leather-bound manuscripts, yellowed with age, were piled side by side. I drew out the one on top. On the front cover, the word *L'oliveto* was stitched into the leather with green thread. The Olive Grove. I rifled through the other books. *The Waterfall. The Redwood Forest.* There was one for each site.

I looked around; Bree was at the last cabinet, unlocking its magic. I waited until she was done. "Hey, what do we do with the stuff we want to take with us?"

She pointed to a small pile of crumpled reusable grocery bags on the floor next to the desk. I grabbed one and was about to put the manuscripts in it when I thought of something. "But aren't they going to notice these things are missing?"

"Leave that to me," she said, moving back to the computer.

Great. I shook my head a little and stacked the manuscripts into the bag. The next cabinet had three drawers, each labeled alphabetically. I opened the top one, marked *A-F*. It was filled with manila folders, a name listed on each tab. I picked one at random—ABRAMS, JEFFREY. There were so many folders jammed in the drawer that it was hard to get it out, so I just jerked it up enough that I could peek inside.

ABRAMS, JEFFREY. Called: July 9, 1997. Animal Form: Mountain Lion. Site: The Waterfall.

And then below it, stamped in large block red letters, one word: *DECEASED.*

I pulled my fingers off the folder as if it had bitten me. I clenched my hands into fists for a moment. Then, quickly, I shoved the folder back in place and pulled out another one.

ARCONI, STEPHEN. Called: February 28, 1962. Animal Form: Cougar. Site: The Waterfall. DECEASED.

I slammed the drawer shut and rolled out the middle one so hard it almost fell off its hinges. A quick trip through the folders in that drawer and the one below told me what I'd suspected after reading Stephen Arconi's file. These were records of all the dead Malandanti from the Twin Willows Clan. I leaned against the cabinet, trembling. Would Jonah someday be one of those files—his life reduced to two lines in black and white?

I breathed in deep through my nose to quell the sudden queasiness in my gut. I swallowed hard and went to the next cabinet. My fingers shook as I reached for the top drawer.

"Finally," Bree said.

"What?"

"I'm in." She pulled a flash drive out of her pocket and plugged it into the side of the computer. "Download in progress."

"Downloading what?"

She crossed her arms. "Nerina might think magic is the way to bring down the Guild, but I think a good old financial reckoning will do the trick." She grinned. "I'm about to have every little dirty financial secret they have in my hands."

It was smart. I had to give her credit. My thinking leaned toward Nerina's, but Bree could be right. And hey, it was my idea to bring her in. So I could pat myself on the back a little bit too.

I turned to the filing cabinet. This one was filled with manila folders too, but they were significantly thicker than the one-sheet folders in the DECEASED file. I thumbed through the tabs, looking for something that might offer a clue to what was inside, but most of them had generic labels, like CORRESPONDENCE or PAYMENTS.

I closed the top drawer and tried the middle one. A dividing tab in the center caught my eye. DISSENTERS. The folders behind it were all labeled with names. I saw it almost immediately. JACOBS, LIDIA.

My fingers couldn't pull the folder out fast enough. The card stock sliced my thumb, but I ignored the stinging pain and flipped the folder open. The first sheet was an overview, with several typed lines:

Did not attend initial meeting
Did not attend supplemental meeting
December 4: Visit paid at home. Resistant. Reason for failure unclear.
December 6: Reckoning
Conclusion: Possible Benandanti connection. Monitoring.

I felt sick. December 6 was the day our barn had been destroyed. They were watching my house. They were watching my mother. Jonah had warned me, but this was black-and-white proof in my hands. I took a deep breath to steady myself. This was why I was here, to find this stuff out so I could protect her. I shoved the folder into an empty bag and dug back into the drawer. I pulled out all the files in the DISSENTERS section and stuffed them into the bag. I didn't stop to look through any of them; it didn't matter whether I knew the people or not. All of these people needed to be protected.

The last filing cabinet was marked CURRENT in spidery handwriting. I opened the bottom drawer. There were no written labels on the tabs, but the folders were color-coded. Three-quarters of the folders were purple, while the rest were green. I slid out a green one. There was a header at the top of each piece of paper in the folder.

WOLFE, JONAH.

My whole body shook. I dropped to my knees beside the drawer. "Bree." It came out as a croak. I cleared my throat, which throbbed with heat. "Bree."

Within a breath, she was by my side, kneeling next to me. She pulled one of the other green folders and shuffled through the papers. In total silence, we each took one folder after another and shoved it into the bag. Bree was about to open the last folder when the computer behind us pinged, making both of us jump. "My download is done," she muttered and got up to retrieve her drive.

As I stuffed the last of the Jonah files into the bag, it hit me. This cabinet was marked CURRENT. If the other one was filled with the previous Malandanti of the Twin Willows Clan, then this one contained . . . the identities of all the current members.

My heart was everywhere in my body, thudding in my throat, my chest, my gut. I reached for a purple folder. As I was about to pull it out, a light beamed in through the door's frosted glass window. Without thinking, I ducked low, flattening myself on the floor.

"Shit." Bree scrambled over to me. "It's one of the guards, making his rounds."

"What do we do?"

She craned her neck to look at the door. The glass was still lit by the guard's flashlight. "He shouldn't even be looking at this room. The spell should repel him."

"Which spell—yours or the Guild's?"

"The Guild's—" She froze. "My spell undid their magic. He can see the door now."

Ice-cold fear flooded my veins. We inched backward on our bellies until we were hidden by the filing cabinet. I barely breathed while the light flickered off the walls. After what felt like an endless number of minutes, the light retreated, and the room was dark again.

"We have to go. Now." Bree jumped to her feet and

hustled to the desk to gather her stuff. I dashed to the filing cabinet and looked at the top two drawers. What secrets did they hold? Who were the other Malandanti? There was no time to look. I grabbed a thick, purple folder out of the bottom drawer at random and rolled it shut.

At the door, Bree stopped me and faced the room. She raised her hands and whispered a few words that sounded strangely like Latin. I felt a shudder pass through the walls and the floor.

"Now they won't see the missing files," she told me. "They won't even know to look for them."

We cracked the door open less than an inch. The guard was nowhere to be seen, but he had to be somewhere on this floor. I focused on the camera down the hall. It faced away from us.

"Come on," Bree whispered.

We ran on tiptoe until we were right under the camera. It felt like the longest minute in the world, waiting for it to change direction away from the stairwell. At any moment the guard could come back . . .

The camera clicked and began to swivel. We covered the distance to the door in two steps. I took one last look down the long, marble hallway before Bree shut the door behind us.

We ran down the stairs at breakneck speed and flung ourselves out onto the street. We didn't stop running until we were around the corner and out of sight of the Guild building. Only then did I slide to a halt and bend over, panting to catch my breath.

Bree pressed one hand to her side, the other against her cheek. "We did it," she gasped. "We did it."

I straightened. We looked at each other. Both of us broke into smiles at the same time and then, to my utter shock, Bree Wolfe hugged me. "Thank you," she whispered.

My face felt hot and prickly. "Hey, you're the one that got us in. All that magic you did—that was amazing."

She pulled away from me and rolled her eyes. The mask of toughness that she always wore fell back down on her face. Still, she had dropped it for that one moment . . . and for me. She peered down the street. "Now we just have to figure out how to get home."

We walked to a bus stop a few blocks away. There was one last bus out of Bangor; it would drop us off a couple of miles out of Twin Willows, but we could walk that. After what we did tonight, we could do anything.

It was only when we were settled into our seats on the warm bus that I remembered the purple folder. My stomach turned over and over as I found the bag it was in and pulled it out.

"What is that?"

"It was the only other file I was able to grab from that last cabinet. I think it's got another Malandanti identity in it."

"Well, don't keep us in suspense." Bree reached for it at the same time my fingers found the edge of the folder. We opened it together.

The words on the front page swam in my vision for a moment before making sense.

Called: June 2, 2001. Animal Form: Raven.

I searched up the page until I reached the header.

WEBSTER, PRATT.

CHAPTER SEVENTEEN
The File

Alessia

It all made sense. The reason he was allowed into all the executive meetings. The way he acted like Mr. Wolfe's boss, instead of his assistant, when they were alone. A long time ago, the Lynx had suggested that Mr. Wolfe was the puppet, and someone was pulling his strings. Now I knew who that was.

We lugged all the bags from the bus stop through Twin Willows and back to the farm. The whole world was hushed at this witching hour, but I still imagined eyes on us everywhere. *Monitoring.* Was someone staking out my house even in the middle of the night?

All the things I'd learned in that room swirled in my head, so many threads of information that I couldn't weave them together at all. The Dissenters . . . Jonah's file . . . the seven ancient books detailing each of the sites . . . and Pratt. Pratt Webster was the Malandanti Raven. Pratt Webster was Jonah's Guide.

When we got to the farm, we headed straight for the

woods and the stone wall. I couldn't keep anything in my house, not if the Guild was spying on us. It was safer to keep it underground in Nerina's lair. I only wondered what she would do when she came home and found her coffee table covered with stolen files.

After we'd dumped everything out, I texted Heath. It didn't seem right to keep him out of the loop. By the time he descended into the lair, we were surrounded by stacks of papers and folders and a pile of the leather-bound books.

"What is all this?" Heath asked. "Where's Nerina?"

"We reclaimed the Redwood site," I said.

"And broke into that room at the Guild," Bree said.

Heath looked back and forth between me and Bree. "I think I need a drink."

We lost track of time. It could have been three in the morning or twelve noon; I had no idea. We worked in silence, carefully passing papers, talking only when there was something vital to say.

I showed Heath the file on Pratt Webster first. It was all there, telling us what we'd suspected. He was the head of the Twin Willows Clan, and Mr. Wolfe was his Guild lackey. He was the boss, even if his official job description was Assistant.

After setting that aside, we started on the DISSENTERS files. Lidia's file was frustratingly thin; if they did have a tail on her, they hadn't had time to record it in the file yet. Three-quarters of the way down the stack, Heath paused. "Alessia."

I looked up. He handed me a file and kept his focus on me while I flipped it open.

SALTER, EDWARD. Owner: Salter Hardware and Dry Goods. Prominent figure in Twin Willows. Well-liked by neighbors. Friendly with mayor. Relationship with Lidia Jacobs (?)—cross-reference with Jacobs file.

Confrontation with Wolfe on December 13. Later that night Salter was seen on the grounds of Lidia Jacobs' farm, tracking the Panther into the woods with a shotgun. The Boar headed him off before he reached the Waterfall.

Visited by the Rabbit on December 14. Memory erased. Disappeared for two weeks as a result of memory loss.

Current status: Has returned to Twin Willows and has not been a problem since.

The Rabbit. Was that their code name for their mage? Had his true identity been in the top two drawers of that last cabinet, the drawers filled with answers we would never get to? It couldn't be helped. The odds that we'd ever get back into that room were about as good as a snowball's chances in hell. But now I knew exactly why Mr. Salter had been targeted. He'd seen Jonah that night, the night of the blizzard when they were both snowed in at my house. And he'd probably heard a noise, the sound of Jonah leaping from the guest bedroom window onto the roof of the garage and then to the ground . . .

I swallowed hard. As a non-Benandante, Mr. Salter wouldn't have been able to see Jonah's silver aura. All he would've seen was a huge deadly panther skulking around the house of his best friend. He'd probably gotten the shotgun from his truck, the only thought to protect me and Lidia, not knowing he was really hunting a human being.

I rubbed my face. It was an awful thought, but the Rabbit had actually done us all a favor by erasing his memory.

"There's a file on the mayor here," Bree said.

"What does it say?" Heath asked.

Bree ran a finger down the page. "Name, personal stats, how long she's been mayor . . . Well, well." She raised an eyebrow. "She filed a letter of complaint against the Guild with the EPA."

"Really? But she's always kissing up to your dad."

"She probably wanted to cover all her bases," Bree said. "If the plant went through, the Guild would see her as an ally. But if it didn't, she could say she was against it the whole time."

"But they found out about the letter anyway," I pointed out. "Are they watching her too?"

Bree read down the page. "No. It says, 'the Rabbit paid a visit on December 12. No trouble since then.'" She looked up. "Who's the Rabbit?"

"I think that's their mage," I said. Heath jerked his

head up and snatched the file from Bree. "I think he's the one who killed Sam Foster."

"The Rabbit." Heath ran a hand through his hair, his shaggy blond locks sticking out every which way. "But who *is* he?"

"Whoever he is, that's a really stupid code name," Bree said. "Rabbit, as in 'pulling a rabbit out of your hat'? It took a real genius to come up with that one."

Heath snorted and bent back over the handful of files in his lap. My fingers itched to reach for the Jonah files, but I couldn't quite make myself do it yet, so I reached for another DISSENTERS folder. I flipped it open. My blood ran cold.

Across the top of the one piece of paper in the folder read the name JACOBS, TOM.

It was my dad. My dad had a folder at the Guild.

The black print swam on the page. There was hardly any information there, just his name and address and the following two lines:

December 27, 2013: Mr. Jacobs seen at the Waterfall.
Current status: DECEASED.

I touched that last word as though somehow it could connect me to my dad through the ether of heaven and earth. Why was there a file on him? Was it simply that he was seen at the Waterfall and deemed suspicious? Or was it something deeper? The question that was always inside me rose to the surface again. *Did my dad know about the Benandanti?*

But the only two people I could really ask were Nerina, who had made it clear she wasn't answering the last time it had come up, and Lidia. And I definitely couldn't ask her.

I slid the file off to the side, beneath the pillows that surrounded me. Someday, someday, I would have the truth. But whatever it was couldn't help me now.

"Find anything good?" Bree asked without looking up from the paper she was reading.

"Nothing relevant." It wasn't a lie. I watched her and Heath for a moment, until I was sure they were completely absorbed in what they were reading. Then I finally reached for one of Jonah's files. I couldn't wait any more. I had to know what the Guild was saying about him. If he was on probation, as he'd told me, there might be something in these files that could protect him.

My fingers clenched the thick green folder. Why was I trying to protect my enemy? I shouldn't care that he was on probation. I shouldn't care if they were angry at him for not killing me. I should leave him to their mercy. After all, he had put himself in this situation.

I opened the file and splayed my hand flat against the paper.

I couldn't feel that way, even if he hadn't told me he wasn't sorry. Even if he hadn't had that look in his eyes, that look of missing me, of wanting me. I'd realized a while ago that I couldn't hate Jonah. I might not be allowed to love him, but I couldn't hate him.

The first folder contained nothing I didn't know. Age, birthplace, Social Security number, passport information, previous addresses. The second folder had details about some of the other places they'd lived. I noticed the information stopped at the place they'd lived before Fairfield, Connecticut—where they'd moved to Twin Willows from. I glanced at Bree, but she was entranced by whatever she was reading. I slid the third folder into my lap and opened it. Sure enough, the header at the top of the first page read FAIRFIELD.

My throat dry, I carefully read each page. It contained a story I'd heard before, but it was fascinating to read it from the Guild's point of view.

Female twin approached and Called. Refused the Call. Extremely disagreeable and unsociable. Not likely to divulge existence of Malandanti to anyone.

Risk factor: Low.

I snorted quietly. As clever as the Guild seemed to be, they'd really missed the mark on Bree.

Assessment of male twin: unmotivated, unfocused, cavalier. Possible drinking problem. Probably easily manipulated.

My heart started to beat faster, harder. There was a time stamp on the page: September 15. That was a little over a month before the Wolfes came to Twin Willows. I turned the page.

Subject will be at a high school party on September 20. Will likely drink heavily.

It is believed that guilt will be the best possible motivator.

And then below that:

Vehicle brakes tampered with. If unsuccessful, we will involve the Rabbit.

I closed my eyes. In my mind, I could see Jonah's face when I had suggested to him that the Malandanti had caused the accident that had caused his ex-girlfriend Emily to lose both her legs. White-hot anger and absolute denial etched deep in his features. I had never mentioned it again, despite my deep suspicion. Now I had proof.

I shuffled through the rest of the papers in the file. It was all documentation of the accident's aftermath, the steps they had taken to keep Jonah out of jail, the bribes they had given the Fairfield police and the press, a detailed record of all payments made to Emily's family. And the magic the Rabbit had performed to make everyone agreeable.

"It's nearly six," Heath said. I started; I had almost forgotten their presence beside me. Bree began to neaten up the papers that covered her lap and the floor around her. I slid the Jonah file away from me and all the way under the sofa, which I was leaning against. I would come back later to retrieve it and my dad's file and keep them in my room. All I knew was Bree wasn't ready to see Jonah's file. She would fly off the handle and storm to Jonah, wave the papers under his nose, and rant. We couldn't afford that. Jonah couldn't know we'd broken into the Guild. I had to find some other way to tell him what the Malandanti had done, how they had manipulated him.

As we walked up the stairs to the outside world, I noticed that Heath was carrying three of the leather-bound manuscripts. "What are you hoping to find in those?"

"I don't know. Maybe something we didn't know about the magic at each site. Something that can help us regain the ones we don't control. And I want to call Nerina and find out if she knew about these books."

"Don't do that," Bree said.

Heath raised an eyebrow. "Why not?"

We emerged into the early-morning chill, the forest blue and grey all around us. Bree scratched her face as she looked at Heath. "Um, she kinda told me to wait until she got back to break into the Guild."

Heath threw his hand up. "That's great, Bree. Now I have two teenagers who can't follow directions." He sighed heavily. "Fine. But you're going to have a lot of explaining to do when she gets back." He pulled his phone out of his back pocket. "Hopefully she can tell me when that will be." He parted ways with us when we reached the fence.

Bree and I headed over the hill toward the house. "I

don't know how I'm going to climb back in my bathroom window without my mother seeing," she said.

I raised an eyebrow.

"It's the only way to sneak in and out of my house. But I figured I'd be coming back at night so it would be no big deal."

"So don't go home." I bit my lip, but it was too late to take the suggestion back. "Just tell them you spent the night at my house. We'll tell my mom you showed up late last night to work on that project."

Bree kicked at the ground. "I don't have a change of clothes."

"You can borrow something of mine."

"I don't know." She curled her lip. "Someone might actually think we were friends if I did that."

"Heaven forbid." I bumped her side. "Don't worry. I'll let you tell everyone I snore."

When Jenny saw me walking up the road with Bree, she dropped her bag to the ground and stared. I knew Jenny wouldn't buy the line I had sold my mother—about Bree and me working on a school project together—so I scrambled to think of something else to say. Luckily, Bree beat me to it.

"Your friend is pretty pathetic," she told Jenny. "She called me up last night and lured me over to her house with promises of baked goods and then grilled me for hours about my brother. I wound up having to spend the night."

Maybe it wasn't so lucky that Bree had spoken first.

"Lessi, you have got to get over him." Jenny slung an arm around me and squeezed my shoulder. "He is so not worth it." She tossed a glance to Bree. "No offense."

"None taken," Bree said cheerily. "See you in government, Alessia!" And she walked on ahead of us, her gait so bouncy she was almost skipping.

Jenny dropped her arm off my shoulder. "Seriously, Alessia? Now you're hanging out with *Bree Wolfe*? I just don't know what to think anymore. It's like you're a different person."

I am! I wanted to shout. I wanted to tell her everything. I wanted her to be the understanding, supportive friend she had always been. And suddenly I was angry—so angry—that I couldn't tell her. It wasn't fair. The one part of my life that I so desperately needed, I was expected to sacrifice. "You know what, Jenny? Maybe I am a different person. Maybe you just don't know me at all."

She stopped and put her hands on her hips. "You're getting mad at me?"

"Yeah," I said. "Yeah, I am. You have no idea what I'm going through."

"Then tell me!" She threw her hands up. "Tell me what you're going through. Let me help."

"You can't." My breath came in fast, shallow gasps. I had to stop soon or I would start crying, and I really didn't want to do that. Not here, in the middle of Main

Street. "You can't help. Sometimes there are just some things you can't fix, okay? Sometimes you just need to be a friend no matter what."

"I am—"

"No, you're not." Pinpricks started at the backs of my eyes. "You're planning trips to Massachusetts without me. You've got this whole other life going on, and you're shutting me out."

Jenny's own eyes were bright, and two little spots of red appeared on her cheeks. "You shut me out way before I did. I was pounding on that door, and you just wouldn't answer."

We stared at each other for a long moment.

She hung her head. When she raised it again, I thought she was going to apologize. But instead, she picked up her bag, turned on her heel, and walked the rest of the way to school without me.

"I wanted to answer," I whispered. I watched her back retreat farther and farther away. "But I must not speak of the Benandanti."

CHAPTER EIGHTEEN

The Discovery

Alessia

Jenny didn't speak to me all morning. When I walked into second-period French class, she and Carly sat together, whispering furiously. They didn't even look up when I sat down, and I distinctly heard my name twice.

I folded my arms and sank way down in my chair. I hoped against hope that Jonah would skip, but just before the bell rang, he skulked into the classroom and took his seat behind me.

Now that he was there, I found myself waiting for a note to land on my desk. After fifteen minutes, I wanted that note so bad my stomach hurt. But no note appeared. I risked a glance over my shoulder. Jonah was focused on his French book, reading the chapter Madame Dubois had assigned. I stared at him. Really? *Really?* All of a sudden he was a model student?

I guess it was Ignore Alessia Day. I dropped my head into my hands and rubbed my temples. My insides felt all twisted and tangled, everything out of place. I couldn't sit in this room surrounded by people who were mad at me. I dumped all my books into my bag and marched up to Madame Dubois. "I need to go to the nurse," I told her in French. I figured if I spoke in French, she'd let me go easier.

Without protest, she handed me a hall pass. "Feel better, dear."

I couldn't remember the last time I'd been in the nurse's office. I rarely got sick, and when I did, I opted for a tough-it-out approach. The nurse took my temperature (slightly elevated) and asked me when I last had my period (ew). She made the required phone call to Lidia, who I knew was out all day at one of the farms where we'd boarded our goats. In a bigger school, I might have been made to stay there until Lidia could pick me up herself. But in Twin Willows, where everyone knew everyone, the nurse wrote me an excuse and sent me home by myself.

Small-town life had its advantages.

When I got home, I dumped my bag on the couch in the living room, went to the kitchen, and made myself some coffee. While it was brewing, I texted Heath.

Meet me at Nerina's.

What are you doing out of school?

was his immediate reply.

Tell you when I see you. Want some coffee?

> *Yes and FOOD. Starving.*

It made me smile, a hard feat considering my mood. I filled an old lunch bag with apples, cheese, biscotti, half a loaf of bread, and some jam. I pressed the plunger down on the French press and divided the coffee between two travel mugs.

Heath was already in the lair when I got there, one of the leather-bound books open in his lap. I handed him his coffee and settled down on the floor next to him. "How'd you get out of school?" he asked after taking a sip from his mug.

"Told them I was sick." I pulled one of the other manuscripts over to me.

"Are you?"

I shook my head. I could feel his eyes on me as I carefully opened the book. The pages were thick and brittle. My eyes itched, and my throat grew hot. I wasn't going to cry, not for the second time in as many hours. But it couldn't be stopped. I bent in half, my head meeting my knees.

Heath slid the book off my lap and scooted in close to me. "Alessia," he said, his voice gentle, "what's wrong?"

I couldn't answer. The tears came all at once, drenching my face, and my throat was too thick for me to talk. I felt Heath put his arm around me, but he didn't say anything. He just let me cry for a long time.

"It's just everything," I finally said with a hiccup. Then it all came out in a big rush. "Carly and Melissa have forgotten I exist, and now Jenny's not talking to me, and Jo—Jonah's over me, and my only friend is *Bree Wolfe*, which is just ridiculous because she's not friends with anyone, and I can't talk to my mom, and she's gone all the time with Mr. Salter anyway, and . . . and I miss my dad." I blinked while the last of the tears fell from my eyelashes. My tearstained cheeks felt tight.

"Wow. That's a lot."

"Yeah." I sniffled and wiped my nose with the back of my hand. "I'm a mess."

"Alessia, every new Benandante is a mess. It's a really hard adjustment." He squeezed my shoulder. "And you've had to deal with a lot more than most."

I snorted. "Yeah, I guess most Benandanti don't have a Malandante for an ex-boyfriend."

"You just have to take it one day at a time." His blue eyes were wide and serious.

"Is that what you do?" I asked quietly.

"Yes," he whispered. He cleared his throat and slid the book I'd been looking at toward me. "And what we have to do today is read through these books."

I ran my fingers across the embroidered title. *The Redwoods*. The text inside was an antiquated form of Italian. I had to turn a lot of the words over and over in my internal translator. The words we absolutely couldn't understand, Heath and I wrote on a piece of paper to give Nerina.

Every book was a detailed account of the magic contained at each site and a history of which side controlled it. The last entry still recorded the Malandanti as being in control of the Redwoods. I took a pen out of my bag and carefully wrote the date, followed by the words, in Italian, *Regained by the Benandanti.*

"Now we have two," I murmured.

Heath looked up, and I showed him what I had done. He smiled. "Now we have two," he agreed. "Baby steps back to seven."

I knew he was trying to be positive, but it was so agonizing. It felt like such a steep hill to climb, especially when the Malandanti were so organized and so power-ful. Where were the Benandanti's hallowed marble halls? Where was our room sealed off by magic and filled with our detailed, documented history?

I jerked my head up. "Nerina's home in Friuli—the one that was destroyed. Is that where the Benandanti kept our version of these files?"

Heath closed the book he held—*Angel Falls*—and rested his hand on top. "We've never had these kinds of files."

I squinted at him. "No records of past Benandanti or anything? Why not?"

Heath looked meaningfully at the papers spread all around us. "So no one would ever be able to steal them."

My lip curved up. Maybe the Malandanti weren't so clever after all.

For three days and nights, Heath, Bree and I met after school in the underground lair and worked side by side poring over the books and papers. We kept ourselves plied with coffee from Nerina's fancy machine, home-cured salami from our basement, and fresh loaves of bread Lidia had baked. We emerged only for meals and to tend the chickens so Lidia didn't get suspicious.

We had worked our way down to the last few folders and had taken to reading them simultaneously instead of passing them back and forth to one another. As Bree and I peered over Heath's shoulders at the paper he held up, his phone buzzed in his pocket. He pulled it out.

"That thing gets texts?" Bree asked, looking at the antiquated cell phone.

"I keep telling him to get an iPhone," I said.

"I don't need an iPhone," Heath muttered. "I don't need to check my e-mail every five minutes."

"Do you even have an e-mail address?" Bree said.

Heath ignored her and held up the phone so we could read the text.

> *Griffin is winging east.*

"I suppose that's code for she's getting on a plane."

"That's a really dumb code," Bree said. "Any idiot could figure that out."

"Do you think they rescued Dario?" I asked.

Heath bit his lip. "I hope so. Nerina is a little paranoid about electronic communication, obviously," he added, waving the phone, "so she hasn't told me. But I don't think she would come back unless he was okay."

"Unless he's dead," Bree murmured, taking the paper from Heath's hand and replacing it in its folder.

"Bree!"

She looked up at me. "Sorry," she said, shrugging. "But that's a distinct possibility, isn't it?"

"Yes, but—"

"All right, let's all just think positive," Heath interrupted. He reached for the next folder in the pile, the very last folder we had managed to steal from the Guild. I looked around at all the progress we'd made. Everything had been separated into piles according to their usefulness. I thought of the folder with Jonah's name on it, currently hidden between the mattress and the box spring in my room. I didn't know how useful it would be to the Benandanti as a whole, but it was precious to me.

Heath spread out the few papers in the folder on the table in front of us and shifted so we could all read them at the same time. The papers were old and yellowed, the handwriting on them faded from time. My gaze moved across the text, not quite taking in what I was reading at first. Next to me, Bree drew in a sharp breath. On my other side, Heath seemed to have stopped breathing. I looked back at the first page and carefully read it all again, my heart skipping beats with each line.

We all seemed to realize at once what we were seeing. I gripped Heath's knee, my fingers digging in hard. Bree slid off the couch to kneel on the floor, her hands splayed over the papers.

"It's the spell," she whispered. "The spell that makes everyone agree with them."

If we had the spell, surely we could figure out how to break it. I closed my eyes. It wasn't just the spell. It was the answer.

CHAPTER NINETEEN
The New Mage

Alessia

As badly as I wanted to skip school the next day to wait for Nerina to get home, I had tests in both French and government, and I didn't want to give Morrissey any reason to call a conference with Lidia. I walked to school holding my notes in front of my nose, trying to absorb them by some sort of magic. But all I could think about was what we had found in the Guild papers. I knew the enormity of the discovery would erase any anger Nerina might have about me and Bree breaking into the office without her permission. It could truly be the turning point in the war with the Malandanti. Focusing on school was the least of my priorities, but I couldn't draw suspicion to myself by doing badly.

I spotted Jenny ahead when I passed the turn-off to her house. Ever since our fight, she purposely hadn't waited at the corner for me, and I'd been forced to stare at her back while we walked the last few blocks to school in silence. It was ridiculous. I tucked my notes into my bag and jogged to catch up to her. "Hey."

"Hey," she said without looking at me.

I fell into step with her. "Seriously? How long are you going to keep this up?"

She still didn't look at me. "Until you apologize."

"Jenny, come on." I stepped in front of her, forcing her to stop and look at me. "I tried to say I was sorry, and you just walked away. I *am* sorry, but I was really hurt."

Jenny's gaze darted all over the street until it finally rested on my face. "How 'bout we both say we're sorry and call it a day?"

"Deal." I reached out to touch her arm. "I'm really sorry. I've just been going through a rough time."

"I know. I'm really sorry, too." She dropped her bag to the ground and pulled me into a hug. "I should've been more understanding."

We walked to school slowly, our steps in sync once more. "We're still saving a spot for you," Jenny said. "On the girls' weekend. If you want to go."

"I do." I bit my lip. "Are you sure Carly and Melissa want me there?"

"I think if you show up at lunch today and grovel a little, they'll be okay," Jenny said, grinning. "Have you mentioned it to your mom?"

"No."

Jenny groaned. "Well, you'd better do that before any of us get our hopes up. Maybe my mom should call her."

"Maybe." It wasn't Lidia I was worried about, though. There was no way Nerina and Heath would let me out of

Twin Willows, not with our hold on the Waterfall hanging by a thread and the promise of victory over the Guild so ripe in our hands.

The French test wasn't fun, but somehow I made it through even though I was very aware of Jonah bent over his own test paper behind me. When lunchtime rolled around, I clutched my lunch bag to me as I approached. Jenny smiled and waved me over. Melissa and Carly looked up, tight smiles on their faces. I guessed Jenny had said something to them.

"Hey, guys."

"Are you ready for the government test?" Carly asked.

I rolled my eyes. "Not even a little bit."

She scooted over and gestured to the notes spread out in front of her. "Let's cram."

I slid in next to her, and we bent our heads together. Melissa and Jenny chatted while Carly and I studied. The normality of it filled me with relief. I didn't care if I failed the test. Getting back into my friends' good graces was worth more than any grade.

When the four of us emerged from the front doors at the end of the school day, everything seemed to be restored. "I already scheduled a tour for us at Williams," Melissa told me, "so you have to talk to your mom ASAP."

"I will, I will."

We walked across the lawn toward Main Street. A

huge black SUV idled at the curb. Josh Baker and Bree stood next to it, having what appeared to be a heated conversation.

"Trouble in paradise," Melissa said, nudging me.

I watched them for a moment, snatches of their words carrying on the light wind. "You can't expect me to drop everything for you," Bree was saying.

"But it's been like four days," Josh whined.

I moved a little closer to eavesdrop, my friends at my heels. "Get a grip," Bree hissed. "I am not on your hook like the other girls in your harem."

Carly whistled low. "You go, girl."

"He's such a player," Melissa said. "It's about time someone gave him a taste of his own medicine."

Bree moved away from Josh, but he grabbed her arm and swung her to face him. I took several fast steps, but before I could reach them, Bree had pulled out of his grasp. "I never said we were more than what we were," she said. "I was just playing by your rules."

"You're just a little whore, aren't you?"

"Hey!" I shouted. I broke away from my friends and jogged over to Bree. "We're still on school grounds, you know. I'd be happy to report you to Morrissey for harassment."

Josh sneered. "Whatever. Good luck getting anyone to touch you with a ten-foot pole after this, Bree."

"As if I care."

Josh climbed into his car, revved the engine, and

pulled away from the curb without looking.

A little hatchback coming down Main Street had to slam on its brakes. Bree tossed her hair and looked at me. "Thanks."

"He's been an asshole since the second grade," I said. I turned back to Carly, Melissa, and Jenny. "Right, girls?"

For a moment they looked between me and Bree. "He tried to feel me up when we were eleven," Carly said finally.

"His dad pinched my mom's ass," Jenny said. "She gave him a black eye."

"I think I like your mom." Bree laughed. The sound caught my friends off guard, as if it reminded them she was a human being with feelings too. I grinned. Nothing like boy troubles to bond girls.

Jenny, Bree, and I said good-bye to Carly and Melissa and headed down Main Street. Bree turned down her street with a quick wink at me. I knew she'd double back as soon as we were out of sight. Now that school was over, I couldn't wait to get to Nerina's. I wondered if Heath had already told her about our discovery. And I wanted to know what had happened in California.

"So you'll talk to your mom?"

I started. "What? Oh, yeah. Definitely."

"Let me know if you need my mom to call." Jenny narrowed her eyes at me. "Promise?"

"Promise." I swiped my fingers across my chest. "Cross my heart."

I waited until Jenny was out of sight and broke into

a run all the way home. I bypassed the house and headed straight for the woods. Along the stone wall, through the hidden door, down the secret stairway . . . I skidded to a halt when I emerged into the living area.

Heath and Nerina stood entwined on the calfskin rug, unaware that I'd come in. He held her face in his hands like a precious object, his lips moving against hers as if he were a man starved. Her fingers dug into his shoulders and back, her body molded to his as though they were made for each other. And with an intake of breath, I realized they were. How could the *Concilio* keep them apart?

I backed up the steps on tiptoe. My cheeks tingled with heat as they disappeared from my view. I closed the door quietly. A twig snapped behind me, and I spun around.

"What's up?" Bree asked.

"Jeez," I breathed, pressing a hand to my sternum. I leaned against the wall to catch my breath.

"Aren't we going in?"

"Ah . . . let's give them a few minutes."

Bree raised an eyebrow and grinned. "Heath's finally getting some?"

"*Ew!* No!" I shuddered. "Could you be any more crass?"

"Well, yes. Yes, I could."

"Well, don't." I curled my lip. "Gross."

"But they are—"

"They're making out. Okay? Are you happy?"

Bree rubbed her hands together. "Excellent."

"Look," I said, launching myself away from the wall, "I don't want them to know I saw them. They're not supposed to be together—the *Concilio* ordered them to be apart. It's complicated."

"Why? Because she's immortal? That's insane."

"Yeah, well, in Italy if your family orders you to do something, you do it." I glanced at the closed door. "Maybe we should go in."

"Are you kidding?" Bree grabbed my arm. "We should give them at least an hour."

"Bree!" I pulled away from her. "Don't you want to know what happened at the Redwood site? And tell her about what we found?"

"And don't you want your Guide to get laid?"

I held my hand up. "Don't make me vomit."

Bree laughed. "Come on. I bet your mom has some biscotti lying around." She took me by the elbow and guided me away from the wall, but at that moment, the door shifted open, and Heath appeared.

"Oh—hey," he said. His lips were raw and red, and his shirt was untucked.

"Hi." I slid my arm out of Bree's grasp. "We were just coming to see you guys."

"Nerina's inside," Heath said. He glanced down and shoved his shirt back into the waistband of his jeans. "I was just, um, leaving."

"What? Don't you want to stay and tell her what we found?"

"I did." Heath walked away from the wall, back toward the farm.

Bree threw her hands up. "*I* wanted to be the one to tell her!"

"Sorry," Heath tossed over his shoulder. "See you later, Alessia."

I watched him go, my insides a little twisted. "Something must've happened between them," I muttered. "I mean, after I walked in."

"Let me guess. It went something like this. 'Oh, Nerina, I love you so much,'" Bree said in a mock-Heath voice. "'But *caro*, we cannot. The *Concilio*—'"

I had to stifle a laugh. Bree's imitation of Nerina was pretty dead-on.

"'Damn the *Concilio*! I want you!'"

"'They are my family! Do not make me choose between them and you!'"

"'Because you choose them!'"

"*And scene.*" She took a little bow and descended the stairs into Nerina's lair.

I followed her, shaking my head. I was certain that was how it had gone down, too. That was the only thing keeping them apart, even with the *Concilio* so far away. Nerina's duty to them always came first, even over her own heart.

When we came into the living area, Nerina was sitting in the oversized chair, a sheaf of papers in her hands. She was looking at them, but I could tell she wasn't seeing them. Her lips, too, were swollen, and her eyes were red-rimmed. She looked very much like the teenager she once was, small and vulnerable.

Bree cleared her throat, and Nerina started. "Oh, there you are, girls. Come in, come in." She set down the papers and stood to hug us both. "I am so very proud of you. You were naughty to go without my permission," she added, wagging her finger at us, "but it paid off. Sit, sit."

We settled on the couch. I tucked my feet underneath me. "What happened in California? Is Dario okay?"

"*Sì.*" She sighed and leaned delicately into the back cushions of the chair. "He was hurt, but he will recover. The Redwood Clan is caring for him."

"Did he give up anything?" Bree asked.

"No. He held strong."

I swallowed. I didn't want to know the extent to which he'd been tortured. I wasn't sure if I could hold strong under the same circumstances. "And the Redwood site is safe?"

"*Sì.* And just before I left California, I received even better news." A smile danced across her lips, lightening the redness in her eyes. "Pakistan has been recovered too."

"So we have three sites in our control now?" I gulped in a breath and reached for a folder that lay on the coffee table in front of me. "And with this information, we can bring down the Guild. This is great, right?" I looked from Nerina to Bree. "Right?"

"Yes. It is fantastic." Nerina pressed her palms to her

cheeks. "But we cannot stop to celebrate. We are winning battles. But we have yet to win the war."

"But this could help us!" I waved the folder. "We're getting close." I shoved aside the niggling thought in my brain, that if we won the war, I could leave the Benandanti. I could have a normal life. Heath had promised. But another thought sliced through that one. If the Benandanti won, where did that leave Jonah?

"And I have an idea to bring us even closer," Nerina said. "I spoke to Dario about it and was able to convince him, too."

I met her gaze. "The mages."

"*Sì*." Nerina brushed a hand over the papers on her lap. "It's time we have our own Rabbit. And I know just the person." Her razor-sharp gaze settled on Bree's face.

Bree shrank into the corner of the couch under my and Nerina's stares. "What, me?"

Nerina stood. "Yes, Bree. *You*."

Chapter Twenty

My Super-Awesome Jedi Mind Trick

Bree

I dropped my head back against the couch cushions, letting out a loud sigh. "Seriously?" I said to the ceiling. "Every time I think I'm out, they pull me back in."

"Out?" Alessia said. "How could you think you're getting out?"

"I did my part!" I sat upright and waved at the stack of books and papers we'd stolen from the Guild. "I spied on the Guild; we broke into the magic office and got the stuff. I thought I was done."

"You're in too deep to be done," Alessia said in such a matter-of-fact tone that I wanted to punch her. "We need you now more than ever. Isn't that right, Nerina?"

I could actually feel my hand flexing into a fist, and I had to sit on it so I didn't slam it into her jaw.

Nerina obviously saw that I was on the edge, because she came to sit between me and Alessia. "She's right, Bree," she said, resting a hand on my knee. "You are invaluable to us, and we cannot lose you."

"But a *mage*? Why me?"

"I told you, *cara*. You have magic in you—powerful magic. It could be the single greatest weapon we have to use against the Malandanti."

Me, a weapon? Uh, no thank you. "I don't want to be a weapon. I want out."

"How can you be so freaking selfish?" Alessia yelled.

My mouth dropped open. I'd never heard her volume go above five.

"Do you have any idea how much I want out?" she said. "But I can't get out. Maybe, just maybe, there is the tiniest sliver of possibility that if we win back all seven sites, I can."

I shot a glance at Nerina, whose eyes were wide. This was obviously news to her too.

"Heath promised," Alessia said. "He said if we got back all seven sites I could get out."

Nerina opened her mouth.

Alessia held a hand up. "I don't want to hear *no* right now. I need to know there's the slightest chance it could happen. I need to have hope." She looked at me again. "And without you, there isn't any. So stop thinking about yourself for once."

A hot, white rage bubbled up inside me. "I wasn't thinking about myself." My voice shook with the effort to not scream. How dare she? How dare she, when she knew who I was really doing all this for? My gaze lasered straight into Alessia's eyes. Her face paled. After a moment, she blinked and looked away. Yeah. She knew exactly who I was thinking about.

"You would be helping Jonah as well," Nerina said. I swung to face her. "If we destroy the Guild, if we take down the Malandanti, he will be free too."

"If he doesn't die in the process," I snapped.

Nerina tilted her head. Her calmness irritated me so much my palms itched. "And as a mage, you could make sure that didn't happen. You could protect him."

My chest heaved. I stared right into her eyes. "I will choose him over the Benandanti. If it comes down to it. You should know that up front."

"*Cara*," Nerina said. This time the softness of her tone melted my rage a little. "I would never expect anything less. Your first loyalty is always to your *famiglia*." Her voice broke over the word, and she turned away. I thought of the little scene I'd just performed aboveground for Alessia, and my cheeks burned. It wasn't funny. It was tragic. God, between the three of us, we had Shakespeare beat.

I swallowed hard. My throat felt jagged and raw. I was between a rock and a goddamned hard place, and the only way out was to get down on my knees and crawl through the scariest opening, the one covered in spiders and scorpions.

"Okay." The word was rotten on my tongue. *So that's what betrayal tastes like.* "I'll do it. But I get the same deal as Alessia. We regain all seven sites, and I'm done."

I stuck my right hand out. After a moment, Alessia

walked over and put hers on mine. A long minute passed. Nerina laid hers gently on top. I noticed that she'd started biting her cuticles since the last time I'd seen her.

"Deal," she said quietly, and we dropped our hands.

We stood there looking at each other in awkward silence.

I crossed my arms. "I need a cigarette."

I was having a dream about sleep. In it, I got to sleep for hours and hours without anyone bothering me.

"Miss Wolfe?"

Go away, I thought.

"Miss Wolfe!"

"What?" I said crankily without opening my eyes.

"Miss Wolfe, if you do not wake up this instant, I will send you to the principal's office."

I cracked one eye open. The entire class was staring at me, and Mr. Tanner stood over me, his little piggy eyes squinting at me. I sat up. "Jane Austen was making a commentary on society."

Mr. Tanner folded his arms. "That would be a relevant statement if we were discussing Jane Austen. However, we are discussing *Jane Eyre*."

"Gothic feminism."

"Miss Wolfe, if you fall asleep in my class once more this week, I will start deducting one grade point for each minute of naptime."

"Then keep me awake," I muttered, but he had already headed back to the front of the class. I missed Mr. Foster. He would've kept me awake or at least ignored me while I was sleeping. I sighed and stared out the window. It was snowing—*again*. It seemed as if that was all it did this time of year in Maine. I wished Mr. Tanner would just send me to Morrissey and be done with it. Maybe I could even get suspended. Then at least I could get some sleep. I snorted to myself. Unlikely. Nerina had kept me captive in her underground lair for the past five days, all afternoon and evening, only stopping for twenty minutes to eat dinner. I thought eating a meal in under two hours was sacrilege to Italians, but apparently I was wrong. I was just lucky my mom had decided to go away for a few days. And my dad had barely blinked when I'd abruptly quit my internship. He was hardly ever home these days.

The bell rang, and I vaulted out of my seat and into the hall before Mr. Tanner could harass me again. The rest of the day dragged until my final study period, which I usually skipped. But I was actually going today. Only I wasn't going to study schoolwork.

I slid into a desk in the back corner of the room and pulled my hoodie up. As kids filed in around me, I took out the book Nerina had given me to work on from last night's session. It was written in a really old, really dead language—not Italian, not Latin, not Greek or Aramaic or Hebrew or anything that remotely resembled words. Nerina thought it was a secret code, and even though I

NICOLE MAGGI

knew she was probably right, I was kinda hoping it would turn out to be some alien language from another planet or dimension.

I opened the book, which was easier said than done because the pages weren't paper; they were bark. The book creaked as I laid it flat, and I glanced around to make sure no one was watching me. They weren't. Most of the other kids in study period were losers too busy carving loser-band logos into their desks to notice my creaking book, or they were do-gooders who were, you know, *actually studying*.

Just like the other book Nerina had shown me, this one hummed when I pressed my palms onto the bark pages. The letters seemed to shift beneath my touch, as if they were trying to tell me something. I could sense that the book wanted to be known, but I was missing something, something I needed to give it before it would reveal its secrets. I closed my eyes and felt my way into the book. It was like stumbling down a pitch-black hallway, bumping into walls and chairs as you went. I pushed further, and the book pushed back. An electric shock jolted through me. I yelped and fell out of my chair.

A couple of the do-gooders looked over at me, annoyed that I'd interrupted their nerd session. The teacher at the front of the room didn't even glance up from his laptop. Fifty bucks he was surfing porn. I climbed back into my chair and smacked the book. "All right, bitch," I muttered, "if that's the way you want it."

I touched the book again, but this time I didn't force my way in. I tiptoed, cajoling it as if I were a guy trying to talk his virgin girlfriend into having sex. Now the pathway into the book was lit by a single lightbulb, swinging crazily from a loose cord, casting shadows on all the walls. But in between those shadows were doorways. I just had to know which one to push open . . .

"Hey."

I shook my head, blocking out the noise around me, and pushed at the closest door. It didn't budge.

"Hey!"

My eyes opened a slit.

The nerd in front of me had turned around and was leaning on my desk.

"What," I said through gritted teeth.

"Um," she said, "you're talking to yourself."

"So?"

"So I'm trying to *study*."

"Yeah, well, so am I."

Her gaze dropped to my book. "What kind of a textbook is *that*?"

My fingers gripped the edges of the bark pages. "It's a none-of-your-goddamned-business kind of textbook."

With a huff, she spun around.

I smirked at her back and closed my eyes again. It was easier this time, sliding down into the deep, dark hallway, passing over the first door. No, that wasn't the right one; of course it wasn't . . . I passed by one door, two, three . . . None of those were right either . . .

This one. It called to me, faint but sure. I put a hand on the knob and turned. It swung open and light poured out, an unearthly green glow that flooded out into the hallway, filled all the corners, *filled me.* I could feel its aura in every pore of my body, alternating warm and cool, like stepping from sunlight into shadow and back again.

My gut twisted, telling me to pull away, to shake the light off me like a bug, but I forced myself to stay. This was what Nerina and I had been working on: not running away from my power. Apparently, I had commitment issues. *No shit, Sherlock*, I'd told her. The trembling started at my toes, trying to get me to run, but I kept myself rooted. If for no other reason than to show Nerina I could.

The light made me glow . . . I could see through my skin, see my blood running through my veins, see my lungs expanding and contracting, my heart pumping. The light spiraled up, up, up, into my head.

My eyes flew open.

Everything in study hall was exactly the same. Only now, every human being in the room wore a halo of the same green light. I held my hands up in front of my face. Same green. "Whoa," I breathed.

The nerd girl turned around again. "Look, if you don't shut up, I'm going to say something to Mr. Curtis."

Obviously she couldn't see I was too busy glowing to shut up. "Chill out," I muttered as I examined my green hand.

Her halo flickered and turned back on, brighter than

before. Her face slackened, and she slumped in her seat. "No worries, dude," she said in a mellow-yellow voice. I stared. She seemed way too Type A to say stuff like *dude*. Then she picked up her pen and started doodling on her arm.

Whoa.

I stood and moved to the loser guy two desks ahead of me. "Ask Mr. Curtis if he's on the *Big Boob Blowout* or the *Pussy Galore* website today."

The guy's halo flickered and brightened just like the girl's. "Hey, Mr. Curtis," he called to the front of the room. "What's the site of the day? Big Boob Blowout or Pussy Galore?"

Mr. Curtis slammed his laptop shut. "*Excuse me*, young man?"

"He didn't mean anything by it." I met Mr. Curtis's gaze across the room. "You should just dismiss us all early."

Mr. Curtis scratched his nose. "Why don't you all take off early? Day's almost over."

Holy shit, I was Obi-freaking-Wan Kenobi.

I grabbed the book and my bag. When I got to the door, I couldn't help it; I raised my hand just as Alec Guinness did in the movie and gave it a little wave. "You don't need to remember any of this," I said, and all the halos in the room flickered.

The halls were empty; everyone was still in classes. I passed the office and peered through the glass windows. Sure enough, all the secretaries inside wore halos.

Everyone in the world was my bitch.

Moments later, the last bell rang, and green-haloed kids poured into the halls, hundreds of chess pieces just waiting for me to move them. I wove in between them. The possibilities made me lightheaded.

I stopped the bitchy senior girl who'd said my lipstick made me look like a whore on my first day here. "You should tell your boyfriend you're cheating on him," I told her.

She nodded and walked away with purposeful strides.

Josh Baker brushed past me, knocking my shoulder with intentional force. I caught his elbow. "You need to tell your mother you have herpes."

"Okay," he agreed, a goofy smile on his face.

God, it was like eating an entire chocolate cheesecake and not gaining a pound. The light fed me with every halo flicker until I glowed so bright I looked radioactive. I soared through the doors onto the lawn, buoyed by power. It was still snowing, and while most everyone else huddled under the building's eaves or jumped into cars waiting at the curb, I stood in the open, my arms stretched wide, tasting the cold flakes on my tongue. I owned the world . . . or at least, everyone in it.

Jonah sidled up to me. "What's with you?"

I dropped my arms and squinted up into his face. Could he see the light? Did being a Malandante give him that power? But no—his eyes were clear as ever, save for the shadows that always lived there. His gaze shifted to something beyond me. I turned.

Alessia hurried across the lawn, her blue wool hat pulled down tightly over her ears.

I rolled my eyes. "You two need to figure this out already."

Jonah's halo flickered.

I straightened. "In fact, I think you should meet tonight and talk."

Jonah blinked at me. "I have to go."

He set off in Alessia's direction. I jogged a step behind. When he reached her, I brushed behind her and murmured, "Say yes," into her ear. I only had time to hear him ask her to meet in "their new place"—wherever that was—before I was out of earshot. I didn't need to hear her say yes. I knew she would.

I stumbled to the Jacobs farm, tripping over my own feet with drunken glee. Wait until I told Nerina. I could do anything. I could order the Guild to turn themselves in. I could command the Malandanti to stop attacking the Waterfall. I could tell Pratt Webster to go fuck himself. *I could tell my dad what I really thought of him.*

I opened the door in the stone wall and hopped down the stairs. "Nerina!" The aroma of freshly brewed coffee filled the air. She stepped out from the kitchen, an espresso cup in her hand. As soon as she saw me, her eyes widened. The cup smashed to the floor, splattering coffee onto her dove-grey pencil skirt.

"What the hell did you do?"

CHAPTER TWENTY-ONE

The Reunion

Alessia

Candlelight danced against the walls of the emergency shelter when I stepped through the door; Jonah had gotten here first. I shut the door behind me with a snap. Movement in the corner caught my eye, and Jonah emerged from the shadows. My breath hitched. His green eyes were muddied and sunken, as though he hadn't slept in a long time. "Are you okay?" I whispered.

He swallowed and sat down on the floor in a pool of dim light. I hesitated. The last time we'd been here, it hadn't been pretty. And I knew I still couldn't be with him. But his posture—his head bent, his shoulders hunched—made my heart twist.

I sat across from him, our knees inches away from touching, and set my backpack beside me. "What's going on? Why did you want to see me, now, after all this time?"

His gaze was fixed on the old braided rug that covered the floor, but he glanced up at me from under his lashes. "I don't know. I just knew I had to." He flexed his fingers. "I miss you."

The last time we'd been alone, Jonah had seemed a little conflicted about his role as a Malandante, but he'd still been defiant, still sure he was on the right side. Now, sitting so close to him, I thought he seemed . . . broken. I watched his face, how the shadows moved across his skin. I wanted to touch him so bad my fingers itched. I clenched my hands into fists. "I miss you, too," I allowed.

"You and Bree have gotten kinda chummy." He picked at a loose thread on the rug. "Is it—does it have anything to do with me?"

Just like a boy, assuming everything was about him. "No."

He met my gaze. I had to bite back a gasp at the darkness I saw there. "Does it have anything to do with the Benandanti?"

"You know I can't—I won't—tell you that."

He held his hands up. "I'm not asking to spy. I just want to know what's up with you. What's up with Bree. I . . . hardly ever talk to her anymore."

"I'm still not telling you."

His posture bent even more, if that was possible. "I don't blame you. For not wanting to tell me things. But I'm not going to tell *them*. I promise."

"Jonah, I'm not worried about you telling them willingly. I'm more worried about them forcing it out of you." I thought of Dario, about how he'd *stayed strong*. He was immortal, with hundreds of years of training to withstand torture. I didn't know anything about Jonah's training, but I would bet he wasn't *that* well trained. I knew I wouldn't be able to do what Dario had done.

He looked past me to the posters on the wall, chewing his bottom lip.

I narrowed my eyes at him. In the past, he would've jumped down my throat for a comment like that. "Jonah? Are you okay?"

"No." If it hadn't been dead silent in the basement, I wouldn't have heard him. "I'm not okay."

My rib cage tightened so much I couldn't breathe. I couldn't stand it; I reached forward and touched his knee. He didn't move, didn't look at me, but he covered my hand with his. "Talk to me. Tell me what's going on. I won't say anything to anyone. I promise."

His fingers curled around mine and squeezed. "I think . . . I think you might be right."

"About what?"

"About them. The Malandanti." He made an involuntary motion, as if he were checking to see if one lurked in the corner. "Maybe I am . . . on the wrong side."

I think time stopped for a moment. Even the dust particles hung suspended. The only thing moving was my brain, whirring from side to side. *Did he really just say what I think he said?* Somehow I found the ability to speak. "Why? Why do you think that?"

"I've heard things," he whispered. "Things that are impossible to misinterpret."

I fought the urge to shout, *What things?* If I pushed, I knew he would bolt. I turned my hand beneath his and stroked his palm. He closed his eyes. I wanted to kiss away the pain I saw on his face.

"It's funny you should mention them forcing things out of me," he said. "I overheard them talking about doing that to someone. In California?"

I nodded. "At the Redwood site."

"They're going nuts because you guys have reclaimed it and the one in Pakistan. That each of your Clans now has a member of your *Concilio* with them."

"But why don't they just do the same with your *Concilio?*" It was what my own Clan had been anticipating, anyway.

"Because they think it would scatter their power. I guess they think they're better off working together from wherever they are." He sucked in air and looked at me.

I pressed my palm onto his. "It's okay. I promised I wouldn't tell anyone, and I won't." Not even Nerina, I swore to myself.

His shoulders relaxed. We sat in silence for a few minutes.

Jonah swallowed. "I heard my Guide talking to someone. I don't know who it was, but it wasn't a Malandante. But they were talking about Mr. Foster. About *what they did* to Mr. Foster." He wouldn't look me in the eyes. "About the magic they used to kill him."

My throat was hot. I could see again the life force leaching out of the Lynx, his aura flickering out like a dying light. "Angel Falls," I said. "It's the magic from Angel Falls."

"Yes." Slowly, Jonah raised his gaze to mine. "You were right, Alessia. They killed him. We have a mage, and he killed Mr. Foster."

I shifted onto my knees and leaned toward him. "Do you know who the mage is?" Jonah shook his head. "But you just said you heard them talking. He's not a Malandante, so he was in human form. Who was he?"

"I couldn't see him. He was in shadow, and the second my Guide sensed me, he vanished. Like, actually vanished."

I sat back. "Yeah, I saw him do the same thing when he attacked me and Mr. Foster. Neat trick."

"I didn't know," Jonah said. "You have to believe that I didn't know."

"I know you didn't." I pulled my backpack into my lap. "I have to show you something." I unzipped my bag and drew out the green folder with his name on it.

Without a word, I handed it to him. Whether he was ready to see it or not didn't matter anymore; he *needed* to see it, to know the truth. I watched his face as he read it. First, his eyes narrowed; then they widened. His breath came in short, loud puffs. He jerked his head up to look at me. "Where did you get this?"

"I can't tell you that. But it's legit. I swear."

"I know it's legit. There are details in here that no one else could know." Jonah slid his hand from mine and slammed it against the folder, creating a puncture in the middle of the green expanse. "God, how fucking stupid am I? You even saw it. Remember?" He hauled himself to his feet and strode in a wide circle around me. "The night you—found out about me. You said you thought they caused the crash to make me join. And I said no way." He shook the folder above his head. "And here's proof. You could see it, and I couldn't."

My heart twisted for him. "Sometimes when you're on the outside of things, you can see more clearly than when you're on the inside," I murmured. I wished I could make the truth easier for him to swallow, but he had to taste its bitterness for himself.

Jonah dropped back onto the rug next to me. "They crippled an innocent girl for life, just to get me to join." He threw the folder. It rippled for a moment before floating down outside the small pool of light that contained just the two of us. "God, what have I done?" He bent forward until his elbows were on the floor, his face buried in his hands.

"Jonah." I put my hands on either side of his head and drew him up. "You didn't know. You couldn't know. You were manipulated. You can't blame yourself."

His eyes were full of anguish. My hands shook as I wove my fingers into his hair. "Maybe not for that," he whispered. "But everything that came after. Mr. Foster . . . God, even the bus crash that almost killed you . . . That's all my fault."

"You weren't there," I protested. "At the crash, or when Mr. Foster died. It's not your fault."

"But I made them stronger." His voice broke. "When

I joined, they became a complete Clan again."

"If you hadn't joined, they would've found someone else. And everything would've happened anyway."

"But maybe it would've taken them longer. Maybe—"

"Jonah." I put my fingers over his lips, trying to ignore the shiver that ran down my spine. "It doesn't matter now. What matters now is what you do going forward."

He grabbed my hand and pressed his lips to my palm. It was like a fiery brand, imprinting my skin. Breathing hard, he said, "I want out. I want out of the Malandanti." His face softened. "Will you help me?"

In the weeks since I had learned Jonah was the Malandanti Panther, I hadn't let myself think about what if. Deep down, I knew this was my truest wish, that Jonah would leave the Malandanti. But I didn't allow myself to think it could ever come true. Now it had. I felt as though I held a precious glass bubble in my hand, and one false move would make it shatter. I slid closer to him and touched his cheek. "Of course I will help you. Whatever the cost."

We were so close to each other now that our breath mingled. I slipped my arm around the back of his neck and inched toward him. His face blocked out all the shadows of the room. When his lips finally met mine, there was only light.

It was as if we had been lost in a desert for days without food or water and had just found an oasis. With one urgent tug, he pulled me onto his lap. I poured myself into him and wrapped my legs around his waist, his hands like fire on my skin beneath my sweater. His lips moved to my throat, and I moaned, tilting backward but held fast by his strength.

"Alessia," he whispered against my skin. My pulse below his mouth quickened. "I love you. I love you so much."

I trailed feather-light kisses along his brow until I reached his ear. "I love you too," I said, so quietly the only way I knew he heard me was from the way his hands tightened on me.

In a graceful arc, we fell backward onto the rug. He pressed the length of his body into mine, and I arched up into him, wanting more than I knew I should give. I lost myself in him for one sweet, beautiful moment longer. With an awful, ragged breath, I pulled myself away. "We can't. Not tonight."

"I know." He held me, his hands gentle. "But a guy can dream."

I laughed and sat up. He rolled onto his back and stared up at the black ceiling. I eased down until we lay side by side, looking up into the nothingness. In the darkness, I found his hand. In the quiet, all I heard was our breath. I wanted to stay there forever, inside our precious glass bubble. I knew the moment we left this basement, it would break.

"Is there another way out of this room?" Jonah asked.

I looked at him. "Yeah, through the upstairs. Why?"

He turned his head toward me. "In case there's

someone watching the basement entrance. One or both of us could've been followed."

The glass was already splintering. As happy as I was in that moment, as glorious as it was that Jonah wanted out of the Malandanti, the cold, stark facts lay bare before me. He wasn't out yet. We could not be seen together. If it got back to Heath, I would be dead in the figurative sense. If it got back to Pratt, Jonah would be dead in the literal sense.

We lay there for a long time, letting the quiet speak for us. When at last we left—he through the back door, I through the front—the night was still full and black. But there was one tiny piece of light on my horizon. Because even though I'd been through every scrap of paper we'd stolen from the Guild, there were books I hadn't read, books made out of bark and leaves in ancient languages that I couldn't read. And I was sure—not because I knew, but because *there had to be*—that in one of those books was the way to set a Malandante free.

CHAPTER TWENTY-TWO

In Which I Get Bitch-Slapped

Bree

Nerina was *pissed*.

She stepped over the shattered remains of her espresso cup and stalked toward me, her stiletto heels rapping on the floor. "*What did you do?*" she repeated in a hiss.

Shit. I fought the urge to turn tail and run. "I unlocked that book you gave me. You told me to work with it—"

"I told you to study it, not use it." She seized my arm, her fingers digging deep into my flesh.

"Ow! Hang on—"

"You stupid girl! How many people saw you?" She shook me, her face less than an inch from mine. Okay, so apparently Nerina had a bad side, and now I was on it.

"Nobody saw me," I said through gritted teeth. I tried to pull my arm away, but damn, girlfriend obviously worked out. "Well, maybe a few people, but I took care of that—"

"You took care of it?" She dragged me into the living area and threw me into a chair. She slammed her hands down onto the arms of the chair on either side of me so I couldn't get up. Not that I was going to try to get up. She was *that* mad. Her eyes looked as if they were going to spit fire and melt off my face. "In my four and a half centuries, my gut instinct has been wrong once, Bree. Once. And my gut told me you are our next mage. My gut told me to trust you. Was my gut wrong for the second time in almost five hundred years, Bree? *Was it*? Did I choose the wrong mage?" She leaned in. "*Did I*?"

Oh, my God, she was playing the I'm-disappointed-in-you card. Coming from my parents, it had never worked on me, but Nerina had had four hundred fifty freaking years to perfect it. I felt about as big as an ant. "N-no," I whispered.

"Then I must be a terrible teacher. Because I thought I made it clear that the magic is never to be used for fun, for sport, for personal gain, or in a random manner. Did I say that? Or did I imagine telling you that?"

Um, no. She hadn't imagined that. I had just kinda sorta conveniently forgotten about that little instruction. I remembered the way the magic had taken hold of me, with such a firm, sudden grip. There was no way I could've remembered Nerina's instructions at a time like that. "It just happened. The power . . . took over me. I couldn't help it . . ."

"You could help it." Nerina balanced herself in a squat in front of me. She was like a goddamn yoga master. That's probably all she did here alone in this dungeon—practice yoga in four-inch heels and tight pencil skirts. She pointed a long forefinger at me. "That magic was not controlling you. You controlled that magic wholly, and you know it. You chose to use it in the way you did." She arched an eyebrow. "Perhaps there is more Malandanti in you than I thought."

Cheap shot. I crossed my arms. "I would never use magic to kill people."

"Do you know who the original Malandanti were?" she asked, ignoring me.

I shook my head.

Her nostrils flared. "The original Malandanti were Benandanti, Bree. They wanted to use the magic to control people, to manipulate them into doing their bidding. Their fellow Benandanti disapproved and exiled them. So they went rogue." She searched my face, her eyes piercing every inch of my skin. "At this moment, you are no better than they were."

Dammit, she was right. I thought about how drunk I'd felt, making that bitchy cheerleader break up with her boyfriend for no reason. Making Josh humiliate himself. And for what? Petty revenge. I slumped back into the chair. I wasn't any different from the Rabbit. I deserved her wrath. "So what are you gonna do to me?"

Nerina gave a satisfied nod before she stood and walked to the couch. She settled herself on the edge and crossed her legs. "Well, I was going to take you to the Waterfall tonight to test you out with the Clan, but you are clearly not ready for that." She eyed me up and down. "We obviously have more work to do. You need to learn the fine art of subtlety, my dear."

I sat up a little. "You're not going to punish me?"

"What good would that do? Besides, we haven't the time. The Malandanti will attack the Waterfall any day now in retaliation for our winning back Pakistan and the Redwoods. You need to be ready for that." She rose and came to stand over me again. "But if I ever see you using magic for your own personal fulfillment—a fulfillment I find rather twisted, I might add—be assured you *will* be punished. And not by me. By the *Concilio*. We have rules, Bree, and you broke half a dozen of them today."

I picked at a nonexistent tear in the chair. "Sorry."

"Well." A faint smiled cracked across Nerina's lips. "She *is* capable of apologizing."

I snorted. Then I looked up at her. "How did you know? That I'd used the magic?"

"Oh, please. It seeps from every pore in your body. Anyone who has used the magic before can sense it. I would have been able to smell it a mile away had I been aboveground." She tilted her head. "Can you still feel the magic?"

I held up a hand in front of my face. Wisps of green light still shone around my skin, but they were faint now. "A little."

"Give me the book back, please."

I dug into my bag and handed it to her.

"I'm assuming the people you used it on won't be bothering us?" she asked as she set the book down on the coffee table.

"You mean, did they have any idea? I doubt it. I mean, unless you think my pervy study hall teacher is a Malandante."

"He could be, Bree," Nerina snapped. "That's the whole point of not using the magic—how you say—will-nill?"

"Willy-nilly," I muttered.

"*Esattamente.* Willy-nilly. You never know whom you are using it on." She picked up another book whose pages were made of soft green leaves. "But I am assuming you did not use it on anyone you knew to be a Malandante? Or a Benandante?"

Craaaap. I squirmed a little.

The movement was not lost on Nerina. "Bree . . ."

"I'm sorry, okay? I didn't know what I was doing. I didn't even mean to do it. I just said something, and he took it as an order, and then I kinda—I don't know— nudged it along, I guess."

"Nudged *what* along?"

"It is *so* not a big deal."

"Bree."

"Okay, okay." I blew a strand of loose hair off my face. "I kinda told Jonah and Alessia that they should figure out whatever is going on between them."

Nerina pressed her palms to her temples and dropped

back onto the couch. "They *cannot* be together. *Ever.* I thought she was finally getting over him."

Seriously? I made a face at her. "I don't know where you're getting your information, but Alessia is not in any way, shape, or form over Jonah. And he's not over her. Those two are moon-faced idiots when it comes to each other." I shrugged. "Maybe I helped them finally cut the cord."

Nerina jabbed a finger at me. "I certainly hope that's what's become of your little prank. Because you've pushed them closer together—"

"Yeah, yeah. I know. You'll sic the *Concilio* on me." I stood up. "Look, we can't do anything about it now, so let's just see how it plays out, okay? And now I'd like to get to work. Apparently, I have some subtlety to learn."

"Not just subtlety," Nerina said, getting to her feet. She click-clacked to the stairs and grabbed her fur-trimmed coat from the coat rack. "Control. You need to learn control." She poured herself into the coat like a Slinky and whirled to face me. "Because every time you lose control like that, every time you use the magic for yourself and not for others, the magic corrupts you."

I stopped dead in my tracks. "Excuse me?"

Nerina's eyes glinted. "Yes, dear. The magic will corrupt you, if you let it. That is what happened to the original Malandanti." She started up the stairs, her voice floating back to me. "It is my job to see that does not happen to you."

I wanted to hate Nerina. I really did. But every time I thought I hated her, she would do something like pour me a cup full of rich dark espresso from her thermos and hand me gourmet biscotti. It wasn't Lidia's biscotti, but it was close. She dusted off two tree stumps, and we sat side by side drinking our coffee in the moonlight. It was like something out of a Bertolucci film. While we sipped, she told me stories about the *Concilio* in Friuli. "The last time we had a mage was two hundred years ago," she said. "Gemma. She was very powerful."

"What happened to her?" I asked. The coffee was so good it made up for the last three hours of torture Nerina had put me through. But we had cracked another book, and I had added another skill to my résumé. I was pretty sure I'd redeemed myself after the whole magic-for-personal-gain incident the other day.

"She was killed in battle," Nerina said softly. Her gaze met mine. "Every mage we have ever had has died in battle."

Okay, now I hated her again. I tossed the remains of my biscotti on the ground. "Really? Why would you tell me that? Why not just lie?"

"I don't believe in outright lying to make someone else comfortable. The truth is always better, no matter how hard." Nerina flicked an imaginary crumb off her coat. "Being a mage is not for the faint of heart."

"Hey, I've been accused of a lot in my young life but never of being *faint of heart*." I crossed my arms and curled my lip at her. "I spied on my own father. I broke into the Guild. And I agreed to be a mage even though it meant going up against my own twin. *What* about any of that reads as faint of heart?"

"You don't need to point out your attributes to me." Nerina rose in a long, fluid motion and walked in circles around me. "But before I waste any more time training you, I need you to know exactly what you are getting into. You were not born into the Benandanti, not like me or Alessia or Heath. You were recruited by the Malandanti and, though you refused, they are still the side that chose you, not us."

I narrowed my eyes at her. "But *I* chose *you*."

Nerina held a finger up to quiet me. "This is the moment when you need to make the same commitment that a Benandante makes when he is called. That you will lay down your life in the line of duty. That the Clan comes before all else."

"I told you I would choose Jonah first."

"And I will make that concession for you." She stopped right in front of me, her dark gaze fixed on my face. "But can you make that commitment to me? To the Benandanti?"

For once, I kept my mouth shut and really thought about that. Could I? I thought about how miserable Alessia was, the Benandanti ruining her life. Did I want that?

What did I care if the Guild built a hydroelectric power plant in Twin Willows? As soon as it was done, we'd be off to a new town anyway. I chewed my lip. Nerina's eyes were still on me, but I ignored her. What she was asking was between me and myself alone. If the Benandanti brought down the Guild, what would that mean for my family? Would it send my mother into a deeper depression? Would it make my dad even more of an asshole? Or . . . maybe it would change everything for the better. The possibility of that was like touching a bruise that hadn't quite healed. Better to leave it alone, in case it never happened.

And then there was Jonah. That wound would never mend, no matter what I did. If the Benandanti were ruining Alessia's life, the Malandanti were destroying Jonah's. Not just his life but him. I could see him crumbling before my eyes, like in one of those rapid-aging commercials on TV.

Nerina was right; I wasn't born into this. This wasn't my fight. But too many forces around me—my father, my brother—had made it mine. My father . . . He could go to hell for all I cared. But my brother . . . I lifted my gaze to Nerina's. "Yes," I said. "Yes, I can."

She nodded once. "Good. Now you are ready."

"For what?"

"To meet the Clan."

I opened my mouth to ask how that was going to happen—weren't they all animals?—but before I could say anything, a ghostly blue light filled the little clearing where we had been working. Nerina dropped to the ground. I stumbled back. The light hurt my eyes. But just as suddenly as it had appeared, it was gone. I blinked, spots clearing from my vision.

Nerina lay on the ground and a . . . a . . . *creature* stood next to her. "What the . . ." I breathed. The thing looked like a lioness but had wings like an eagle's. It was not real . . . "Nerina?" I whispered.

The thing nodded, and then I understood. She was immortal, a member of the *Concilio* . . . Of course she wouldn't turn into something as mundane as a falcon or a panther. No, a mere mammal wasn't good enough for Nerina; she had to be mythical. I squinted. "A griffin?"

She nodded again and padded away from me. I followed, stepping carefully over her human form. As I did, I saw the glimmer of burnished gold near her neck. A locket, similar to the one Alessia wore that kept her caul safe.

I could tell Nerina was dying to fly; she kept flexing her wings, furling and unfurling them, but she stayed on the ground to lead me through the woods. Miracle of miracles, it had stopped snowing. Now it was just cold. I followed her into a cluster of birch trees, their limbs white and bare in the moonlight. The sound of rushing water filled my ears. Nerina stopped. She swung her huge head toward me. It was totally unreal to see her eyes in the depths of the red-gold fur that covered her face. She stamped one giant paw into the snow, which I took to mean, *Stay here.* I stayed. I wasn't about to argue with a *freaking griffin.*

Nerina gathered her haunches and launched into the air, her magnificent wings blotting out the sky above me. Damn. Girlfriend was impressive. No wonder Heath was so hot for her. She disappeared into the night. I hugged myself against the cold and realized I was going to have to buckle against my better fashion sense and get a puffer coat.

The woods here were dead quiet. After a few minutes, it got spooky. I glanced around, trying to figure out where Nerina was, but everything was dark and shadowy. There were no birds or squirrels or deer—nothing except the sound of water. I stilled. Of course. We were near the Waterfall.

A twig snapped behind me. I flattened myself against the trunk of a birch tree, as if it would really do anything since my coat was bright red. A hulking white wolf crept past me. *Jesus*. I grappled against the tree—could I climb it?—but the wolf shook its head. Eyes wide, I took in the faint blue glow that haloed its whole body. It wasn't a wolf. It was a Benandante. A bird called softly above me. I jerked my gaze up, away from the wolf. Alessia soared over the treetops, her outline just visible against the darkness.

The Clan was gathering.

It felt like ages before Nerina returned.

"I think my toes might've fallen off. I'm pretty sure I have frostbite," I told her when her unearthly form reappeared. "Does the Benandanti have health insurance?"

She tossed her head, her breath white in the frozen

air, and turned away. I followed her out of the birch trees, through some brush I had to practically Indiana-Jones my way through, and to the shores of a deep, clear stream.

I was so not a nature girl, but the sight of the Waterfall could turn me into one. The water flowed, end over end, tumbling down rocks into a glittering pool below. Blue light haloed the entire thing; that had to be the protection to keep the Malandanti out. The Malandanti . . . I whirled in a circle, peering into the forest all around us. "Isn't there usually a Malandante here, watching us?" I asked Nerina.

She shook her head.

I threw my arms into the air.

She couldn't exactly answer me in the form she was in. Seriously, how did the Clan talk to each other when they were transformed? Charades?

Nerina urged me forward with a jerk of her head. I stepped through the protection bubble. My skin tingled with the magic, and I felt a surge of power down my spine. Maybe someday I'd be capable of magic this potent. Maybe tomorrow.

I stopped on the shore of the pool. Nerina led me around the edge of the pool to the other side, where I could see the Clan waiting. Alessia perched on a branch that hung out over the water. A huge, fierce-eyed Eagle sat next to her. Beneath them were the White Wolf and a Stag, its antlers shimmery in the moonlight. I swallowed. They were missing one. Mr. Foster. Alessia had told me he transformed into a Lynx. Even though I had never really known him, I could feel the Lynx-shaped hole in the cluster of animals in front of me.

The Stag and the Wolf trotted out. Alessia and the Eagle fluttered down so the four of them formed a semi-circle. Only then did I notice a glowing line in the ground. Nerina nudged me toward it with her nose. I flashed her a look—*What the hell am I getting myself into?*—but she was maddeningly unresponsive. I edged toward the line until my toes met it. Nerina pushed her head into the small of my back, and I stumbled over the line.

My whole body lit up with blue light, filled me with warmth I hadn't felt since we'd lived in Florida. The Clan closed in around me. Something bubbled inside me, something like when Jonah and I were kids and we would talk to each other in our own made-up language and no one else could understand us—we were our own world. I felt that now . . .

Belonging.

My throat tightened. *No, no, no . . . don't cry, don't cry*, I told myself. But I couldn't help it. Tears squeezed out of the corners of my eyes. *Dammit.* Why did Alessia have to be here to see this? I buried my face in my hands.

I didn't know . . . I had no idea. The Clan was a family, just like me and Jonah. And they'd just let me in. I was part of them now. I was part of something bigger than myself. Yeah, I'd known that before. But now I knew it to the core of my being, as deep as I knew the language that only Jonah and I spoke.

Welcome, Bree.

The voices echoed in my head. I slid my hands from my face to my temples. "What the hell?"

This is how the Clan communicates.

I looked wildly amongst them. "What, you read minds?"

Not exactly. That voice—male—it was familiar. The Wolf stepped forward. Heath. I was sure of it. I almost said his name out loud, but his blue eyes pierced into me, and I remembered. I wasn't supposed to know their identities. Except now they all knew mine . . .

We can speak to each other with our minds, the Wolf said. *But we can't read any thoughts beyond what we want the Clan to know.*

You can open or close it at any time. That was Nerina; her voice was unmistakable. *Don't worry; you'll grasp that soon. But if the Clan is Called, you will be, too.*

"But now you all know who I am," I said.

Yes. The Stag tossed its head. Its voice was deep, unfamiliar. He and the Eagle were the only ones whose real names I didn't know. *But you are a member of our Clan now, and we are sworn to protect any and every Clan member with our last breath. Knowing your identity will never change that. By stepping into this circle, you have sworn the same oath.*

I fought for my breath, trying to control it, but I sounded like a dog in heat. I couldn't speak, couldn't even think clearly—God, could they hear the jumbled thoughts inside my head?

Alessia flew to me and landed gently on my shoulder. She pressed her feathery face to mine. Despite the cold, she was warm. *We all know what you've sacrificed, Bree. We all know the danger you're in by being here.*

And we are all grateful. It was a new voice, soft and maternal. By process of elimination, it had to be the Eagle.

I turned to Nerina. "But I thought you said I wasn't ready."

Ready or not, we all have to be prepared. The Malandanti will attack, especially now that we are one member short.

I felt the ripple of sorrow that shuddered through the entire Clan. Whoa. It was like a hive mind. "This is weird," I muttered.

Alessia's wing brushed my hair as she launched off my shoulder. *You get used to it.*

"So do we all sing 'Kumbaya' now or what?"

I could swear the Stag laughed. Thank God one of them had a sense of humor. Not surprisingly, Nerina ignored me. *We cannot stay here long.* She paced between each member of the Clan. *I cast a spell to keep the Malandanti away, but it is fading. My magic is not as strong as our new mage's.* She blinked her dark eyes at me. *From now on, Bree and I will be training here at the Waterfall. She will learn to mask herself so she cannot be identified. And when the Malandanti come, we will meet them with our new power.*

I shivered. The Malandanti would attack, and I would fight them . . . including the Panther that was my brother's soul.

CHAPTER TWENTY-THREE

The Time Traveler

Alessia

I caught up to Bree just beyond the stone wall, swooping low. *Can we talk?*

She nodded. "But can we do it someplace warm? Unlike you, I haven't been covered in feather down for the past hour."

Meet me at the Cave. I'll be there after I transform. I soared toward the farmhouse. A faint blue light tinged the edge of the horizon. It would be dawn soon; we would have to hurry.

My body was bone tired when I slid back into it. I'd been Called the instant my head had hit the pillow. *No rest for the wicked*, I thought, tiptoeing downstairs and out the back door.

Bree was waiting against the little hobbit door of the Cave. "I should buy stock in coffee," she muttered.

"It's amazing how well I've learned to function on no sleep since joining the Benandanti," I said, unlocking the door.

Inside, the Cave was warm and close. The pungent smell of cheese tickled my nose. I pulled out a tray of goat's cheese and put it on the table. "Want some?"

"Yes, I'm *starving*." Bree reached for the knife I set next to the cheese. I found some bread in the little fridge beneath the counter and set that out, too. "So, um, that was intense."

"Yeah." I hauled myself onto a stool. I rolled my ankles and wrists, my joints crackling. "But that's not why I wanted to talk to you."

Bree swallowed and leaned against the table. "Okay, look, I'm really sorry. I was being stupid and power hungry, and I didn't think anything would come of it."

I squinted at her. "What are you talking about?"

She froze. "Nothing. What are *you* talking about?"

"Nuh-uh. What did you do?"

"Fine." She sighed. "Nerina gave me this book to unlock, and when I did, it gave me the power to control people."

"Like what the Rabbit did to Mr. Salter?" I asked through gritted teeth.

She nodded, not looking at me.

"And then what happened?" I was getting an itchy feeling in my gut.

"I kinda told Jonah to just figure out this thing with you guys already—"

"Bree! What the hell!" I jumped off the stool. "Is that why he wanted to meet?"

"Did you guys meet?" Bree asked, her eyes wide.

"What happened?"

"None of your business."

"Did you guys do it?"

"Oh, my God! That is so not any of your business, but no." I slammed around to the other side of the table.

Bree had this little smirk on her face that made me want to hit her.

"I can't believe you did that. I hope Nerina gave you a long and boring lecture on how wrong that was."

"Yeah, yeah, she did." Bree popped another cheese-slathered piece of bread in her mouth.

I wanted to scream. But even if she'd pushed us together, what had happened in the basement was just between me and Jonah. She didn't manipulate that.

I pressed my hands flat on the table. "Okay, whatever. That's not why I'm here." I took a deep breath. "I promised Jonah I wouldn't tell anyone any of this, but I also promised him I would help him, and I can't do that alone. So I'm going to tell you something, and you have to swear on anything you hold sacred that you won't tell anyone. Okay?"

"You should know by now that anything involving Jonah is my business, too. And that he will always come first. You can trust me."

"I know, and that's why I'm coming to you." I ran a hand over my face. "He wants to leave. The Malandanti. He wants out."

Bree stilled, holding the knife just above the table.

"That's not possible, is it?"

"I don't know." I blew a long breath out. "But if it is possible, the answer must be in one of those books we took from the Guild. And you can read them now, can't you?"

"Not all of them—"

"But you just said you unlocked that one book—"

"Yeah, *one* book." Bree dropped the knife. It thunked on the gnarled wood. She pushed the cheese plate away. "But there're six more. Plus countless documents and stuff. And I have no idea what my training with Nerina will look like now that I'm a full member of the Clan. We might not even deal with the books anymore."

"But if the books contain the magic of the sites, I'm sure you will." I leaned toward her. "Even if you don't, you have to get into them. You have to see if there's something in there about this."

"I will. I promise. Because if there's a chance he can get out . . ."

I stretched an arm across the table to her.

After a moment, she took my hand and squeezed my fingers. I now had the Benandanti mage working with me. If that couldn't help Jonah, I didn't know what could.

"Alessia?"

The sound of my mother's voice made my elbow slide off the table. I jolted awake. "Huh? Sorry, Mom."

She crossed the kitchen and ran a hand through my

hair. "*Cara*, are you feeling okay?"

"Yeah, I'm fine. Just tired." I gave her hand a gentle push and dug into the oatmeal she'd just set in front of me. "Thanks for breakfast."

She didn't answer, just slid into the chair opposite me and picked up her cup of coffee. I felt her gaze on me over the rim of her mug. "You haven't been sleeping well," she said. It wasn't a question.

I shrugged and shoved another spoonful of oatmeal into my mouth.

"You're working too hard."

I stilled for a split second before recovering and gulping down more oatmeal. Not for the first time, I wondered how much Lidia knew about the Benandanti. She'd lied all those weeks ago when I'd asked her about the amulet; I was sure of it. I took a sip from my own cup of coffee. "School's hard this semester."

A shadow crossed her face, and she looked away as she nodded. "I wish I could afford to give us a holiday," she murmured. "It would be nice to get away for a few days."

My heart skipped. Had she really just given me such a perfect opening? I put my spoon down. "Actually, Mom, I wanted to ask you about that."

She looked back at me, her eyes wide. "*Sì, cara?*"

"Well, Jenny and Carly and Melissa are planning to go away for a few days to look at colleges in Massachusetts." I hunched my shoulders. "I'd really like to go with them."

Lidia raised an eyebrow. "What colleges?"

"Williams, Amherst, and Mount Holyoke. Jenny's already called and set up tours."

"And when are they going?"

"Next weekend." I finished my oatmeal, hoping to look casual even though my heart was racing.

"And whose parent is going with you?"

Thud. My heart slammed to a halt. "Um, none. We were planning to go by ourselves."

Lidia's mouth opened.

Before she could speak, I held my hand up. "Mom, I'm almost seventeen. So is Carly. And Jenny and Melissa are already seventeen. We're old enough, and we'll be fine. I'll check in three times a day, I promise. And it's only for two nights. We're going to stay at this cute, little inn that's run by an old retired couple. Talk to Barb about it if you want," I added.

Lidia closed her mouth. I could practically see the wheels turning in her head, all the reasons she wanted to say no. But as the long minutes stretched on, and she wasn't saying no, I wondered again what she knew. Did she know I had been Called? And if I was old enough to handle the Benandanti, wasn't I old enough to go away for the weekend with my girlfriends?

At last, she picked up her mug and downed the rest of her coffee. "You know, Alessia," she said, setting the cup gently down, "ever since your father died, you have been a big help in running this farm. You've risen at dawn without me dragging you out of bed, and you've never complained." She swallowed. "And I've been preoccupied lately—with Ed, with helping him out—and still you've done your chores and your schoolwork without me looking over your shoulder."

I half-smiled at her. Where was she going with this?

"What I'm trying to say is—you deserve a little vacation. You have proven to me that you are mature and trustworthy. So, okay." She reached out and patted my hand.

"I can go?"

"You can go."

"Oh, thanks, Mom!" I jumped out of my chair and hugged her. She laughed and kissed my cheek.

Just before I pulled away, she held me closer. "You are a good girl, *cara*. I love you so much," she whispered into my ear.

"I love you too, Mom." And I let go of her with a pang, wishing once again that I could tell her everything.

It was only on the way out of the house, my heart light with the thought of how Jenny would react when I told her, that I remembered the real person I needed to get permission from wasn't Lidia.

"Crap," I muttered, shaking my head. There was no way Nerina was going to let me leave Twin Willows for a weekend—not with the Malandanti closing in. Up ahead, at the bend in the road, I spotted Jenny, her hot-pink peacoat like a flower blossoming in snow. My steps grew heavy.

"Did you talk to her?" Jenny asked by way of greeting.

I nodded. "She said yes."

Jenny squealed and jumped up and down a few times before she noticed my face. "So why do you look like Ryan Gosling just died?"

"I'm still not sure I can go," I said. Jenny's jaw tightened. I grabbed her arm and started walking toward school. "Look, things are still really hard at home, with the fire and the goats gone. I just feel really bad taking off right now."

"Lessi." Jenny laid her head on my shoulder as we walked. "You are like the goodiest of all the Goody Two-Shoes I know. That's really sweet. But your mom said yes. And I'm sure she'll be okay for three days. Not even. Like two and a half."

"Yeah, I know. Okay, okay. But if I have to cancel at the last minute, *please* don't be pissed."

"You won't." Jenny squeezed my elbow. "Carly and Melissa are going to be so psyched!"

I let her chatter my ear off as we got closer to school. Maybe I would be able to go. Maybe everything would be quiet at the Waterfall. Maybe we'd defeat the Malandanti, and the war would be over. Maybe I could talk to Heath, and he'd see how hard I'd been working and say I needed a vacation too. I almost snorted out loud. Of those three maybes, the last one was the least likely.

When I shed my skin and headed for the Waterfall that night, Nerina's voice intruded into my mind. *Come to the*

forest just beyond my place. I need you to help me with Bree's training.

But I'm on watch tonight.

I've Called the Eagle to take over.

I veered over the charred remains of our barn and glided lower, past the stone wall and into the bare trees. Now that the leaves were gone for the winter, the forest didn't provide the same kind of shelter, save for the towering pines that populated the woods. Spotting Nerina's soft blue glow through the dense pine needles, I slowed. Nerina hovered just above Bree's head. Bree's arms were raised, a harsh white light emanating from her palms. As I approached, the light flashed out in a circle.

I was blasted backward, blinded for an instant. When I could see again, everything around me was haloed in shimmering light. The trees shone bright with gold and red leaves, foliage lush and full. I blinked. Leaves? The forest looked like it had months ago, in the ripeness of autumn . . .

What—?

A moment later, the light flickered and went out. Bree dropped her arms and fell to her knees, her chest heaving. The barren trees once again surrounded us.

I fluttered down next to Bree. *What the hell was that?*

Nerina landed with a soft thud. *Pakistan.*

It was only then that I spotted the book at Bree's feet. It looked as though it was made of stone, with Arabic letters etched into its face. The site at Pakistan—which we had just regained control of—had the power to manipulate time and space.

I cocked my head. *Did we just time travel?*

We didn't, Nerina answered. *The trees did. Bree turned them back to autumn.*

"Just . . . for . . . a minute," Bree gasped.

Don't talk, Nerina scolded. *Save your breath.*

Bree! That's amazing!

She shrugged, but I could tell by the slight curve of her mouth that she was pretty proud of herself.

She is doing very well, Nerina said. *This girl is quite powerful.*

Okay, okay, stop making me blush. Bree got to her feet. *What's next?*

We've been transporting objects through time and space, Nerina said. *It's time to progress to people. That's where you come in, Alessia.*

We both swiveled to her. *What?*

It'll feel odd, but it won't hurt. Nerina padded in a circle around us. *This is a very powerful tool, Bree. If you can hone it, you will be able to transport an attacking Malandanti during a battle. Not permanently but enough to get them out of your way.*

Hang on. A wheel turned in my mind, clicking a series of images into place. *Is this how the Raven makes himself disappear?*

Yes. I believe so.

So he's not turning off his aura like I thought, I said. *He's actually moving in and out of time?*

That's not important right now. What is important is for Bree to master this. Nerina halted in front of Bree, her fierce, dark gaze on Bree's face. *Are you ready?*

Bree spread her feet and raised her arms. *Yes.*

Good. Alessia, fly.

Hang on, I said, fluttering over Nerina's head. *This isn't going to, like, break down my molecular structure or something, is it?*

You've been watching too much science fiction. Of course not.

You better be right. I took off into the air and circled the treetops.

Keep flying, Nerina instructed me. *She needs a moving target.*

I did as she said, dipping in and out of branches. A couple of times I felt Bree's light touch my tail feathers, but I was too fast for her magic. I glanced down. Their conversation didn't include me, but I could tell it was intense. Nerina sat on her haunches just in front of Bree, her lion's head upturned, their eyes locked on each other. I focused on their bent heads. Nerina nodded once and backed up. Bree raised her arms again. I sped up; the Malandanti wouldn't make it easy for her, so neither would I.

Light shot into the air, beaming through the trees and up to the stars. It caught me and turned me upside down. When I righted myself again, the pine trees were gone. Below me, the Waterfall rippled over rocks. Sunlight gleamed off the water and dappled the deep green leaves of the willow tree that hung over the pool. I spun.

Something was wrong. The barrier over the Waterfall was dark and silvery, the halo of the Malandanti . . . Oh, God, had they come while I was with Nerina? Had we lost it again? Heart in my throat, I flew into the protective copse of birch trees where I had first seen the Waterfall with Heath.

Twigs crackled below me. I looked down. The Lynx slunk on his belly through the birches, his eyes focused on the Malandanti-controlled Waterfall . . . No, it couldn't be. The Lynx was dead . . .

I froze in midair. The Lynx. The Waterfall. I blinked up at the sky. Sunlight . . . daytime. Green leaves . . . I ruffled my feathers. The air was warm and sticky. Humid. Summertime. Bree had sent me back all the way to summer.

The incredible reality of it barely had time to register when the light flashed again, and I was back amongst the pines. Below me, Bree stood in the clearing, a white glow draining from her fingertips. I shot down to her. *You did it, Bree. You did it!*

What did I do?

You sent me to the Waterfall during the summer. I jerked my gaze to Nerina. *It was still controlled by the Malandanti. And the Lynx was there. It was definitely in the past. She did it.*

Shaking, Bree sank to the ground. The light had left her. Her skin looked ashen in the moonlight. With trembling hands, she dug out a bottle of water from her backpack and gulped down half of it.

Are you okay? I asked.

I will be.

Her strength will only grow. Nerina stretched her wings wide, then tucked them in close to her body. *The more she practices, the greater her magic will become.*

I thought you said the more I used the magic, the more it would corrupt me, Bree said, shoving the water bottle back into her bag.

I looked between them.

No, Nerina corrected, *what I said was if you use the magic for personal pleasure, it would corrupt you. Using it to defend the Benandanti will make it grow.*

God, there're too many rules. Bree got to her feet. *I can't possibly keep track. Come on, let's go again.*

Over and over, Bree sent me through time, just a few months or so. I found myself above Main Street on the first day of school or outside our still-intact barn in the still of summer. As the light flashed once more and brought me back to the pines, I had a sudden thought. Could Bree send me back to the time before my dad died? Could I see him one more time?

But that would be using the magic for personal reasons, and I couldn't ask her to do that.

Finally, Nerina allowed me to return. I landed hard on a low branch. Bree stood in the center of the clearing. She didn't look tired or even out of breath anymore. Instead, she was radiant. She was lit from within, her skin practically glowing. And there, just tracing her outline, was the faint blue aura of the Benandanti. She looked . . .

otherworldly. Like the blue-skinned Hindu goddess Jenny's mom had a statue of. Nerina was right. The magic was making her strong.

That's enough for tonight, Nerina said. *Tomorrow we work on the Redwood power.*

The power to heal? Bree asked, wrinkling her nose.

Yes. We followed Nerina as she loped through the trees, back toward the stone wall. *And if you keep this up*, Nerina added, clearing the stone wall with one graceful bound, *you might just save us all.*

I left them at the edge of the farm and soared back to my open window. My skin stretched tight and possessive around my soul when I flooded back into my body. I sat up. Bree? The savior of the Benandanti? Okay, fine, I couldn't deny she was powerful. I couldn't imagine tapping into the kind of magic she was accessing. My own magic was different, and it was one kind of magic that Bree would never have.

There were still a few hours before daylight, but there was no way I could sleep. My brain still felt wobbly from being buffeted through time so much. I tugged on my boots and a thick sweatshirt, wound a scarf around my neck, and tiptoed downstairs. The world outside was black and grey. Moonlight reflected off the snow so that a soft light shimmered just above the ground. I crunched over the hard, snowy grass. I had the thought to go to Heath's cabin, even though he was still on duty. I just knew if I stayed in my room, I'd go out of my mind.

The ruined remains of the barn loomed in the darkness like a charred, broken-down Stonehenge. I paused at what was once the sliding door and looked up through the skeletal walls to the stars. Too bad Bree couldn't send me back to just before the fire. I could take out that damned Raven once and for all. My fingers gripped at the splintered wood. Could she do that? Send me back long enough to change something?

Soft footsteps echoed over the snow. I peered into the night. Bree was heading back from Nerina's. I slid into the shadows of the barn, but she had already raised a hand to wave at me. I waited while she broke into a jog and skidded to a halt in front of me.

"Shouldn't you be catching up on your beauty sleep?" she said.

"I don't sleep anymore." I was too tired, and my nerves were too raw to do the sarcastic wordplay thing with her. I stepped away from the charred beam. "See you at school."

"Wait." She fell into step with me. "Where are you going?"

"To Heath's."

I felt her glance sidelong at me. "What's with the 'tude?"

"Really, Bree?" I stopped so suddenly she almost stepped on me. "I just spent the last four hours being thrown around in time. I'm a little out of sorts." I started walking again, so fast she had to jog to keep up with me.

"Hey, I wasn't the one who volunteered you for the job," Bree said. "Take it up with Nerina."

"Maybe I will."

"Maybe you should."

We were almost at Heath's cabin. The windows were dark save for the soft gleam of moonlight off the glass.

Bree bolted in front of me and blocked my path. "You know what I think? I think you're jealous."

"What? You're insane." I folded my arms and looked at her, not quite meeting her gaze.

"Yeah, I don't think I am on this one." Bree stuck the tip of her tongue out of the corner of her mouth. "I think I just swooped in and stole your thunder. Not to mention your special little *Concilio* friend."

"What does that mean?"

"I mean, Nerina came here, to *your* farm, but now she's spending all this time with *me*." Bree planted her hands on her hips. "And you're jealous. Which is really unfair, since *you* were the one who dragged me into this. I didn't ask for any of it."

"Yeah, you keep saying that, Bree," I said, jabbing my finger at her, "but you certainly aren't turning any of it away. The lady doth protest too much, methinks."

"Oh, whatever." Bree rolled her eyes.

But then she looked right at me, and I looked at her, and we stared at each other for a few long minutes. Finally we both rolled our eyes.

"Okay, maybe we both a have a point here," Bree said, sitting down on the step outside Heath's door.

I squeezed in beside her. An unnatural warmth

emanated from her. Now that I was right next to her, I saw the faintest blue trace of light around her. The magic still clung to her.

"I guess I am a little jealous." I kicked at a little clump of snow below the step. "I mean, I'm just a Benandante. You can do all this other cool magic."

"But I'll never be a Benandante."

"You kind of are. I mean, you're a member of the Clan."

"But I'm human." Bree looked up at the stars. "Do you know how intimidating it is to be surrounded by these huge, powerful animals? You guys are *impressive*, man."

I shrugged, but I was smiling. "I guess. But doesn't the Tibetan site have the power to separate your soul from your body? So I bet you'll get that power, too."

"I'll be able to 'shadow-walk.' That's what Nerina called it. My soul can travel, but it won't take on the form of an animal. Not like a real Benandante."

"Still. That's cool." I bumped her arm. "I guess we're even. You get to do all this magic . . . but you'll never know what it's like to soar above the trees like me."

Bree coughed and looked down at her feet. "Actually . . ." she muttered.

I straightened. "What?"

"Um." She glanced over at me. "When I was Called, before I Refused, I transformed. I mean, you know that. All Refusers transform once."

"Oh." I blinked. "I guess I never realized that."

"Yeah, well, they do."

She didn't say anything, so I nudged her.

She sighed. "Look, don't read too much into this, okay?"

"Okay . . ."

She pressed her lips together and looked up at the sky again. A pale line of light was forming on the horizon. "When I was Called, when I transformed, I turned into a Falcon. Just like you. So I do know what it's like to fly. But just that once."

I stared at her. Was there one thing—*one thing*—I had and she didn't? She had magic. She had Nerina. God, she even had Jonah. She got to see him every day, sleep in the room next to him . . .

I swallowed hard and looked away. It was idiotic to be jealous. She couldn't help what she had transformed into. I certainly didn't choose to be a Falcon. But now that I was, I wouldn't choose anything else.

"That's weird," I said at last. "Why didn't you turn into a Panther, like Jonah?"

Bree shrugged. "I guess I have more falcon in me than panther." She tucked her hands into her pockets and shivered. She swallowed hard and met my eyes in the silvery dawn. "What's going to happen, Alessia?" she whispered. "What's going to happen when I have to fight him in battle?"

My throat closed tight. I couldn't answer. I just sat with her, and together we watched the grey light break over the barren trees.

CHAPTER TWENTY-FOUR

Dipping My Toe into the Dark Side

Bree

Alessia and I left Heath's cabin before he even got home. She ducked back into her house, and I trudged on toward home. The thought of going to school in a couple of hours seemed pointless. I mean, what could they teach me there that would outdo what Nerina was teaching me? Every time we unlocked a book, I felt its knowledge flow into me. There wasn't a teacher on this planet who could do that.

The pink fingers of dawn grazed the street as I walked along. My skin still hummed from the remnants of magic clinging to it. Tomorrow—actually today—I'd learn how to heal. And maybe the day after, I'd unlock the book that would tell me how to save my brother.

I turned the corner onto my street. A house and a half away, I heard the yelling.

Crap.

My mom's voice echoed into the outdoors as I crept around the back of the house. She couldn't have extended her little trip to wherever another few days?

"You are on thin ice, mister. If I catch you sneaking out one more time, you're going to be grounded until summer."

I didn't hear Jonah's muttered reply, but it obviously wasn't an apology.

"What did you just say to your mother?"

Oh, shit. Dad was home. I pressed myself against the house. My heart beat faster than it ever had during the night's training.

"Apologize to her. *Now.*"

"No." Jonah's voice roared through the walls. "She's been at the spa for the past week. I could've blown up our street and she would've been too deep in a mud bath to know. And now *she's* trying to ground *me* for sneaking out?"

I clenched my hands into fists.

"You say you're sorry *right now*—"

"Travis, it's okay—" Now my mom's voice was placating. I could picture the scene—her hand on my dad's chest, trying to keep him away from Jonah. He'd called out her crappy parenting, and she knew he was right, but my dad would rather die a fiery death than admit his son was right.

"You know, I don't think either one of you has ever said to me, 'Don't sneak out.' Until you start to give a shit about me, I don't think it's any of your damn business what I do."

The sound of flat palm against cheek rang out into the backyard. My mom shrieked. Jonah yelled something

I couldn't understand until another slap silenced him. My hand was on the door; I was ready to run into the kitchen and fling myself between Jonah and my dad . . . and I froze.

I didn't care about getting caught sneaking out. My dad might hit Jonah, but he had some weird fifties-sensibility about hitting a girl. I could handle him. It was Jonah who couldn't know I had been out.

Because the magic still tinged my body the faintest Benandanti blue, and his Malandanti eyes would see it.

And if he knew now that I was working for the Benandanti, I might not get the chance to save him later.

I felt like the most cowardly piece of turd, climbing up the branches of the tree and in through the bathroom. They were still yelling downstairs by the time I changed into my pajamas, messed up my hair, and checked the mirror to make sure the magic was gone. I stumbled into the kitchen, rubbing my eyes. "What's going on?"

"Your brother was out all night." A cigarette perched between my mother's fingers. Its light pulsed as she sucked a breath on it. I itched to snatch it out of her hand and take my own drag. Then I realized I hadn't smoked since I started training with Nerina. Huh.

"Nice." I hopped onto a stool and pulled the bowl of fruit toward me. "Hope she was worth it."

"Bree." My father dropped his coffee mug into the sink with a clatter. "I've had enough from the two of you."

Really? Hadn't I just gotten there? I gave him a simpering, sweet smile. "Don't you have to go to work, Papa Dearest?"

Dad either didn't hear the sarcasm in my voice or chose to ignore it. He squinted up at the clock on the wall. "Oh—you're right. See you later, dear." He pecked my mother's cheek. She didn't even look at him as he did it. Just before he left, he turned and jabbed his finger at Jonah, then me. "I expect a good end-of-the-year report from all of your teachers, or there will be consequences."

"Like what? We'll move again?" Jonah muttered, but Dad was already out the door.

Mom stubbed her cigarette out in the sink and eyed the both of us. "Is it too much to ask for you to behave for a few days? You have no idea what I'm dealing with." She brushed a lock of ginger hair off her face. "I know you don't believe this, but I am on your side. No matter what happens with your father." She grabbed her laptop and her cell phone off the counter and shot us a shrewd look. "Can I trust you two to get yourself off to school please?" And without waiting for an answer, she disappeared upstairs.

I plucked an apple from the fruit bowl and bit into it. "Nice going, Jonah. Was it Alessia again?"

His eyes pierced my face. "You know it wasn't." He waved in the direction that Mom went. "Any idea what that was about?"

"Nope." I took another bite of apple. "You look a little tired, Brother Dear. Maybe you should talk to your Guide about getting some time off. I'm sure the Malandanti would be very understanding."

"Shut up, Bree. I'm really not in the mood." He skulked out of the kitchen. I heard his footsteps thud up the stairs. A moment later, his door banged shut.

"I guess I'll just have breakfast by myself then," I called out to the empty room. I tried to eat the rest of the apple, but its taste had turned rotten in my mouth. There was no sound from upstairs. Mom was . . . doing whatever she did all day, and Jonah was giving her a big middle finger by skipping school.

I jumped off the stool and tiptoed upstairs, then showered and dressed quickly. I couldn't wait to get back to Nerina's. Her home might've been underground, but this house was the real tomb. Everyone inside it was dying, and I wasn't going down with them.

A little while later, when I appeared at the bottom of her stairs, Nerina said, "Shouldn't you be in school?"

I shrugged. "Seems pointless, when this is so much more important."

Nerina narrowed her eyes at me. "Normally, I would disagree; your education is very important. But we are in a precarious situation, so I will allow it." She lifted a bloodred book from the coffee table. "The Stag will be joining us tonight to work on the Redwood magic. So let's jump ahead to another site since we have more time."

"Goody." I rubbed my hands together. "Where are we going today?"

She held the book up. The surface of it seemed to shift and change, as though it were wrapped in mist and written in sand. I reached for the book. There *was* mist, undulating around the cover like a snake. "Venezuela."

I froze, my hand an inch from the book. I felt its power vibrating toward me. "*Angel Falls*," I whispered.

"The power to suck out a life force."

I snatched my hand back. "I'm not using the same magic that killed Mr. Foster. No effing way."

Nerina held the book closer to me. It was now a hair's breadth from my fingertips. I didn't want to touch it, and yet I could feel its power inside me, uncoiling in my belly.

"Fight fire with fire, Bree," Nerina said. "This magic is dangerous, *sì*. But I will teach you how to use it so you will only stun a Malandante, enough to take him out of commission. Not to kill. We are still angels, and they are demons."

I swallowed. *Jonah is not a demon*, I wanted to say, but I couldn't. He hadn't been out all night at the library. And if I could use this power to remove him from battle before he got hurt, it would be worth taking a step over to the dark side.

I skipped school for the next three days. I created an elaborate ruse to cover my ass on all sides. I had Nerina call the school and pretend to be my mother. "Bree has the flu," she said in a dead-on American accent. Then I called my mother and told her I was staying at a friend's house because I couldn't handle the drama at home. I had

Nerina pretend to be Alessia's mom. "Bree is welcome to stay here," she said in a roughed-up version of her own Italian accent, "but I'll send her home the moment you ask." It played perfectly into her motherly guilt, which I was betting she got over pretty fast and would be more relieved than guilty to have me out of the house.

I turned off my phone so the calls from Jonah didn't distract me. I lost track of time. Whenever we emerged from Nerina's lair, I wasn't quite sure what color the sky would be. Sometimes Alessia was there, and sometimes she wasn't. Sometimes we used Heath as our guinea pig; sometimes we used the Stag. Sometimes we went to the Waterfall and watched the movements of the Benandanti within and the Malandanti without. On one occasion I saw the Panther creeping along the top of the stream, his green eyes fixed on Alessia as she swooped in circles inside the protective barrier. I gave Alessia a hard time about a lot of things, but I had to give her credit for how well she ignored him.

Sometimes we spent hours in Nerina's lair, trying to unlock the secrets of the spell that kept the true nature of the Guild from the rest of the world.

Nerina taught me how to mask my identity so it looked like I was always in shadow. I got so good at it that once when Alessia came to train with us, it took her like twenty minutes before she saw me. I snuck up behind her as she hovered just above Nerina's head. "Boo!"

She fell out of the air, and I nearly died laughing. Nerina was not amused.

When at last we went to bed, at the ass crack of why-am-I-awake o'clock, we'd lie in the dark talking. Sometimes we discussed the work, the books, the stuff we'd stolen from the Guild. Sometimes Nerina would tell me stories about the Benandanti from long ago, including the years when the Roman inquisition investigated them. "We had three mages working around the clock to cloak the Olive Grove from them," she told me. "Back in those days, we always had more than one mage working for the Clans."

"Why did it change?" I asked.

"It got too dangerous for the mages. I've told you about that before."

Yeah, she had . . . but there was some sick need in me to know more, like how exactly each mage died. What spell had brought them down? Which magic had the Malandanti mage used to destroy them? Was it the magic from Angel Falls or something else? As though knowing this would help me prevent it from happening to me.

And sometimes Nerina would leave me alone. If she had to go to the Waterfall to meet with the Clan, she'd give me a bunch of homework before she left and test me when she returned. Usually, it took me the length of her absence to master whatever it was she'd told me to do. But sometimes, I'd grasp it early, and then it would just be me, alone in her lair with the books.

I hadn't forgotten what Alessia had asked me to do. It was one of the reasons I kept ignoring Jonah's calls. If I heard his voice, I might blurt out that I knew, that I was coming to rescue him, that I would save him as I'd failed to do in Fairfield . . .

I'd managed to get through every book except *Angel Falls*. That book scared the living crap out of me. But I forced myself to sit on the floor with the book in front of me. The deep red mist swirled around it, like blood that had evaporated into air. "All right, bitch. It's just you and me now," I whispered. I glanced at the clock. Nerina had been gone for over an hour; she could be back at any time. Better work fast.

The mist covered my hands when I touched the book, numbing them cold within seconds. I ignored the prickling pain and closed my eyes, forced myself into the book's dark corridors. *Are you in there?* I asked it. *The answer to the question I need answered?*

One by one, the doors along the corridor swung open. I already knew what was inside most of them— how to suck out a life force, how to do it just enough to leave a Malandante crippled, how to use a Malandante's aura to bend their will to yours. But there were doors I hadn't explored, like how to destroy a life force completely. I paused at that one. I could see it in my mind, how it would go, how I could do it, but when I pictured it, I saw the Lynx as my victim, and I couldn't go there. I wouldn't do to another soul what they had done to Mr. Foster.

The chill from the mist had gone into my bones now, and I couldn't feel my hands. *Screw you, cold.* I went deeper, and the magic pushed back, wrapping my wrists in invisible bands of freezing iron. I was trapped outside the last unopened door, unable to go backward or forward.

There was a place inside me, like a safe haven. I pictured it as the house where we'd lived until I was ten, before Dad got the job at the Guild, and we'd started moving around. A little brown-and-white Tudor with a low white fence around the yard. My best friend, Diana, and I would sell lemonade just on the other side of the fence. Now that house was just a memory. But when I'd first started training with Nerina, she told me that once I unlocked each book, its magic would be in me forever, and I had to keep it contained somewhere. She left it up to me to decide what that container was. I chose the old Tudor house, and now each book's magic rattled around in there like a family of ghosts.

I summoned the house and the ghosts inside, calling forth the magic from Tibet. The power to separate my soul from my body. Inside the *Angel Falls* book, my body stood rooted in the hallway. I pulled my soul apart and shadow-walked through that last door. I tricked the Angel Falls magic into thinking it had me caught, when really my shadow was bouncing off its walls like Peter Pan.

The answer to Jonah's problem smacked me in the face. The full impact of it darkened my shadow skin as I drank it in; it filled me like too much vodka, and I stumbled back into my body. With a hard tug, I wrenched my hands off the book. My skin was red and raw, as though I'd been shoveling snow without gloves. I flopped onto my back, panting. *Shit.* Now I had to tell Alessia what I'd found. *Double shit.*

Bree!

Nerina's voice ripped through my head. I clutched my ears even though I knew I couldn't block her out. *Get to the Waterfall! Now!*

What the—?

The Malandanti. They're here.

CHAPTER TWENTY-FIVE

Take That, You Motherfuckers

Bree

I didn't think; I just acted. That was how well Nerina had trained me. I didn't need to plan out what I was going to do; I just did it. I wasn't much for plans, anyway.

I plucked myself out of Nerina's lair and transported through time and space to the birch trees by the Waterfall. Shadows poured out of me. I wrapped them around my body and plunged through the trees to the water's edge.

It was chaos.

Frozen for an instant, I didn't know where to look first. Screeches and howls filled the air. At the edge of the protective barrier, Heath and the Malandanti Coyote rolled in the water, their jaws locked on each other. Across the stream, the Stag had the Boar backed up against a tree. Using his antlers like horns, he stabbed at the Boar, who feinted from side to side to avoid getting gored. My gaze swung wildly around the perimeter of the Waterfall. Where was Jonah?

Inside the barrier, Alessia dodged and swerved in the

air. A huge form loomed from the pool below, blocking her from my view.

What the hell—?

It's one of their Concilio. *The Harpy.* Nerina's voice was raw with rage. *She cracked the barrier with her magic and got in.* I spun around and spotted Nerina up the stream. She galloped through the water, a dark shadow on her tail. My gut turned over. Jonah.

Nerina wheeled and swiped Jonah across the nose. He fell back, and she rose, bursting through the barrier to help Alessia. I ran into the water toward Jonah.

Bree. It was Nerina.

I stopped.

Get down to the base of the pool, she instructed. *Focus on the Harpy.*

I glanced back at Jonah. He was on the other side of the stream now, loping toward the Boar.

Bree!

I'm coming, I'm coming. I made my way down the rocks. Spray from the Waterfall dappled my cheeks. *Where's their mage?*

I don't see him yet. When he gets here, take him down.

I took a deep breath and crossed into the barrier. The outside world was muffled. My toes touched the edge of the water, my shoes sinking deep into the cold mud. Above me, a battle raged between all the winged creatures of the Benandanti and the Malandanti. The ocean-blue auras of Nerina, Alessia, and the Eagle mingled with the silvery glow of the Raven and the Harpy.

Now that I was just underneath it, I could see the god-awful ugliness of the Harpy. She looked like a cross between a vulture and the scary-ass velociraptor from *Jurassic Park*. I had no idea how I knew it was female, but I knew, the same way I could spot the Mean Girl Queen Bee on the first day at a new school. The Harpy stretched her black wings, blotting out the moon, and craned her scaly neck. Her yellow eyes bulged out of their sockets as she looked right at me.

I shrank back into my shadows. She couldn't see who I was, could she? No, I was fully cloaked; I was sure of it.

Still, those neon eyes pierced me as if they knew me to my core. She flexed her talons, six-inch-long nails gleaming in the darkness. Quicker than I could blink, she swiped one of those deadly talons at Alessia, who darted out of the way just in time to save her belly from being ripped open.

All right, you fugly bitch, I thought, *it's on*.

I pulled the first trick out of my hat and sent the Harpy to another time and place. But as soon as I released the power into the air, the Harpy pushed it right back to me. I had to jump out of the way. In an instant, it landed on a fallen log next to me, setting it on fire. I looked up, my mouth open. The Harpy tossed her velociraptor head and let out a cackle.

Well, okay. Fine. *I'm just getting started. Bring it.* I raised both my arms. Bloodred mist spiraled out of my palms and threaded the air. The Harpy dove out of the barrier, but the mist caught the Raven in its wake. *That's for Alessia's barn, you little butt-monkey*, I thought.

The Raven tumbled down and hit the water with a fierce splash.

And this is for my brother. I dragged the Raven up to the shore, the mist binding him to me like a hangman's rope. He flopped on the ground, trying to move his wings, but I held him fast.

When I had practiced this with Nerina and the Stag, neither of them had fought back. It was easy to stop then. But the Raven *fought*. My breath was stolen as he strained against me, my heartbeat quickening. I pressed my magic into him, deeper and deeper, until he couldn't move. A silvery light seeped from his feathers. His life force flowed toward me. I beckoned it . . . *I could take him out right now, and Jonah would no longer have a Guide . . .*

The Raven croaked a pitiful little sound. I blinked. The Angel Falls magic fell out of me. *No.* I wasn't *that* mage. The Raven flew up in an arc over my head. I snarled at him. I wasn't that mage, but I wasn't a saint, either. I flicked my wrist and blasted him out of the here and now. He disappeared with a little pop.

An ungodly sound tore across the Waterfall. The Harpy bore down on me, talons outstretched, her demon-yellow eyes targeting me . . . I threw my arms up and reappeared at the top of the Waterfall.

The Malandanti Bobcat looked up in surprise. It was

perched on a rock in the middle of the stream. Too late I saw the figure behind it, a human shape cloaked in shadow just like I was . . .

The figure took one splashy step toward me and pushed.

I tumbled backward. The barrier swished across my skin as I fell through it. For a long moment, there was nothing but air, my limbs thrashing wildly to grab onto something and finding nothing. When I finally hit the water, I felt as if I had crashed into a pile of bricks. Pain cracked across my ribs, knocking the wind out of me. The force of the Waterfall tossed me in and over, again and again . . . I tried to suck in a breath and got a lungful of water. I fought my way up, up toward the light oh so far above me, but something shoved me down again—some force I couldn't fight. Their mage—their Rabbit—holding me under until I drowned. I kicked and reached, trying to find my magic, trying to find anything to save me. Iron bands wrapped around my chest; red spots popped in front of my eyes. My whole body tightened, trying to get one tiny, lifesaving drop of air. God, I was going to drown, just as Jonah had almost drowned all those years ago in Mexico.

Huge paws appeared above me. With one enormous burst of effort, I grabbed onto them. I rose up and up, pinpricks of light dancing behind my eyelids . . . I broke the surface and opened my mouth. Air—sweet, beautiful air—poured into my lungs. Nerina dragged me to the shore. I rolled onto my side, coughing water out of my lungs.

Bree. Bree. Are you all right? She nudged my face with her dripping-wet nose.

I flopped onto my back, panting. Above me, Alessia and the Eagle circled the Harpy, trying to drive her out of the barrier. What magic did she possess to get inside in the first place? I didn't have time to ask. Every time the two Benandanti Birds got close to the foul Harpy, she screamed and flashed her talons so close to them I was sure their heads were going to come off. I sat up. The Harpy flew at Alessia and the Eagle, pushing them back against the barrier. I knew the rule; if the Harpy succeeded in getting the Benandanti out, all the Malandanti could rush in and retake the Waterfall.

Get up there, I screamed at Nerina. *Don't you see what she's going to do?*

Are you—?

I'm fine. I pushed my wet hair off my face and hauled myself to my feet.

Nerina ran into the sky and rammed the Harpy from behind. Alessia and the Eagle dropped below her, down toward the pool. The Harpy turned on Nerina, the look on her face pure murder. I splashed back into the water, ignoring the chill that crept into my bones, and lifted my arms high. *Party's over, you whore.* Calling on the power of the Redwoods, I sent strength into the barrier. Light flashed out in all directions, so bright they must've seen it in Nova Scotia.

The Harpy screeched with shock; I would've laughed

if the sound hadn't practically tore my eardrums in half. Her Foulness was blasted up about twenty feet. Where she landed, I had no idea, but she was nowhere in sight when the light cleared. The barrier glowed fierce and sure, fortified by a second layer on the outside. Up at the top of the Waterfall, I saw the Bobcat try to break in and receive a jolt that sent it upstream.

Behind the Bobcat, the Rabbit stood tall on a stone jutting out of the stream. Shadows billowed around him. I raised my arms again and realized my shadow-cloak was gone; the water must've washed it away. Panic sliced through me: who had seen?

I couldn't think about that now. I conjured up the shadows and pulled them around me just as a silver streak of light shot at me. I ducked just in time. Behind me a tree exploded.

At the top of the Waterfall, the Rabbit was laughing. "Silly child." His voice sounded as though it were right against my ear. "You think you're any match for me?"

Well, yes, actually I did. I called on the power of the Redwoods again, its golden light molding around my body like a shield. The next bolt of silver light that came at me just bounced off my chest. I brought my hand up, sharp and quick, and the Rabbit's legs shot out from under him.

He landed hard on a rock in the middle of the stream. "Bitch!"

Oh, please. I'd been called worse than that. Even

though I was shivering from my dunk in the water, exhil-aration roared through my veins, power tingled my skin. The Rabbit was on his feet again, and now he had his own shield of Redwood magic around him too.

In the wink of an eye, I displaced myself to the top of the Waterfall, right behind him. "Hello," I said in his ear.

He spun around. Though we were both cloaked in shadow and light, I could see his eyes—dark, dark brown with gold flecks. Somewhere in the back of my head, Nerina's voice was yelling at me to get away from him, but I ignored her. This dude was going down, and I wanted a front-row seat.

We raised our hands at the same time, bloodred mist spilling out of our fingers. Whoever he was, he thought on the same wavelength as I did. But I was using the magic for good, and he for evil. That was the difference between us.

He flicked his fingers at me. Red mist droplets seared holes in my golden shield. Without losing focus, I slashed my hand in the air, slicing a red line across him. Scarlet smoke poured from both of us. We circled each other, our shadow-cloaks dragging in the water, bursts of gold and red and blue and silver light arcing back and forth as we each tried to make the other stumble. But we were too equally matched.

I tried to blast him out of time and space, but he blocked me before the magic was even fully out of me. Silver light crackled at his fingers, but he had barely raised a hand before I waved the light into nothingness. My chest heaved. Maybe we'd just tire each other out to death . . .

Bree. Nerina's voice broke into my mind. I didn't know where she was; I was too afraid to look away from the Rabbit to find her. *End this already.*

I'm trying—

You know what we need. Do the— What did you call it? Super—

Jedi Mind Trick. My lip curved up. I'd been so concerned with protecting myself from the Rabbit's magic I'd forgotten what I needed him for.

Everyone needs to keep the Malandanti busy, I said to the entire Clan. *If they see what I'm doing, they'll ruin it. Got it?*

I reached inside my little Tudor house and pulled out the green magic. The fun magic. It didn't manifest in the air like the other magic; it was invisible to anyone but me. I cocked my head and met the Rabbit's eyes. "You should lower your shield."

The green halo appeared above the Rabbit's head, just like those stupid Stormtroopers that Obi-Wan takes care of with a flick of his hand. His eyes slid a smidge out of focus, and the golden light around him disappeared.

I reached out and grabbed his wrist. He didn't resist, just got this goofy smile on his face as though the hottest girl in school were suddenly hitting on him. "Follow me," I said, and he did.

Out of the corner of my eye, I saw Heath at the edge of the Waterfall, blocking a smaller black figure from me. Jonah . . .

The green halo above the Rabbit's head flickered for an instant, and he blinked. Shit. "We're going inside the barrier," I told him, and the halo stabilized again. I clenched my jaw and blocked out anything but the Congo magic. I couldn't let Jonah be my undoing . . .

We reached the bottom of the Waterfall. I pulled the Rabbit in through the barrier with me. The moment he was inside the Benandanti's magic, the shadows around him dropped away. He stood unmasked before me, and for a long breath, I just stared at him.

I didn't recognize him, not from Twin Willows or from my internship at the Guild. He was young, maybe Heath's age, with mud-brown hair that fell into his eyes. He was shorter than he'd appeared in the shadow-cloak. His shoulders stooped slightly, as if he were trying to fit through a doorway that was too small for him. He looked completely ordinary, unassuming. Was that why the *Concilio Argento* had chosen him? Because no one would think to look twice at him? Not like me, who made a scene in every room I entered.

Everybody, into the barrier now. Hurry, I said. A flurry of movement rustled the air all around the Waterfall at my command. I knew there were only a few Malandanti left who were hanging on, still trying to fight, but even a few would be enough to destroy the spell. Heath leapt inside the bubble a few feet from me, his paws imprinting deep in the snow at the edge of the water. Above me, Alessia and the Eagle swooped around the perimeter of the barrier, joined a moment later by Nerina. *Where's the Stag?*

I'm trying—

I saw him, on the far edge of the pool, his every move toward the barrier blocked by that ugly-ass Boar. *C'mon, c'mon—*

Something struck me between the shoulder blades, and I collapsed to the ground, my side scraping painfully on the rocks jutting out of the snow. I looked up to see the Rabbit looming over me, the green halo gone, shadows spiraling around him once more. "Did you really think you'd get away with this?"

"Yes," I screamed, and this time I fought him not with magic but with my bare hands. I grabbed his ankles before they disappeared in the cloak and yanked him onto the ground next to me.

He started to scramble backward. I punched his stomach as hard as I could. He pulled my hair, dragging me toward him.

Really, with the hair pulling? "What are you, a girl?" I panted and kicked him in the shin.

He yowled, and I congratulated myself on having chosen my pointy-toed boots to wear that night.

I'm here, the Stag shouted.

I hauled myself to my feet. The Rabbit tried to get up too, but I jammed my heel into his chest. "Stay down."

The green halo popped above his head, and he slackened.

I fought for breath, trying to remember exactly what

I was supposed to do.

Bree—now, Nerina yelled.

But I couldn't—not until I knew. My eyes sought the darkness, looking for that sleek black figure. I found him, at the top of the rocks, descending fast. *Get back,* I thought, *get back get back get back.*

A Benandante and a Malandante could not communicate telepathically. But I swore he heard me. Somehow, our twinspeak reached across impossibility. He changed course, heading to the edge of the trees.

Nerina charged toward me, her wings like a super-turbo fan. *Do it,* she shrieked.

I looked down at the Rabbit, like the most pathetic of slaves under my dominatrix boot. The halo flickered. He'd break it soon . . .

I met his gaze. "This is for Mr. Foster," I said very clearly, and with my foot, I shoved him into the barrier.

The scream that tore from him was so horrible I almost backed down. But I knew what I was doing wouldn't kill him. It would just hurt—a lot. The barrier crackled, lines of silver magic fracturing across it. The Rabbit's body fused into the barrier, sharp fractals emanating from his limbs. His magic—Malandanti magic— was joining ours. The two forces twisted together until the blue light of the Benandanti encased the silver of the Malandanti, overpowering it.

I pulled every ounce of power from every corner of my body and soul. "Let the veil be lifted; let the glamour fall," I called out, my voice echoing in every direction. "Let the world see truth, one and all."

A boom like a nuclear bomb went off, an invisible mushroom cloud of power exploding across the far reaches of the Guild. Magic rained from the sky, shards of the false mirror they had been holding up for so long. I wondered what it looked like to the rest of the world. To me, it was the most beautiful thing I'd ever seen.

The Rabbit disappeared with a pop, somewhere outside this time and space. I only hoped that wherever he landed, he was in a shit-ton of pain and would be out of commission for quite a while. The sky cleared, the mirror shards gone, replaced with the serenity of the stars. The Malandanti were gone. The magic had blown them away, back into their hidey-holes to lick their wounds. I hoped Jonah had gotten far enough away and was now safe at home in bed. As soon as I was done here, I'd go home at last and check.

Cold crept up my legs, and I realized I was standing knee-deep in the freezing water. I backed up to the shore and sat down on my butt. My whole body shook, but whether it was from my soaking-wet clothes or the magic still pulsing through me, I didn't know.

Nerina landed lightly next to me. *Go home,* she said. *Take a hot bath.*

I looked her in the eyes. "I just saved your asses, and that's all you have to say to me?" My teeth chattered.

Her laughter tittered in my head. *You are magnifico, Bree.*

She pressed her huge head against mine for a moment. *We could not have done this without you.*

The whole Clan descended around me in a crush of fur and hide and feathers.

"Air, air," I muttered, but I let them smother me. My parents had never shown this kind of pride toward me, no matter how many A papers I brought home.

At last, they released me. I met Alessia's eyes through the fierce bird mask of her face. I could hear her thoughts without her speaking them. She wanted me to make sure Jonah was okay too.

I pushed myself to my feet and walked backward through the barrier. "*In bocca al lupo,*" I shouted, my arms spread wide. They echoed the blessing back in my mind. With a soft pop, I disappeared from the Waterfall and reappeared at the top of my driveway.

A black car idled at the side of the street, exhaust fumes spiraling into the cold night air. I slid into the trees in front of my house, but if they'd been looking, there was no way they hadn't seen me just appear out of nowhere. Maybe the car was empty. Maybe the driver was waiting for my dad. Maybe the Guild had already started to fall apart in the wake of my spell-breaking, and he had to rush to the Headquarters for damage control.

The rear passenger door of the car opened. One black-stocking-clad leg appeared after another, and an impossibly tall woman emerged. Her hair hung about her shoulders in snaky locks. I clung to the closest tree. She looked like Medusa. I swallowed and tasted bile. No, not Medusa. She looked like . . . the Harpy . . . only a human version . . .

"Bree Wolfe?" She advanced toward me, her dark eyes magnetic. I couldn't look away. I tried, and I physically could not do it.

I tried to toss my hair, but it was still wet and clinging to my neck. "Nope. You got the wrong girl."

"I beg to differ."

The driver-side door opened. With superhuman effort, I wrenched my gaze away from the Harpy, turned, and ran. Heavy footsteps pounded after me, closer and closer. My sopping-wet clothes weighed me down. I tried to run faster, but my legs would not obey. Thick arms reached around me from behind, one around my waist, the other around my neck. A beefy hand clamped over my mouth. I kicked and bit, twisting and struggling, but the arms just locked tighter around me. I was dragged backward, toward the car. I summoned my magic, willed myself to disappear and reappear anywhere else, anywhere but here.

Nothing happened.

I tried again and again. Smoky silver light snaked around me, binding me. Not just my body. My magic. They were blocking my magic.

"Please," I said, "I don't know anything. Really. I don't."

I only had time to see the inhuman yellow eyes of the Harpy bitch crinkle with triumphant glee before a hood descended over my face, and I was thrown into the trunk of the car.

CHAPTER TWENTY-SIX

The Getaway

Alessia

The morning after the battle, I headed downstairs for breakfast. I heard the news report before I saw it, blaring from the little television Lidia had on in the kitchen.

". . . shocking allegations of corruption, including slave labor in the communities the Guild Incorporated claims to help . . ."

My heart jolted. It was already happening. We had truly done it. We had taken down the Guild. I stepped into the kitchen and fixed my gaze on the small screen.

". . . an anonymous source has leaked financial records to the *Wall Street Journal* that details years of misconduct . . ."

Bree's download from the night we'd broken into the Guild. *A little financial reckoning,* she'd said. She or Nerina must've leaked it after the battle last night.

". . . and the Hague has announced it is investigating Guild CEO Silvio Debrusco for war crimes in the Congo, where the Guild has several coffee and cocoa plantations. Now for the weather . . ."

Lidia spun around from the stove, a smile spread wide on her face. "I don't think we'll have to worry about that power plant now."

"Guess not." I grinned back. I wanted to dance in circles. Instead, I hugged Lidia around the waist. She smelled like maple syrup and freshly baked bread. "It must've been your signs, Mom."

She laughed. "Sit, sit. I'm making waffles."

That explained the maple syrup scent. We chatted happily while we munched on her thick, doughy Belgian waffles. It was like before . . . before the Benandanti, even before Dad died. He might've been just outside, working in the still-standing barn.

After breakfast, Lidia headed into town to see Mr. Salter. I almost asked her point-blank what was going on between her and him, but the words failed in my mouth. I wasn't sure I really wanted to know. It was just *wrong* to think of Lidia with anyone other than my dad.

Instead I headed to the hen trailers. I collected the eggs, but I left my basket just outside the trailer door. I ducked into the woods, came to the stone wall, and went below to Nerina's.

Before I emerged into her living area, I heard voices and clinking glass. I stepped off the bottom stair. Heath and Nerina stood in the middle of the room but, thank goodness, this time they weren't kissing. They were drinking champagne instead. Several newspapers were spread out on the coffee table, a couple in Italian, all with variations on the same headline: "Allegations of Corruption Will Be the Guild's Downfall."

"Alessia," Nerina sang out. "Come have a glass of prosecco and toast the Benandanti's success."

"Um, it's not even eight in the morning," I said, but Nerina was already pouring me a glass. She shrugged and handed it to me.

"It's five o'clock somewhere in the world," Heath said.

"Your years in France ruined you," I said, wagging a finger at him. I took the glass from Nerina and looked at the bubbles inside. "What's prosecco?"

"It's like champagne, only better." Nerina clinked my glass with hers. "Because it's Italian."

I took a sip. The bubbles floated right up to my head. I took one more sip to be polite and set the glass behind the lamp on one of the end tables. "So, we did it." I picked up one of the newspapers and skimmed the article. Corruption, war crimes, stockholders bailing. The Guild was screwed. "We can breathe easy now, right?"

Both Nerina and Heath snapped their gazes to me. I knew exactly what they were thinking, that I was going to call in my end of the bargain I'd made with Heath all those weeks ago. "We still haven't won the war," Nerina said. "Four sites are still under Malandanti control."

"We need to be more vigilant than ever," Heath added. "The Malandanti will want revenge."

"But they'll be preoccupied with all of this for a few days, right?" I waved a hand over the newspapers. "And shouldn't we celebrate each victory?"

Heath narrowed his eyes at me. "What do you want?"

I sighed. "Fine. I want to go away with my friends for the weekend."

"Absolutely not—"

"*Un momento.*" Nerina held a hand up. She searched my face, her eyes soft. "I think Alessia deserves a little break. How long will you be gone?"

"Tomorrow until Sunday. Two and a half days." I watched her cross to the couch and sit next to me, my heart hopping from one beat to the next.

Nerina took another sip of her prosecco and set the glass on the table. "Go. Be with your friends. Take these few days for yourself. Because," she added, drawing back and touching her red-tipped fingernails to my cheek, "when you return, we must prepare for the battle of our lives."

I hugged her. "Thank you, Nerina. Thank you!"

"You can't let her go! Come on, Nerina. I'm the Guide—"

"And I'm the *Concilio.*" Nerina drew away from me and stood up. "And I say it is all right."

"I'm gonna go pack," I said, dashing to the stairs before Heath could change Nerina's mind. I glanced back just before I headed up. Nerina was looking at Heath from underneath her lashes, a sultry smile on her lips. Apparently she had an ulterior motive for getting rid of me for the weekend. I shuddered. *Ew.*

School crawled by that day. I ducked into second-period French just before the bell. My heart jumped when I saw Jonah already in his seat. He'd made it back okay, then. I suddenly realized I hadn't seen Bree yet, but she was probably skipping school again. She'd been out all week—"sick" —but I'd bet she was home sleeping off the aftereffects of the battle.

Jonah raised his eyebrows as I slid into my seat. I hunched my shoulders, not quite sure how to act. We'd had a huge victory last night—but he'd had a huge defeat. And yet . . . he wanted the Malandanti to fail now, didn't he? I faced forward, the back of my neck hot where I was sure his gaze was. It was too confusing.

Halfway through class, a note landed on my desk.

I need to see you. Tonight, at our place.

I bent over my desk to scribble back.

Can't. Going away for the weekend and leaving really early tomorrow.

We'd gotten permission to skip school, since we had a tour at Williams College in the afternoon. I stretched my hand back beneath his desk. His fingers brushed mine as he took the note.

Within a minute it was back on my desk.

Can I walk you home, then? Alone?

Yes.

The day inched forward. I barely heard Carly and Melissa's happy chatter at lunch. "Do you think my red sweater is too low-cut to wear to the tour?" Carly nudged me.

"Huh?"

"My red sweater?"

"Oh, um, ask Jenny. She's the fashion expert."

"It's too low-cut," Jenny said. "We want to look serious."

"But they usually have college students do the tour," Carly said. "It could be a cute guy."

"Or a nerdy girl. Just wear the black turtleneck."

Carly sat back in her chair with a huff. I glanced around the cafeteria. Jonah sat in the corner; it had gotten too cold and snowy for his usual seat under the bleachers. From across the crowded room, I met his gaze. The noise that separated us disappeared. His eyes were as piercing as the Panther's, searing into me. I gripped the back of my chair.

The rest of the afternoon passed as if we were stuck in honey, trying to swim our way out.

When at last the final bell rang, I burst out through the front doors. Jenny caught up with me on the sidewalk. I spotted Jonah off to the side, that same fierce look on his face.

I put my hand on Jenny's arm. "Um, Jonah's gonna walk me home today."

She glanced at him. "Are you two getting back together?"

"No." She narrowed her eyes at me, and I faltered. "I don't know. It's complicated. Just—please don't give me a hard time about this."

"Okay. He can have you this afternoon only because I get you for the whole weekend." She danced away to where Melissa and Carly stood on the curb. "It's gonna be legendary!"

I laughed. I was still smiling when I landed by Jonah's side.

"What was that all about?" he asked, jerking his chin in Jenny's direction.

"Oh, we're all going away this weekend to look at colleges. No parents."

"Whoa. Your mom went for that?" We started the long walk to my house. It felt easy again, and I had to hold myself back from slipping my hand into his the way I used to.

"Surprisingly, yes. But I wasn't about to look a gift horse in the mouth." I shrugged. "Should be fun."

"Well, you have a lot to celebrate."

I looked sideways at him. "I guess you saw the news."

He met my gaze. "I didn't have to see the news. I felt the spell."

I had to swallow an apology. I wasn't sorry. I was on the right side, not him. I took a deep breath, but before I could speak, Jonah grabbed my hand. The heat of him pulsed through my glove. "I'm glad," he said, his voice hoarse and low. "I want to bring them down, too."

His green eyes were dark with longing. I flung my arms around his neck and buried my face in the smoked-earth smell of him. He held me against him for a long moment before I pulled away.

"I'm working on it," I said. "What we talked about. I'm looking for a way."

He slid my gloves off and raised my hands to his lips, kissing my knuckles first and then my palms. "I know you are, Alessia. I trust you." He held my hand against his heart, and we continued down the street. "I think maybe you're the only one I trust right now." He shook his head. "Ironic, isn't it?"

I leaned my head against his shoulder. "I'm sorry," I said. I had Heath and the Clan and Nerina. I trusted them with my life, every night. And even though I had to lie to them, I always knew if I had to, I could trust my mother and Jenny. There wasn't a time I could remember that they weren't a part of. But Jonah had no one. Even his twin was betraying him behind his back. "Things at home aren't good?"

He snorted. "Things at home are . . . *not good.*" He tucked me in closer to his side. "I don't want to talk about it."

"You can, though. If you want."

"I know." He kissed the top of my head. "And that's enough."

We were at the edge of my driveway. I faced him. "I'd invite you in, but I don't want my mom asking questions."

"I think that's probably best, for now." He glanced behind him, but the street was empty save for the swirls of old snow. I couldn't help looking down the length of my driveway either. The farm lay quiet. Still, I shivered.

"There are eyes everywhere," I whispered.

"I'll risk it," Jonah murmured. He cupped my face in his hands and drew me to him. His face was chilly from the winter wind, but his lips were warm. "When I kiss you, I know everything is going to be okay," he said against my mouth. I caught the words on my tongue and swallowed them to make them true.

A car rattled past. We jumped away from each other. I glimpsed the driver inside; he was talking on his cell phone and didn't even notice us. I reached out and gripped Jonah's hand. "When I get back from my trip, we'll meet at the basement," I said. "Maybe I'll have news by then."

The shadow of a smile crossed Jonah's face. "I'll be counting the hours." He dipped his head to kiss me one more time. As I walked down the driveway to the front door, I felt his eyes on me the whole time.

Our tour guide at Williams *was* a cute guy. Carly shot daggers at Jenny the whole tour, except when the tour guide was looking at her, in which case she smiled so wide I thought her face would crack. At the end of the tour, the guide gave her his phone number. "Call me if you have any questions."

"Oh, I will." Carly tossed her head. "You've been *so* helpful."

"Seriously, Carly, did you hear anything he said?" Melissa asked after the guide had dropped us back off at the Admissions building. "Or were you too busy looking at his butt?"

"*Ew*," Jenny and I chorused, falling into each other with laughter.

"God, I hope our guide at Amherst is female," Melissa said as we headed across the snowy campus to the car. I looked around the sweeping hills and brick buildings, a twist of longing in my chest. I wanted this future. Maybe not here at Williams—I actually *had* been listening to the tour guide and wasn't sure this was the right school for me—but somewhere, far away from Twin Willows. That had always been my dream, to get out of there as soon as I graduated, but becoming a Benandante had shoved that dream to the highest, most out-of-reach shelf. Now, with the takedown of the Guild, that dream seemed a little more reachable.

We dumped off our bags at the little inn we were staying at—me and Jenny in one room, Carly and Melissa right next door—and headed out for lobsters at the little hole-in the-wall shack Jenny's dad had told us we *had* to go to. As we cracked shells and dipped the creamy white flesh into butter, the conversation ricocheted from colleges to applications to finals to the trip to Paris, which made Melissa and I fake cry into our iced teas. Thankfully, no one asked about Jonah. I'd been the last one to get picked up that morning on our way out, and I had a feeling Jenny had told the others to back off.

When we got back to the inn, the chatty old couple who owned the place greeted us with tea and cookies and plied us with the kind of questions adults think kids like to answer over and over. *What do you want to major in? What other schools are you applying to? What do your parents think?* By the time we escaped upstairs to our rooms, it was almost midnight.

Jenny fell into bed, and her breathing deepened into the slow, even breath of sleep almost immediately. I lay awake for longer, staring at the ceiling. Pretty soon, I'd have to have all the answers to those questions figured out. I'd always thought that I would major in creative writing, but my work with the Benandanti had made me rethink that. Something to do with government, or diplomacy. I'd seen how fascinating that could be just from talking to Nerina. But would I even get the chance to explore it? The time was coming soon when I would have to start gathering applications and making decisions, and Lidia was going to be all over me about it. If we hadn't defeated the Malandanti by then, how was I going to explain to her that I'd changed my mind and wanted to spend the rest of my life in Twin Willows?

I rolled onto my side and stared at Jenny's sleeping form. She was so lucky. Her parents had encouraged her independence since she was born. My chest prickled. Lidia would probably be ecstatic if I told her I was staying home to work the farm. The prickling grew hotter. I sat straight up. No. Seriously? I was hundreds of miles away; how could I possibly be Called?

A thousand tiny cracks fractured my body. Before I could break apart, I opened the window. Wind gusted the curtains inward. Jenny mumbled something in her sleep and burrowed deeper under her covers. I dropped onto the bed and let my soul break free.

I soared out the window, opening the channel in my mind to Heath alone. *Um, really? I'm in Massachusetts!*

I know, he answered right back. *We just need you to listen in.*

Is everything okay at the Waterfall?

There, yes. But we have another problem.

I swooped low over hills, in and out of bare trees. Since I had no destination, I worked in circles, gliding higher and higher on the cusp of the cold wind.

The next voice to enter my head was Nerina's. *Has anyone seen our mage?* she asked without preamble.

A chorus of *No* echoed back.

My talons reached out and caught a thick, barren oak branch. I teetered for a moment, thinking back to school. No, Bree hadn't been there. I'd just thought she was skipping.

Are you sure she's actually missing? I asked. Jonah hadn't said anything, but he might not have known. It was typical that one of them would skip school on any given day, and he wouldn't exactly have asked me about her, since he didn't know we were friends. I gripped the branch tight. Were we friends? We were fighting on the same side, working to free Jonah, but I still couldn't count her amongst my circle.

She was supposed to be at my house last night for training,

Nerina said. *She did not show. And she has not been answering my calls and texts all day today.*

Like most teenage girls, Bree was rarely without her phone. I'd seen her answer a text in three seconds flat. And I'd never known her to miss a training session with Nerina. *This doesn't sound good.*

No. It was the Eagle. *I spent all afternoon scouring the town for her. I couldn't find her.*

She hasn't been at home either, said the Stag. *I've had an eye on her house since this morning.*

I didn't want to say it out loud, didn't want to think of the possibility. But the silence that stretched between all of us was too heavy. *Do you think . . . she was captured?*

She was visible, Heath said after a beat. *For a brief moment, after she fell in the water. I saw her. It's very possible one of the Malandanti did, too.*

My heart plummeted. I hadn't seen that happen, but I had been pretty preoccupied with their Harpy. Oh, God, what if the Harpy had seen her? What if she was being tortured right now? I thought about how Dario "held strong." Despite Bree's tough-girl exterior, I wasn't sure she could withstand that. *But she has magic,* I suddenly remembered out loud. *She can protect herself, right?*

Until we find her, we must hope so, said Nerina. She went on to order the Stag to keep watching her house and the Eagle to keep sweeping the town. *The Wolf and I will stay at the Waterfall.*

I closed the channel to the Clan but kept it open to

Heath and Nerina. *Do you need me to come home? I'm sure I can get a bus—*

It might be a good idea, Heath said.

No. Until we know something for sure, we must act as if nothing is wrong, Nerina said. Once more, she was pulling *Concilio* rank. *We will let you know when we hear something.*

Okay, but next time, can you just text me? I launched off the branch and flew back toward the inn. *Not exactly the most convenient time or place to get Called.*

The entire Clan can't have a conversation via text, Heath snapped. *Which is why you shouldn't be away in the first place.*

Heath . . . Nerina warned.

Call me if you hear anything, I cut in before they started bickering. *Good night.*

The pale moon wavered in the dusty dawn as I skimmed the treetops. Ahead, the open window to my room at the inn beckoned. I glided through the window and skidded back into my body. Air flooded my lungs, and I bent forward, pressing a fist to my mouth to keep from making too much noise. When my heartbeat steadied, I straightened. Inhaling deeply, I looked over at Jenny's bed.

She sat on the edge of it, watching me.

My stomach bottomed out. I scrambled backwards on the bed until I hit the wall. "What—? How—? How long have you been awake?"

Jenny pressed her lips together in a tight smile. She

got up and closed the window with a snap. "The cold air woke me up," she said, her back to me.

I watched her climb back into bed, her face hidden from me by her long curtain of blonde hair. She pulled the covers up and hugged her knees to her chest. With a sigh, she rested her cheek on her kneecaps and blinked at me. "So you're one, too."

CHAPTER TWENTY-SEVEN
The Secret Revealed

Alessia

"What? One what?" My heart hammered against my rib cage so hard my whole body shook with the impact.

"Benandanti." The word sounded all wrong coming from her mouth. I stared at her. "I started to suspect when I found you at the top of your driveway."

"How—? How . . . do you even know?"

"I've seen it before." Jenny rubbed her hands up and down her shins. "What it looks like when your soul separates from your body." She hugged herself into a smaller ball. "My dad is one."

Hardly daring to breathe, I crept towards the edge of my bed. "Your dad . . . is a Benandante?"

She nodded, her hair shivering around her face like a veil. "He turns into a stag."

I inhaled so sharply that air whistled against my teeth. "The Stag," I whispered. In my mind's eye, I saw him, his antlers bone-white in the moonlight, his powerful hooves stamping the ground. I heard him in my head, his dry sense of humor, his no-nonsense approach to strategy, and tried to reconcile him with my best friend's father, who posted silly YouTube videos on his Facebook wall.

Jenny smoothed the covers over her feet. "Were you coming back . . . from a fight?" There was fear in her eyes as she lifted her gaze to my face.

"No. A meeting. That's all."

She nodded, not saying anything.

In the room next to us, I heard the toilet flush. I cleared my throat. "Jenny, you can't tell Carly or Melissa. Or anyone."

She rolled her eyes. "Trust me, I know all the rules."

"But your dad— He told you. And your mom, I'm assuming."

"Well, it's kinda hard to hide it from the people you live with," Jenny said. She slid down on the bed and stretched her legs long. "I mean, Lidia knows, doesn't she?"

"No, she doesn't."

Jenny raised her eyebrows. "Seriously? How do you manage that?"

"Um, not easily." I got up and sat at the foot of Jenny's bed. "How long have you known about your dad?"

"About five years." Jenny smoothed a long strand of hair away from her face. "I always knew something was up. Like, he and my mom would be talking about something and then I'd come in and they'd shut up. Or one time my dad was, you know, 'sleeping' on the couch, and I tried to wake him up, but my mom dragged me out of the room. Finally when I was twelve, they thought I was old enough to handle it and told me."

I exhaled a long, slow breath. "I can't believe you had this big secret, and I never knew."

"Um, hello?" She poked a toe against my shin. "Pot kettle black. How long have you—?"

"A few months. Since October." I spread my fingers wide against my thighs, the fabric of my pajamas bunched under my knuckles. "The bus crash. Remember? That was the night I was Called."

"The crash . . ." Jenny jerked her head up. "It was the Malandanti, wasn't it?"

I nodded, then squinted at her. "How much do you know?"

Jenny shrugged. "Not much. I know there's something in Twin Willows the Benandanti are protecting and the Malandanti want. I know the Guild is somehow involved." She looked down at her lap. "I know Mr. Foster was a Benandante. My dad was really upset when he died."

"I was there." I closed my eyes, seeing the scene on the football field behind my eyelids. "I was there when he was killed."

"I'm really sorry, Lessi. That's awful." Jenny gnawed at her lip. "Actually, I kinda thought maybe your dad was one. That that was how he died, and you took his place."

I stared at her. "No. I . . ." My voice trailed off. The question that haunted me rose again. I didn't like to think too much about the fact that I had replaced someone, and the thought that it might've been my dad made my gut clench. "I . . . I don't know. Maybe. I never—"

Jenny touched my arm. "I'm sorry. I didn't mean to bring it up. I'm sure he wasn't."

But I wasn't sure of anything. If only someone— Nerina, Lidia, anyone—would tell me the truth. Maybe when I got home I would demand a reckoning . . .

We sat in silence for a few minutes while the sun grew brighter outside, streaming warmth through the window. Muffled voices seeped in from next door. I knocked Jenny's knee with mine. "I'm glad you know . . . about me. It's really sucked, having to keep it from you."

"Yeah. It has." Jenny's mouth turned up in a rueful half-smile. "Though I think I'm probably going to be in big trouble when my dad finds out I told you."

"Don't tell him." I hated the thought of more secrets, but it wasn't Jenny's fault she was caught in the middle of this. "I won't say anything."

Outside in the hall, a door opened and closed, and footsteps padded on the floor towards our room. Jenny held up a hand, little finger crooked towards me. "Pinky swear."

I hooked my finger on hers. "Pinky swear." A knock thudded on the door, and we broke apart. "Come in."

Carly burst into the room. "Oh, good. You're up."

"We are now," Jenny groaned, rubbing her face as though she'd just awakened.

"My dad told me about this fabulous bakery in Deer-field," Carly said. "But you have to get there super early before they run out of their special donuts. It's right on the way to Amherst."

I looked at the clock on the nightstand. Six o'clock. "These donuts better be worth it."

"They will be." Carly clapped her hands. "Let's meet downstairs in half an hour." She backed out of the room.

Jenny sighed. "I'm sorry. You didn't get any sleep, did you?"

"It's okay." I slid out of bed. The uneven plank floor was cold on my bare feet. "I don't sleep much anymore." Nor would I, until we knew where Bree was. I stared out the window for a moment. She could be anywhere. She could've freaked out after the battle and taken off. I shivered. Or she could be in a basement somewhere, strapped to a chair with a tray of knives next to her . . .

"Lessi?" Jenny came up behind me and put an arm around my shoulders. "Are you okay?"

I shook my head. If nothing else, it was a great relief to not have to lie. "Someone—from our Clan—is missing. That's what the meeting was about."

Jenny drew in a breath. "We'll go home. I'll tell the girls you're sick or something."

"No. It's okay. He—my Guide—said I shouldn't come home. They have it covered. But—" I swiped at a couple of tears that had fallen on my cheeks.

Jenny pulled me into a tight hug. "If they say they have it covered, then they do. One thing I know about the Benandanti—they'll Call you back if they really need you, no matter how inconvenient it is."

I sniffled into her pajamas. "You're right. I just—"

"I know." She shook me a little. "Go take a shower. Maybe a fabulous Deerfield donut will help."

Surprisingly, the fabulous donuts in Deerfield *did* help a little. I couldn't stop thinking about Bree, but our day was so jam-packed that the hours flew by without my realizing it. Before I knew it, we were on our way back to Williamstown.

"What's for dinner tonight?" Jenny asked.

"Anything but lobster," Melissa groaned.

"Italian?"

"Sounds good." Melissa turned to me. "Do you think Lidia will mind?"

"I think she won't mind what she doesn't know," I said.

Melissa laughed and leaned into me a little. "I'm so glad you were able to come, Lessi."

"Me too."

"I'm definitely leaning toward Mount Holyoke," she said, turning back to everyone else in the car. "I didn't think I'd like it as much as I did, but I'm impressed."

"Amherst all the way, baby," said Jenny. She turned the car off the highway, toward our inn. "My mom went there, you know."

"We know," the rest of us said in unison.

"Well, I liked Williams," Carly said. "Plus they have

a great music program."

"I thought you didn't want to go into music," Melissa said.

"I think I want to minor in it." Carly traced circles on the window. "What I'd really like to do is art therapy."

"Wow, Carly." Jenny glanced over at her. "That's really cool."

"Yeah, so noble." Melissa punched her lightly on the shoulder. "You're such a do-gooder."

"Whatever," Carly said. "You're the one who wants to be a doctor. You should be looking at Boston College."

"I probably will," Melissa admitted. "But it would be so cool if we all went to college near each other. Wouldn't it?"

"We could totally see each other on weekends," Jenny said.

I looked out the window at the dark trees. The three of them would be down here, having the time of their lives, and I'd be stuck in Twin Willows. I was stupid to think anything different. We won a battle, but the war still raged on, and now Bree was a casualty. I caught Jenny looking at me in the rearview. She knew. She knew what I had given up. It was the same reason her family had never taken a vacation.

"So, Italian?" Jenny asked. "Or Mexican?" That set off a dinner debate.

I gave her a grateful smile.

"I'm sorry," Jenny said when we were alone in our room. We'd been out late, checking out the college scene in Williamstown, and it was now the wee hours of the morning. "This weekend kinda sucked for you, didn't it?"

"No way." We were both sitting on our beds, deep in our covers to ward off the chill that seemed to seep in through the frame of the old inn. "It was awesome to spend time with you guys. I've missed it. My old life— I've missed it."

"Do you think you'll ever get to college?"

"I hope so." I rolled to my side and propped myself up on an elbow. "I have a deal. If we defeat the Malandanti, I get out. I just don't know . . . when or if that will ever happen." It had seemed so possible just a day ago, but now it was like a faraway dream again.

"It will." Jenny's eyes gleamed in the darkness. "Good always wins, doesn't it?"

"I used to think that," I whispered. "But the things I've seen . . ." In my mind's eye, I saw the light going out of the Lynx's eyes. I saw the Raven flying away from my burning barn. And I saw Bree, working her magic . . . Had evil won over her?

My phone buzzed. It was a text from Heath.

We got her.

I sat up. My fingers shook as I texted back.

Is she okay?

> *She will be.*

Will be? What the hell did that mean?

> *Where are you?*

> *Memorial Hospital.*

> *I'm coming.*

I threw the covers back. "They found her. I have to get home."

In a flash, Jenny was up, too. "I'll wake Carly and Melissa."

"Oh, God." I ran my hands through my hair. "What're you gonna tell them?"

"Don't worry." Jenny opened the door. "I'll tell them my mom had a vision of a car accident on the interstate, and we have to come home."

I almost laughed; Jenny's mom was kooky enough that it could be true. But Heath's text—*She will be*— haunted me. Where had they found her? What state was she in? If she was in the hospital, she was obviously hurt. How badly?

"Sorry, guys," Jenny said for the umpteenth time as she sped up the interstate toward Maine. "I tried to reason with her."

"It's okay." Carly yawned. "Sarah texted me that Mrs. Coppell is springing a test on us tomorrow in chemistry, and I need to study."

"Um, Jenny?" Melissa leaned over Jenny's shoulder from the backseat. "If you don't slow down, *we're* going to be the accident on the interstate."

I glanced at the speedometer; she was pushing eighty. She slowed to seventy-five. I knew she wasn't speeding home just for me. It could have easily been her dad who was missing.

Less than five hours later, we were pulling onto Main Street in Twin Willows. The sun peeked over rooftops, lengthening shadows along the street. Jenny dropped Carly and Melissa at their houses. "Tell your mom she's a sucky psychic," Melissa said as she hopped out of the car.

When they were both gone, Jenny turned to me. "Where to?"

"Memorial Hospital." It was two towns over, twenty minutes away. Jenny peeled onto Main Street and gunned it. We barreled along back roads until she skidded to a stop outside the hospital.

I opened the door and stepped one foot out. "Thank you, Jenny." I flung my arms around her. "You're the best friend a girl could ever have."

"I know, I know." She shooed me away, but her eyes were bright as I climbed out. She waited until I was inside the glass doors, then waved good-bye before she sputtered off.

I texted Heath as I backed away from the door.

Which room?

I didn't want to ask at the desk; she might be here under a different name.

216.

I followed first red, then yellow, then blue lines up to 216. The curtains were drawn. I cracked open the door. "It's me."

"Come in," said Heath.

I ducked around the curtain and stopped short.

Spiderwebs of red lines stretched across Bree's face, as though every capillary beneath her skin had broken. Bruises surrounded each of her eyes. Both hands were bandaged, leaving only the tips of her fingers visible. The neck of her hospital gown was loose, showing the edge of a bandage around her torso as well. I swallowed hard, trying to dispel the lump of bile that had risen into my throat.

"Oh, God, Bree," I whispered.

"What?" Her voice was little more than a croak. "You've never seen someone who's been tortured?"

CHAPTER TWENTY-EIGHT
I'm Fine, Thanks

Bree

Alessia reacted in her typical Alessia fashion—she burst into tears. I tried to roll my eyes, but the bruises in my sockets went bone deep. Everything hurt. "Oh, for God's sake," I said. "I'm alive, aren't I?"

"I'm so sorry, Bree." Alessia sniffled and wiped her nose with the back of her hand. She looked like a little kid who'd fallen off the swings. "I'm so sorry I got you into this."

I sighed and winced as pain radiated across my rib cage. Three broken ribs, two cracked . . . Even breathing was agony. I wished the nurse would come back with more drugs. "Hey, Heath? Can you give me and Alessia a few minutes?"

"Sure." He rose from his chair beside the bed and tucked his hands in his pockets. "I'll be right outside. Keeping watch."

"Thanks." I managed a grateful smile even though it felt as if my skin would fall off. After what he and Nerina had done for me, I wasn't ever going to make fun of him again.

As soon as Heath left the room, Alessia dropped into the chair he had vacated. "What happened? How did they get you out?"

"They were holding me in the basement of the Guild offices in Bangor. There's like a whole labyrinth down there I never knew about." I shifted a few inches. Searing-hot needles pricked my torso. "Heath and Nerina tracked me there and waited until my guard went to the bathroom. They broke in and got me out."

"I should've been there," Alessia muttered. "I'm so sorry, Bree."

"Will you shut up? Seriously, if you say that one more time, I will punch you." I lifted one bandaged hand. "Even though it will hurt like hell."

Alessia snorted. "Okay, okay." She tucked her legs underneath her. "How did the Malandanti find you in the first place?"

"It was that freaking Harpy." I saw her in my mind, her face contorted with sick pleasure as I writhed in pain beneath her. "She saw me, at the Waterfall. I was visible after I fell in the water."

"The water . . ." Alessia snapped her head up. "Did you have a vision? Of the future?"

I pressed my lips together. For sure, one of the things I'd seen was real, a true vision of what was to come, but it was all jumbled with everything they'd put into my mind, all the hallucinatory crap they'd squeezed in there to torture me. I'd seen Jonah, dead on the side of the road, all the Benandanti hanging from the willow tree above the Waterfall . . . I squinched my eyes shut to block it out, but behind my eyelids, the images were even clearer. I opened my eyes again. "I saw lots of things."

Alessia's face was expectant. But I wasn't going to say more. I wasn't going to tell her that all my injuries had come from the Rabbit. Apparently, I hadn't put him out of commission for as long as I'd hoped. He'd used all his power on me trying to get me to talk, all without ever laying a finger on me. I eased back onto the pillows and turned to look at Alessia. "I need to tell you something."

She reached out and touched my unbandaged fingertips. "It's okay, Bree. No one expected you to withstand torture."

I narrowed my eyes at her. "What are you talking about?"

"You told them stuff, right?" She searched my face. "I mean, no one will blame you."

"Are you kidding?" I hoisted myself onto an elbow with a grunt. "I didn't tell them shit."

Alessia stared at me, her mouth open.

"That's why I'm still alive, dummy. If I'd talked, we'd be having this conversation in a morgue." I lay back down. "That's not what I need to tell you."

"Bree—I—"

"Yeah, yeah. You're eternally grateful and all that." I pointed one of my mummy hands toward the door. "I already heard it all from your farm buddy."

"Well, I am. So now you've heard it from me." She pulled the chair closer to the hospital bed. "What do you need to tell me?"

"Right before the battle, Nerina left me alone. With

the books." At the blank look on her face, I gritted my teeth. "The books, Alessia. The ones with all the answers. And I found it."

She rocked forward, knocking against the bed. "You found how to turn a Malandante into a Benandante?"

I started to nod, but a crick pierced my spine. "Yes. But—"

"How do we do it?"

"Would you freaking let me talk?"

"Sorry, sorry." She pressed her knuckles into the mattress. "Tell me."

"It's not good." I met her gaze. "A Benandante needs to die in order to turn a Malandante."

She slumped in her chair. "Dammit."

"That's not all."

Alessia looked up. I knew the hopes I was dashing inside her, because the same ones had been stomped on inside me when I'd read it. "The Benandante has to willingly gift their essence, their aura, to a Malandante. In other words, they have to be on the verge of death—but not quite dead—in order to do it. And they have to *want* to do it."

"Those are nearly impossible circumstances," Alessia said.

"I know." I took a few breaths, deep as my fractured ribs would let me. "It's only been done once in the history of the Benandanti."

We sat in silence, letting the disappointment settle like dust around us.

"I'll keep looking," Alessia said finally. "I'm not giving up."

"Me neither."

Alessia widened her eyes. "You mean . . . you're going to stay with the Benandanti? After this?"

"Hell, yeah." I squared my shoulders and raised my chin. "You think this is enough to knock me out? No freaking way."

She found my fingers again and squeezed. "Thanks, Bree."

"I know, I know. I'm awesome. Now get out of here and let me rest."

But the minute she left, I wanted her to come back, even if all she wanted to do was talk me into a coma. Alone, all I could see were the roiling images the mage had planted in my brain. They played like a movie on a constant loop. And I knew that one of the images was real, that it was the future showing itself before it happened.

But which one it was, I had no clue.

CHAPTER TWENTY-NINE
The Abduction

Alessia

"She's resting," I told Heath when I came out of Bree's hospital room. "But you shouldn't leave, right?"

"Absolutely not," Heath said. He got to his feet and put his hand on the door handle. "Someone will be watching over her at all times."

He pushed the handle down. Just before he opened the door, I threw my arms around him. "Thanks, Heath." He gave my back an awkward pat. I half-smiled and pulled away.

"I was just doing my duty," he said, his cheeks glowing.

"I know. But . . . thanks."

Heath nodded and ducked into the room. I watched him drop into a chair on the outside of the curtain to give Bree her privacy while she rested. I laid my hand on the glass for a moment until my phone buzzed in my pocket. It was a text from Nerina.

I have news. Come to my place.

The red and yellow lines led me out into the afternoon sunshine. It glinted off the icicles that dangled from the emergency entrance overhang. I headed to the taxi waiting stand just to the side, but a voice stopped me.

"Alessia!"

I spun to see Jonah striding up the sidewalk, his dark hair messy and falling over his eyes. My heart seemed to fill again, and I ran to him. But just as I was about to dive into him, he put his hands up.

I stumbled backward. "Jonah?"

"How could you?" His voice was filled with venom, each word a sting. I looked up into his eyes and nearly choked at the hardness in them.

"What are you—?"

"How could you do that to Bree? To *me*?" A couple of EMTs hurried into the building, glancing at us as they passed. Jonah grabbed my arm and dragged me off to the side, out of sight of the entrance. I tried to pull away, but his fingers gripped my flesh like a vise. There was no warmth or softness in him at all. "I trusted you, and all the time you were working with Bree behind my back?"

"That's not what was—"

"Do you have any idea what that was like? Watching my sister be tortured? *Do you*?" His words were punctuated with an anguished sob, his face a contorted mask of fury and fear.

"Oh, my God," I breathed. "You were there?"

"Yes." He let go of me. I fell back against the brick wall. "I was there. I tried to stop it. And do you know what happened? Do you know what they said?"

I shook my head, unable to speak.

Jonah ran his hands over his face and buried his fingers in his hair, pulling at it. "They called me disloyal. They said I was soft. It didn't matter that she was my sister. She was one of *them*—one of *you*. That's all that mattered."

I reached out a hand, let it hover less than an inch from his chest, not daring to actually touch him. "Jonah, I'm so sorry—I never meant for this to happen—"

"But it's your fault. You got her into it—"

"I asked her, but Bree made her own choice." I pointed toward the hospital. "And I know for a fact she would make the same choice, even after this."

"You didn't give her a choice." He stepped in so close to me that I felt his breath, cold and tinged with something spicy. "You told her about Mr. Foster. You said she owed it to him." He leaned in. All I could see were his eyes. "You said she owed it to me."

I couldn't move, couldn't look away, couldn't deny it. "You're right," I whispered. "It's all my fault." This time I dared to touch him and laid my hand on his cheek. "Just tell me what I can do."

He flung my hand away. "Don't you get it? You can't do anything anymore." He stared at me, his skin mottled, his breath hard. "If they are willing to kill my own sister in front of me, what else are they willing to do? What line won't they cross?" Jonah shook his head with a violence that made me shudder. "I can't risk it. I have to fall in line, or they'll kill someone I love." His eyes searched my face as though he were memorizing it. "They'll kill you."

"Jonah—"

"No," he said, his voice almost a moan. "No. There's nothing you can do now." He backed away from me. The harsh sunlight spilled over him leaving him half in shadow. "I will be a Malandante until I die. I can only hope that day is sooner than later."

I squeezed my eyes shut, my body shaking with sobs. When I opened them again, he was gone. Tears spilled onto my cheeks. I slid slowly down the wall until my butt hit the cold, hard ground. Old snow seeped in through my jeans, but I just rocked back and forth, back and forth. I should've told Jonah. That night, in the basement, I should've told him Bree was involved. He could've watched out for her. I lowered my head into my hands and curled into a shivering ball.

It was a long time before I remembered Nerina was expecting me. I peeled myself off the ground and hobbled to the taxi stand, where luckily there was a taxi waiting. The kindly driver turned the heat up full blast while I sat shaking in the backseat, watching the bare trees and gentle hills roll past on the way back to the farm. I gave him a huge tip and climbed out of the cab at the top of the driveway.

Lidia's car was gone; she was probably at Mr. Salter's, as usual. The cab pulled away, and I stood in the driveway, a wind of loneliness swirling around me. It had been convenient having Lidia so preoccupied with Mr. Salter while so much was going on with the Benandanti, but now all I wanted was to have her make me a hot chocolate, sit by the fire with her, and tell her my problems.

But Nerina was waiting for me, and my duty came first.

I crossed the meadow, the grass crunchy with ice and hardened snow. When I neared the stone wall, I stopped.

The door was open.

My insides tightened and twisted. Nerina never left that door open. On faltering feet, I tiptoed to the opening and peered in. "Nerina?" I called in a hoarse whisper.

The only answer was the wind. It blew a sheet of paper up the stairs. I hurried down to catch it.

Webster, Pratt

It was the information sheet on the Raven we'd stolen from the Guild.

I scrambled down the rest of the steps and slid to a stop. The two Italian-leather chairs were overturned. One of them was missing two of its legs. The coffee table had been smashed into pieces, the couch mangled into a mass of stuffing. In the kitchen area, Nerina's fancy coffee machine lay broken on the floor, her dishes and cups in pieces on the counter.

My insides pulled taut like a trip wire. I took a step inside, almost unaware of my movements. Something rolled underneath my feet. I looked down. It was an arrow. A few feet away, beyond two more arrows, Nerina's crossbow lay snapped in half.

She had fought. She had tried to fend them off, but there must've been too many for her. I took another step, trying to quell the rising tide of panic inside me. Something glinted from the ruins of the coffee table. I sank to my knees.

Nerina's locket, the one like mine, that contained her caul.

I snatched it and held it up in the dying light. It swung back and forth, hypnotizing me for a moment. When had they come? How much of a head start did they have over us?

I dropped the locket to the floor and took out my phone. Nerina had texted me an hour and a half ago. An hour and a half. Ninety minutes. A lot could happen in ninety minutes. A Benandante—even a member of the *Concilio*—could be tortured and killed in that length of time.

My fingers slipped as I dialed Heath. It took me three tries to get the number right. "You have to come," I choked out as soon as he picked up. "Nerina's been taken."

CHAPTER THIRTY
The Guard

Alessia

The world lay quiet and snow-covered below me as I soared higher, higher into the stars. On the ground, Heath streaked over hills, leapt over fences and wove in and out of trees. I counted each wing-beat, each heart-beat, each breath as we raced toward Bangor. Our best guess was that Nerina was being held in the same place as Bree had been, and the scent Heath had caught five miles out of Twin Willows suggested we were right.

We didn't speak as we sped behind barns and over houses. It had now been over two hours since Nerina had texted me . . . two hours in which she could've been tortured . . . and ninety minutes of those two hours were my fault. If I hadn't sat in the snow and been completely pathetic about Jonah, I would've gotten to Nerina's sooner. They could've had less of a head start . . . or I could've been there when they attacked, and helped her . . .

And you could've been killed.

I dropped in the air; I hadn't realized I'd opened

the channel and Heath could hear me. *Nerina will be all right. She's* Concilio. *They won't kill her.*

I wanted to believe him, but I could hear how he was telling me this to convince himself. If the Malandanti were willing to kill the sister of one of their own members, surely they wouldn't hesitate to kill a Benandanti *Concilio* member. They'd probably have a party.

I lifted my wings, let the wind fan my feathers. Our only hope was that they wanted to get information out of her and they'd been torturing her for the last two hours. It was a horrible hope, but it was better than the alternative.

Farmland gave way to strip malls and suburbs and the concrete streets of Bangor. Heath wove in and out of alleyways, keeping off the main sidewalks. A huge white wolf in the middle of the city would probably alarm people. I recognized the Guild's building from a block away, its shiny, silver cubic walls rising above the other structures around it. But some of that shininess seemed to have dimmed, in just the few days since we'd taken down the Guild. As we neared, I saw that someone had spray-painted *PIGS* in red across the entry doors.

Around back, Heath said. I veered into the alley behind the building. Heath stood before a set of double doors, their handles looped together by a thick chain. *Ready? On three.*

I moved back to give myself space. *One, two, three.* I flew into the upper part of the doors while Heath slammed into the lower part. A huge crack fractured one of the doors. Heath struck at it with his front paws, and it broke partway off its hinges, enough to let us through. *This way.*

I followed him through dark, twisting halls, like a maze out of Greek mythology. We seemed to be spiraling inward until we came to a room at the very center of the labyrinth. The door was black and solid. There wasn't even a doorknob.

How—?

But before I could even finish my question, Heath rammed the door with his whole body. It creaked but didn't budge. He rammed it again. Blood glistened on his throat. I flew into the door on his third try, tore into it with my talons, but nothing.

Heath fell back, his body heaving. I fluttered around the top of the door, looking for an opening, anything that could give way . . . and then the door swung open.

An unnaturally tall woman leaned against the door frame, smiling at us. "You're right on time," she said. Her voice sent shivers through me. She shook her long, wavy hair, her eyes glinting in the shadowed light, and I knew in an instant she was the Harpy.

Alessia, get out of here. Now.

I'm not leaving you—

Go! It's a trap!

I darted up to the ceiling. The Harpy laughed. What light there was in the hallway dimmed. My vision grew cloudy. Something pulled at me. A sickening sensation flooded me. I looked down and saw the red band wrapped around me, just as it had the night the Lynx died . . .

I fell to the floor, my muscles limp and useless. The hooded mage stepped out from behind the Harpy and dragged me and Heath into the room. Someone was screaming, telling them to stop, but the sound of her voice grew smaller and smaller as the blood rushing in my ears grew louder and louder . . .

"Enough," said the Harpy, the word cutting through the pain inside me. "Lock them in with her."

With a wave of his hand, the mage blasted us against the far wall. A tangled cry escaped me at the impact. A glimmering cylinder of silver light surrounded us. I stretched my talons out to touch it, and an electric shock ricocheted through me. Beneath me, Heath pawed at it, with the same result.

"It's no use."

I spun. Nerina stood an inch away from the light-wall, her arms wrapped tight around herself. Her hair had fallen out of its usual impeccable style, but other than that, she looked unharmed. Heath bounded to her, pushed his head against her hip.

"I'm all right," she said. "They didn't bring me here to torture me."

Then why—?

"They brought me here because they knew you would follow," she whispered and directed her gaze just outside the light barrier.

"That's right." The Harpy's voice was like a thousand tiny nails on a chalkboard. She held up a hand. "Your mage is . . . *not functional* at the moment, shall we say?" She ticked down one finger. "You have one of your Clan watching her, do you not?" Another finger. "And the three of you are here with no way out." She tucked her other three fingers into her palm and held up her fist. "That leaves one Benandante at the Waterfall. And one Benandante is no match for all of us."

And out of the shadows stepped six other figures, all cloaked in dark silvery coats that covered their faces. *Seven figures . . .* I bit back a screech. This wasn't the Clan. It was the *Concilio Argento*.

"Let them go," Nerina begged. "I'm the one you want, Fina. Take your revenge on me and leave them be."

The Harpy walked right up to the glittering cage. Her gaze swept over Nerina, a strange expression of mingled love and hate on her face. "Darling Nerina, always thinking everything is about you. This time, it is not." She waved, and the six *Concilio* filed out the door, followed by the mage. "When we have retaken the Waterfall," the Harpy said, her smile languid, "we will come back and deal with the three of you." She leaned in so that her long aquiline nose almost grazed the bars. "I have been waiting many, many years for this moment, Nerina. Well, of course you know how long. You were there."

"Then why not just deal with us now?" Nerina snapped. "Why keep us alive if you've already won?"

The Harpy ran her tongue along her top lip. "Oh, Nerina. I have always admired your practicality. But sometimes it gets in the way of poetry." She snapped her fingers.

I sensed a rustling at the door but couldn't see what was there.

The Harpy grinned, baring her teeth like the animal she was. "We have a member who seems to be losing his purpose. So we are leaving you in his care until we return, to make sure he knows his place." She strode toward the door.

Just before she disappeared, she turned and blew Nerina a kiss.

I flew forward and peered into the dimness. My heartbeat pounded in every inch of my body. A form slowly took shape as it crept toward us, catlike and black . . . but all I could see was the glow of his emerald-green eyes.